Stupid Spellbound Love

OTHER TITLES BY AMY BOYLES

ROMANCE STAND-ALONES

How to Fake It with a Fae

How to Outwit a Wizard

STUPID LOVE SERIES

Stupid Magical Love

COZY MYSTERY SERIES

Sweet Tea Witches

Magical Renovation Mysteries

The Accidental Medium

The Withering Mysteries

Southern Belles and Spells

Southern Ghost Wranglers

Bless Your Witch Mysteries

Southern Single Mom Paranormal Mysteries

For a full list of books, visit Amy's website: www.amyboyles.com

Stupid Spellbound Love

AMY BOYLES

Montlake

Published by Montlake, Seattle
www.apub.com

EU product safety contact:
Amazon Media EU S. à r.l.
38, avenue John F. Kennedy, L-1855 Luxembourg
amazonpublishing-gpsr@amazon.com

ISBN-13: 9781662536236 (paperback)
ISBN-13: 9781662536243 (digital)

Cover design by Hang Le
Cover image: © Successful girl, © bulatova, © i_fleur, © Dumith Pramodaya, © DniproDD, © overlays-textures / Shutterstock

Printed in the United States of America

For Wilfred Guillory, my dad in heaven. You carried your Creole heritage with quiet dignity. With this book, I hope to honor those roots and let them shine. I pray I've done you proud.

Chapter 1

COCO

The morning I start my dream job, my mom calls to remind me of something: She's forgotten I exist.

"Brittany just hit one million YouTube subscribers," she gushes about my sister while I sit on the roadside in my Camry, the engine idling.

"That's fantastic."

I try to match her enthusiasm, but all I can think is, it's the first day of my new job and Mom has forgotten about the details of my life—*again*.

"We're throwing a big party for her Saturday. I need you to bring the potato salad." That's me, the potato salad daughter. "How do you make it so good?"

"Pickles," I remind her, deflating.

My family likes the crunchy pickles.

"Great. Talk soon!"

She hangs up, leaving me with a hole in the pit of my stomach.

And that's when all hell breaks loose.

Okay, I'm exaggerating.

But it *is* when my hands decide to act like living sparklers. Painful pops of magic flicker from the tips of my fingers.

"Ouch! No!"

To stop the fire, I pop my fingers into my mouth. The taste of pennies zings on my tongue, and my throbbing fingers smart for a second before the power fizzles out.

Here's the thing no one tells you about living in a town that recently reclaimed its magic: Sometimes it comes back *in* you. And while everyone's cool with unicorns and piggycorns (pigs with unicorn horns) prancing around, they're not so keen on humans with magic.

Surprisingly, that's where the townsfolk draw the line.

I tap the GPS screen until the stupid thing comes back to life and nose my Camry onto the two-lane highway that runs out of Mystic Meadows, Georgia—my hometown.

The landscape blooms on both sides with green meadows, rolling hills, tall pines. And running over them all, standing out like an accent pillow in a perfect living room, are ley lines.

These are rivers of power that shimmer like gold. They snake over the earth, crisscrossing one another and tumbling on top of rocks, down hills, and weaving around trees.

As I pass a glowing thread of power dancing alongside the road, my phone rings.

It's Mom again! This time she's calling because she remembered, for sure. I clear my throat like I'm preparing to give my Oscar acceptance speech.

"Hey! Did you forget something?"

"Did you get your grandmother's engagement ring sized yet?"

I glance down at my left hand to the antique emerald-and-diamond ring that fits loosely on my finger. It was a gift from my grandmother and swivels every time I move, so I'm having it sized for my right hand—my non-engagement, single hand.

"I'm dropping it off at the jeweler's today."

"Great. Can't wait to see how it fits you." There's a pause. "Honey, is something wrong?"

Worse than being forgotten is coaxing someone into remembering you. So I say, "Nope. I'm all good."

"Well, see you soon. Bye!"

First Brittany, then the ring. Not me. Not how I am.

It's fine. It's totally fine. I'm used to it.

Even though I try giving myself the pep talk to end all pep talks, it must really suck, because a familiar ache bubbles inside me, pushing up my throat like I've swallowed a rock.

My fingers spark again. As I shake my hands to snuff out the magic, in the distance one of the ley lines turns red and pulses weakly.

My lack of control is not good. I've got to get this power under wraps before someone finds out and my life and job are ruined.

Or worse.

For the past few months, my fingers have put on a fireworks show when I'm angry or sad or frustrated—anything but *happy*. The one emotion maybe they *should* celebrate, they ignore like it's the last shirt on a sales table, the dingy SpongeBob SquarePants tee nobody wants.

As soon as my emotions pull back together, the humming power in my fingers dies and the red ley line returns to its normal state—a dim, yellowish-white strip of magic.

I take a deep breath and focus on why I'm here in the first place. "Okay, where is this site?"

The GPS dings for me to take a right at the next stop sign. As I slow to a halt, a John Deere tractor approaches on the opposite side of the road.

Clarice Sinclair bounces atop the seat. She's older, easily in her seventies, though I'm not sure of the exact number. She has a curly mop of silvery hair that's mostly hidden today by a Braves cap. She wears jeans and a jacket to shield herself from the bite in the early-spring morning.

"Hey, Clarice!"

She rumbles to a stop. "Morning, Coco. Where're you headed?"

Finally. Someone I can humblebrag to! "I'm going to the Maddox resort on the hill."

Her eyes brighten with intrigue. "That's right! You're in Zoning now. Didn't you tell me that?"

"I sure did!"

See? Clarice remembers. Why is it easier for her to remember than my own mother?

The older woman rubs her chin, reminding me of a sinister villain strategizing her evil plan. "Speaking of the Maddoxes, now that Rowe married Pane Maddox, it looks like you're the most eligible bachelorette in town. The Collins boys are still looking for girlfriends." She pumps her brows excitedly. "The oldest got rid of his acne. Except for his back. He still has that problem, but I'd be happy to set you up with one of 'em. Maybe two. How old are you?"

"Twenty-seven."

"Is eighteen too young?"

"Bye, Clarice."

As I roll up the window, she shouts, "Just think about it!"

The last thing I'll consider is a boyfriend who's barely out of high school. No thank you.

But she did have a point about the Maddoxes. It was big news several months ago when Pane arrived in town. His mother wanted to name the next CEO of the Maddox Group, the family's chain of luxury hotels. To win the company, Pane competed against his brother to see who could best save a dying business. He wound up rescuing a struggling piggycorn farm that belonged to his now wife, Rowe.

So Pane won, but from what I understand, he left the company and, alongside his brother, decided to open a resort in town.

Which is where I'm headed for the first assignment of my brand-spanking-new job.

Have I mentioned how excited I am?

As the sedan climbs the hills outside Mystic Meadows, the resort reveals itself from behind a curtain of trees—steel beams, loud construction equipment, men in hard hats.

And standing just off-center is a tall guy with good, strong shoulders, the kind that could hold a steel beam for hours.

With me sitting on top.

Not that I'm fantasizing. But . . . um, I might be a little bit. I shake my head to clear the cobwebs and notice he wears a pair of Carhartt pants and a blue button-down shirt with the sleeves rolled to the elbows. Even from this distance, his forearms appear solid.

Wisps of sandy hair peek out from under his hard hat. My gaze drifts and I recognize some of the men on the site—Isaac from Sparkle Bar, and Ron. Ron's wife, Jennifer, owns the pharmacy.

But what's sitting at the man's feet makes my breath catch. A small, woolly creature with a delicate golden horn erupting from the center of its forehead takes a step, loses its balance, and falls against the tall man's shin.

Oh my gosh.

Is that a *lambicorn*?

Chapter 2

STONE

"Boss, you gotta see this," Ron calls from outside the trailer.

I slam a fist down on my desk. "Dammit!"

"Okay, we'll leave," he shouts.

"No, not you." I rub my face with both hands and groan. On my phone is an image of the original vinyl recording of *Saxophone Colossus*—an album that just slipped through my fingers.

CollectorPrep561 beat me in the auction.

Again.

How do they keep doing that?

One day I will track down this person and make them a scathingly obscene offer for every vinyl in their possession. They won't hesitate to sell, and I'll finally win the albums they've technically stolen / not stolen out from under me.

I slip the phone into my pocket. "Come in!"

The trailer door swings open and Ron and Isaac enter. Isaac tips his hard hat to me, while Ron pulls his off as if he's stepped into a church.

They oversee the resort construction, hired by my brother because they're his friends. Decent guys. Smart. Honest. Honesty is a good thing.

It's the *best* thing.

I grab my hard hat from the desk and put it on. "What's up?"

Isaac smooths a hand down the braids that fall over his shoulder. "You need to see this."

"What? Did something happen? Did the shipment not come in?"

They exchange a charged glance and Ron smirks. "Nothing like that. It's different."

"Okay, show me."

Outside, workers jackhammer, steel beams go up, and the Summit at Mystic Meadows is being framed out. It's the first solo project my brother and I have taken on, and my future rides on it.

We pass a pile of bricks that was unloaded in the wrong place. "Isaac, get those bricks moved. Whoever told the delivery guy to put them there should have known better."

"Yes, sir."

My phone rings while we're walking and I pull it from my pocket.

The name Sylvia flashes on the screen.

Mom.

My step falters. It's been months since she called, and I hoped she'd given up trying.

Before I can steel myself, the sharp cut of betrayal washes over me. It's so profound, so sudden, it feels like my chest is being ripped open. It takes everything I've got to push it aside, to breathe through it and not let rage worm its way inside me.

She lied to me for the better part of my life and somehow thinks a simple phone call will solve everything.

I push the button to end the call before it can even begin.

There's nothing she can say to change what she did.

The guys stop and it's only then that I realize I'm not walking. "Sorry."

"We found it over here," Isaac tells me as we reach a line of trees that hasn't been cleared.

"Found what?"

"This."

Ron steps into the brush and when he comes out, he cradles a small white creature with a stubby golden horn shooting out from the middle of its forehead.

Isaac gestures to it like a game show host. "We present your very own lambicorn. Found on-site and now the property of one Stone Maddox."

"No thanks."

My brother discovered one the night he got married. Wasn't *that* enough? Why does Mystic Meadows need two of them?

Besides, the creature looks like a tiny wet goblin. "Sorry, guys. Not interested."

Ron pets it lovingly. "But it's a magical creature that just appeared. You gotta take it, Stone. Give it to Pane and Rowe."

"First"—I tick points off on my fingers—"my brother and his wife are on their extended honeymoon. Second, I wouldn't know where to put it. Third, I'm not interested in the responsibility. What if I let it down? What if it thinks I'm its real father and years later discovers the truth, that I've been lying to it its whole life?"

I admit that last part sounds pretty bitter.

The men's mouths fall open.

"What?" I shrug.

Isaac blinks. "Not a thing, boss."

Ron gazes at the creature lovingly. See? He's a natural Dr. Dolittle. Unlike me.

"I can't take it, either. Jennifer will kill me. Have you seen how much these things poop?"

"All the more reason for you to put it back where you found it. How'd it get here in the first place?"

Isaac hitches one shoulder. "How do any of the creatures get here? The unicorns? The piggycorns? They just appear."

"Next thing you know, magical people will be walking out of the bushes."

"No, boss." Isaac crosses his arms. "Mystic Meadows has a strict no-people-with-magic policy. The town won't tolerate them."

"Why's that?"

"Something that happened a long time ago. But"—he grins, showing off a row of gleaming white teeth—*"lambicorn."*

I shake my head. "Why don't you take it?"

"Because I don't have time to watch it—between being here and the bar, there isn't space to nurture it the way it should be."

They stare at me expectantly. "And what makes you think I have time to do this?" Both men glance at the trailer and then back at me. "Oh no. I'm really bad with living things. The last plant I had? It died a slow death—and that was a cactus. Do you know how hard it is to *kill* a cactus?"

"You'll be fine." Ron pushes the lambiwhatever—okay, fine, *corn.* He pushes the lambicorn into my arms. "It'll drink goat's milk. Be sure to warm it up."

Then they walk off, leaving me alone with the baby.

I put it down and follow the men. "I don't want it."

Ron shoots a look over his shoulder. "Looks like *it* wants *you.*"

I turn back to see the lambicorn following me. Or *them.* It *could* be following them. After all, Ron did touch it first. Maybe it imprinted on him and now believes Ron to be its slightly overweight and balding mother.

I head back to the trailer. Not my lambicorn. Not my problem.

I open the door and walk through. I turn to shut it behind me and—

"Baaaaaaaa."

It looks up with big brown eyes that will not make me fold. "Listen, kid, I'm not your mom. Or your dad. I'm not interested in complications. I want to build this resort, make my money, and move on. Got it?"

"Baaaaaaaa."

What is it with this sheep? Can't it take a hint?

Just as I'm about to shoo it away—I mean, really shoo, like actually push the creature into the woods where maybe it can find another lambicorn and live happily ever after—a car drives up the red-clay landscape and comes to a halt.

I figure it's one of the workers showing up late, but when I peer closer, it's a woman.

At a construction site.

Don't get me wrong, plenty of women are fixtures on construction sites, but not this one. This is an all-dude affair.

When she exits the car, the first thing I notice is how her dark hair is slicked up into a tight, perfect bun. She's wearing jeans, a flowy shirt, and heels. But it's the bun that grabs my attention. It gives her this whole librarian vibe that's very alluring.

And her legs—they're astronomically long. Wow.

The urge to meet her is like a punch in the face.

She hauls a stack of papers from the car and shuts the door by bumping it with her rear end—which is quite round and very attractive. Then my date with destiny takes a long look at the steel beams and the poured foundation.

Impressive, I know.

She frowns. At my construction site. Peers again. Takes off her sunglasses and stares.

"Can I help you?" I ask, approaching.

She spins toward me, startled, and every piece of paper slips from her grasp. They plummet to the ground like a waterfall, and she drops to her knees to gather the scattered sheets.

"Oh my gosh, I'm so sorry. I didn't mean to . . ."

I bend down to grab a few of the pages and hand them to her, wiping off the dirt first.

"Thank you."

"You're welcome."

The woman, still crouching, looks at me and smiles. Freckles constellate her red cheeks and she has big doe eyes. Long, dark lashes. She appears a bit younger than my thirty-five years.

"Can I help you?" I repeat, rising.

She clears her throat nervously and unfolds. "I'm looking for—"

The lambicorn bleats and she gasps. "It *is* a lambicorn! I saw it from the car. Where did you get it?"

Her eyes flash up to me. They're hazel—gold and brown. Warm.

Before I can answer, she shoves the mess of papers into my hands, picks up the lambicorn, and hugs it. "She is so sweet. Is it a she?"

"No idea. It just showed up."

"Where?"

"In the woods. It's yours if you want it."

She rubs her cheek against its head. "*Awwwww.* You are so sweet." The sheep closes its eyes, clearly enjoying the affection. "I've heard they imprint on one person and that becomes their mom."

"This is your lucky day, because it looks like it's imprinting on you."

The woman grins at me again, and I find my own lips tipping skyward, all thoughts of my mom forgotten. She puts the lambicorn down and gives its head another stroke.

"Let's see who it goes to." She steps away and the lambicorn pads over to me.

Great.

"The lambi has spoken. You are her new daddy."

I rub my cheek. "It'll be the first time someone's called me that."

"That's good." Then she quickly adds, "Unless you want someone to call you daddy. If that's the case, then I take back my previous statement."

"No one's calling me daddy. You're good. I mean, I don't know if you're good, and when I say that, I'm not trying to be suggestive. I just met you, obviously. I have no idea if you're good. *Wait.* Does it feel like I'm digging an actual hole with my mouth, or is it just me?"

She laughs, and our gazes latch for a beat. She looks away first, and when she does, my pulse skips in a way I haven't experienced in a long time.

I've been so focused on the resort and, before that, the competition with Pane that there hasn't been time for stopping to smell the roses.

Some people might say I've buried myself in work to avoid other things (looking at you, Mom). But it's almost impossible for outsiders to understand the burden that comes with the last name Maddox.

Failure is not an option.

But this sensation—feeling my heart like this—is good and, sadly, foreign.

I plow my fingers through my hair, trying to tamp down this sensation swirling in my rib cage. "But really, lambicorns and construction sites don't mix."

"Not unless you want them to," she tells me. "If you want anything to work, it will. All it takes is a little commitment."

"Is that a poster with a cat on it?"

"Sounds like you're an expert. You must have one in that trailer of yours."

"I may allow a lot of things, but I draw the line at cat posters."

"Too bad. I'm a sucker for them." Our gazes lock again and hold a beat too long. She breaks first. "Even if you don't believe it, I bet you'd be a great dad to this little guy."

A great dad.

Those three words encase my chest in ice.

"If you only knew," I mutter bitterly, and curse myself because she wasn't supposed to hear that.

But she does, and she peers at me as if peeling back my wards, catching a rare glimpse of the dips and valleys carved in my heart.

"Trust me," I say dismissively, in an attempt to take control of the narrative, "there's nothing I want more than to be unconditionally loved by this little guy. But I'm afraid my life isn't conducive to lambicorns." I offer my hand. "I'm Stone Maddox, by the way."

"Coco Higginbotham." She shakes my hand. It's warm, like her eyes.

"Higginbotham? That's a mouthful."

"Yes, it is. I'm from the Department of Zoning and Development. I'm the new magical land coordinator."

I frown. "What exactly do you do?"

She lifts her chin and says proudly, "I review development permits, ensure projects are in harmony with the town's environmental zoning, and act as the town's liaison for 'sustainable integration,' which includes symbolic preservation of magical sites—like where the unicorns and piggycorns first showed up. And now that you have a lambicorn, I guess here, too."

I shoot her a grin. "That's even more of a mouthful than your last name."

"It is," she replies, laughing. "But it really just means I'm here to sign off on the resort."

"Let me get you a hard hat and we'll walk the site."

I grab an extra hat from the trailer, but when she tries to put it on, her bun is in the way.

"Is that a pencil sticking out of your hair?"

"Yeah." The tops of her ears redden in embarrassment. "Sometimes I do that."

"Let me get it for you."

I gently remove the pencil and Coco shakes out her hair. The wind catches it, and I stare, mesmerized as ebony strands flip, then spill over her shoulders.

Coco blushes, and it's . . . adorable.

Dammit. No complications. No ties. No lambicorns. No tangled emotions. I'm here to build a resort and that's it.

"Here you go." I hand her the pencil. "Unless there's some other place you'd like to put this? Maybe through a buttonhole?"

"No. Thanks, though."

"All right." I clap my hands, inwardly scolding myself for saying something so dumb. *What the hell, Stone? Does flirting now include using props like hair accessories?* "Let me show you around."

As I lead her through the construction site, she stays right beside me. "Watch your step," I tell her as she nears a mound of clay.

She steps over it while studying the site, eyeing the machines and the men sharply. But when we get close to the building, she stops.

Coco approaches one of the beams and touches it. Tips her head like she's listening to fairies whispering from inside the steel or something.

"You okay?"

She doesn't respond but moves through the space, continuing to touch and tip her head.

"Ms. Higginbotham?"

She blinks, sucks in a deep inhale.

"Are. You. Okay?"

"No, I'm not."

Please don't vomit. The last thing I need is for her to throw up and then have the lambicorn eat it. Oh, God. I'm going to be sick.

"You look a little pale. Do you need to sit down? Drink some water?"

"No. It's not me. It's this building." She runs a hand down a beam. "It isn't right."

"Excuse me?"

"Just what I said." She hugs the papers to her chest and shivers. "You have to stop construction right now. You can't build this resort—not like this."

"What do you mean, I have to stop building?"

She eyes the steel beams and the workers. The sounds of construction are thick in the air: warning alarms as machines reverse, rocks being dumped in the background, men talking.

Coco's expression becomes grim. "Because if you don't, you'll destroy the magic in this land."

My jaw tightens, and only one thought flashes in my mind: There's no way in hell I'm changing one damn thing—*magic or not.*

Chapter 3

COCO

It's the ley lines.

I saw them right after I arrived.

They run like a spiderweb down to the site, rivers of milky threads humming with magic. Before they enter the construction zone, they're strong, almost sentient, alive and thrumming.

But as they race under the poured concrete, I feel a shift. The ley lines deaden. Their energy falters, becoming dim, flat. They struggle to breathe. It reminds me of a clogged pipe or artery. Something is in the way, blocking the path. That something can only be the materials Stone Maddox is using to build his resort.

Which means he is killing the magic—magic that only recently reappeared. Magic my town is banking on to bring in tourist money.

It's only been a few months since the piggycorns received their power to generate electricity. Even now, there are rumors that unicorns are once again being born with power.

Magic is back and I can't let it die.

Stone Maddox, however, doesn't appear to appreciate this.

Worse, there are no laws or regulations regarding materials for ley lines. Legally, he's not doing anything wrong.

But magically? That's a different story.

Officially, I'm supposed to base permit approvals on town records and topography reports. Unofficially? Since today is my first assignment, I'm pretty much going with what I see, and what I see is not good.

But I can't admit this to anyone. If my supervisor discovers I'm using magic in my decisions, I can be fired, branded unstable.

Or worse. Much, much worse.

Stone scowls and when he does, his anger seems to make him grow, and I feel the familiar urge to disappear.

"What are you talking about, we've got to stop?" he demands.

I run my hand down a beam, searching for a hum of power and receiving a weak whisper. "What materials are you using?"

He taps his fingers to his belt impatiently. Behind him, the lambicorn bleats. "What do you think I'm using? It's reinforced concrete and steel beams."

I nod to a spot where the men are paving an outdoor pavilion. "And the stone?"

He drags his gaze from me to them. His jaw flexes, unflexes. "It's synthetic. Look, everything is state of the art, efficient. Eco-friendly."

"But it's not *ley line* friendly. These aren't—"

"'Ley line friendly'?" He laughs in my face. "That's the stupidest—What's that even supposed to mean?"

My hackles rise. *Stupid? I'm not being stupid!*

Power builds in my hands. One of the lines running out from under the resort pulses red.

Not again.

I curl my fingers and exhale to get my emotions under control. I can do this. I can prove to Stone Maddox this is important—for the city.

"The materials must be different when you build around ley lines," I lie.

Hopefully, he's not familiar with the city zoning ordinances.

Stone rubs a hand down his face. "What are you talking about?"

"Just as I said."

"Look . . ."

Something wars in his eyes, and I get the feeling that whatever is causing this reaction, it's bigger than me dropping this news.

He speaks slowly, as if every word pains him. "No one said anything about the materials and the ley lines. That is a lambicorn. *Lambicorn.* We literally just found it, so I'd say the ley lines are doing fine. Besides, how would you know if they're not? Can you *see* them or something?"

"No, of course I can't see them," I snap. "Why would you even ask me that?"

"Because you're talking about them as if you know they're here."

"Well"—I throw my hands up—"they're everywhere in Mystic Meadows. Everyone knows that. It's common knowledge."

He folds his arms. "Really? Common knowledge? Hey, Isaac?"

Isaac puts down the two-by-four he's carrying. "Yeah, boss?"

"Did you know ley lines are everywhere in Mystic Meadows?"

"No, sir. I did not."

"And did you know that if we build here, we have to use different materials than what we're already using?"

Isaac scratches his head. "Say what?"

"Exactly!" Stone turns back to me with his lips quirked in a triumphant look. "See? No one knows this. How do I know you're not making it up?"

I straighten to my full height of *short* and grind out, "I am an official from Zoning. I would not make this up."

He bends down and I get a prime seat to his jade-green eyes—eyes that might make another woman swoon but make me want to kick him in the shins.

He pokes my collarbone. "You know what?"

"What?"

"I think you're a little bureaucrat trying to feel big, and I'm not biting. Go take your bullshit somewhere else. Better yet? Go push some more pencils into your head. Maybe they'll give you some brains."

The papers I'm holding fall from my hands and plop to the ground. I cannot believe he just talked to me like that.

He spins on his heel, showing me his back. "I'm not helping you clean those up."

"I don't need your help."

He waves as he walks off. "Next time, send someone who knows what they're talking about. Someone who can actually *do* their job."

Then he dismisses me like I'm a big nobody idiot.

Well, I'm not a big nobody idiot.

I collect the mess of papers and chase him down, feeling like a stupid Stone Maddox fangirl who doesn't know when to go home.

I jump in front of him. "Down there."

"What?"

I point down the hill. "There's a dark patch of earth."

"And what's that got to do with me?"

"See? The earth is *dying* because the lines are affected by your materials."

He stares in the distance with a baffled expression. "What are you talking about?"

I point again. "Over there."

"First of all," he counters, "I know for a fact the ley lines originate near Wadley Farms."

"There's more than one set," I argue.

"And how do you know that?"

"Because . . . everyone knows that."

"No, they don't. Even if you *think* what you're seeing is a dark patch of earth because the ley lines are getting scrambled or whatever, you're not. That's normal earth. A *normal* patch. If everyone blamed brown grass on ley lines, we'd all be crazy."

"Maybe I'm crazy."

He comes nose to nose with me. "Maybe you are."

But I'm not.

An ache blooms in my temple. I rub it to ease the throb. "I bet that if I snooped around, I would discover the magic is beginning to deaden in town. Magic needs nature to thrive. It needs natural things. All of this"—I gesture to the concrete, the synthetic materials—"is killing it. I'm sure we can come up with some alternatives, something that will work."

He walks backward, nearly stepping on the lambicorn, who bounds away just in time. "Do you have any idea how much money we've already spent? How much more material we've ordered? You're asking me to destroy hundreds of thousands of dollars' worth of building and start over. Have you lost your mind?"

I flinch. His words slap. I've dealt with nasty people before, but his insult stings.

I open my mouth. Close it again.

Then I reply coldly, "I don't appreciate you talking to me that way."

"And I don't appreciate being told by a pencil-pushing bureaucrat I'm supposed to bow down to some *theory*. This! This is *all* my brother and I have to prove we can succe— *Dammit!* Why do I say too much around you?"

His words strike me hard and there's a beat where our gazes lock, our breathing syncs, and the pulsing ley lines hum through me.

It feels like a purr rippling through my veins, and for once, my fingers aren't sparking. Just stillness. Just him and me.

God help me.

And as quickly as the sensation flares, it vanishes.

Stone's jaw tightens, instantly reminding me that we are two people on opposite sides of this argument.

"Please," I murmur quietly. "We only just got the strengthened ley lines back in Mystic Meadows. We can't lose them again. My town's future hinges on this."

Stone's voice is restrained when he speaks, as if he's holding back from shouting. "I am building a multimillion-dollar state-of-the-art facility in anticipation of how much tourism will rise here. I'm investing everything I have into this. So is my brother. So is my cousin. This is everything we've got, and you're telling me I'm supposed to bust it all up and start over?" His jaw clenches. "No. You can *get lost*."

Stone storms off, gravel crunching under his boots. The lambicorn bleats pathetically as it follows. The poor thing's probably starving.

Stone opens the trailer door and slams it shut behind him, leaving the lambicorn outside.

Lava rolls through my veins. What a jerk. Obviously, I didn't give Stone good news. I own that. But the poor lambicorn is innocent. The creature can't help it picked the worst mother in the world to nurture it.

Trust me, lambi, I know the feeling.

I charge over, scoop up the lambicorn, and bang on the door.

It flies open and Stone sticks his head out. "What?"

I press the baby into his arms. "I present your lambicorn."

He pushes it back. "Take it. You have a mothering instinct—the kind of helicopter personality that'll keep it bound in Bubble Wrap until it's twenty."

He slams the door in my face.

I open the door and walk in.

Stone whirls around and fumes, "What are you doing?"

"I'm giving you your lambicorn. Clearly the creature has terrible taste, but it picked you as its mother, so here you go."

I place the lamb on the floor. Stone has removed his hard hat and set it on a desk—which is very neatly put together, I might add, with files organized, the surface, uncluttered. It even smells nice in here, like sand and sea spray.

"It's not mine." He closes the space between us. His body thrums with anger, and it wafts off him in sheets of heat that warm my skin. "How many times do I have to tell you?"

"It's yours." I poke his arm. "How many times do I have to tell *you*?" There's a long pause where it feels like the air has left the room. I lower my voice, doing my best to tamp down my frustration. "I'm sorry we got off to a bad start, but I'm here to help, to work with you. Someone should have come out sooner, but I only recently got hired to replace my predecessor. If you would just let me show you what I think—"

"No," he snaps, venom lacing his voice. "I'm not changing the materials, and neither is my brother. We're pushing forward. There's a deadline. Supplies have been ordered. We're doing what we're doing, and that's it."

I brush hair from my face, and his gaze lands on the antique ring. His eyes narrow. "Nice ring. Did you destroy that guy's life, too? Tell me, was it before or after he proposed?"

I want to scream. "Not that it's any of your business, but this is my grandmother's ring. A man didn't give it to me."

He smirks. "Not surprising."

"For your information, I date plenty."

"I bet you do."

"I do." We stare at one another, and as if the ring has heard us, it slips from my finger and lands on the floor.

Stone stares at it for a long beat. So do I. I glare at him until he bends over, picks up the ring, and hands it to me. "For you, princess. May you hook the best fish in the sea."

I snatch the ring from his grasp. "Like you're some catch. You've got money, but the personality of a piece of plywood."

His jaw clenches. "I sure do."

The tension in the room defuses and I sigh, tired of fighting. "For the sake of our town, please change the materials."

He shoots me a condescending look before rubbing a hand down the scruff on his cheek. "For the sake of this town and the tourism that's coming, I think I'll keep it the way it is. Now, if there's nothing else, you may leave."

He turns around, steps behind his desk, and plops into his chair with a heavy sigh. Conversation over. Just like that. He's decided we're through.

But we are not through.

I tap the top page of the bundle of sheets I'm still holding and tell Stone Maddox in the most determined voice I can muster, "Unless you change the materials you're using, I'm shutting construction of the resort down—*indefinitely.*"

Chapter 4

COCO

Mystic Meadows began as a lumbering community, but when industry died, the founders needed a way to revitalize it. Just as they erected new buildings, the first unicorns arrived.

The creatures had power—could heal, imbue you with love, all of it. Unicorns became big industry for one farmer, giving him a monopoly. With unicorns came tourists, people willing to pay hand over fist to see the majestic no-longer-fairy-tale creatures.

A few years later, the first piggycorns appeared. But they arrived as the magic waned, as unicorns started being born *without* power.

All of this magic, we discovered recently, is tied to a plant—starfizz berries. Growing them reactivated long-dormant ley lines just like the ones that run directly under the Maddoxes' resort.

But no amount of starfizz berries could fix this situation, because these lines are buried under concrete, not sitting flush with the soil.

This is about my town thriving. The piggycorns *finally* received magic, and I'll be damned before I let everything return to the way it was. When grime covered the buildings on Main Street and before . . . before I, the current I—the one who can see ley lines—existed.

Even if I can't tell anyone that I do.

I storm over to my car and spot Isaac from Sparkle Bar opening his lunch box.

He gives me a thousand-watt grin. "Hey, Coco. What's up?"

"I'm shutting the place down." I open my trunk and push aside a tire-inflation kit, an emergency battery charger, a severe-weather poncho, and a flare gun, until I finally find it.

I grab the tape and slam the lid. If Stone Maddox won't listen to me, then maybe this will get his attention.

Isaac cocks his head in confusion. "You're doing what?"

"Shutting it down." I grab the stack of paper from the ground where I put it, and show him the first page and my signature. "Right here. I signed right there, and I'll be filing this today."

He takes the paper in his free hand and shakes his head. "Why?"

"Ask your boss."

He eyes what's in my hand. "What are you doing with police tape?"

"Making sure my filing is obeyed."

"With that," he deadpans.

"With this," I confirm, even though he looks at it and me like we're both whack-job crazy. Well, maybe I am, but I'm determined to do this job right. "If you'll excuse me . . ."

I march across the construction site, minus hard hat, which is violating all kinds of rules, and head straight to the resort, picking my way over huge clumps of red dirt as I go.

When I reach the interior, Ron looks up in surprise. He stops talking with some of the guys and scratches his chin as I wind the Do Not Cross tape around one of the beams and walk it to the end of the building.

"Sorry to tell you this, boys, but we're shutting her down. Better pack up for the day. There's nothing else to be done here." When they don't move, I say again, "Grab your tools and head home before I call the police and have y'all escorted off."

Can I actually do that? *Will* the police do that? People in this town love Pane Maddox—like, they *really* love Pane Maddox. He's a hero for not only saving his wife's farm but also for helping Mystic Meadows reclaim its magic.

If he knew the materials he and his brother are using will destroy the magic again, then he would absolutely approve of my drastic measures.

Right?

I tell myself this as I wind the tape around another beam. Ron still gapes at me.

"What are you waiting for, Ron? You'd better get going before you're arrested. You'll have hell to pay with Jennifer if you wind up booked down at the station."

Jennifer takes no shits, and if the fear bulging in his eyes is any indication, he's terrified of her. "You heard the lady. Let's go, guys."

A thrill of satisfaction zings up my spine. It quickly evaporates when I spot Stone Maddox exit his trailer just as the men pile into trucks and cars and leave for the day.

His gaze whips around until it finds me. The confusion in his eyes quickly dissolves into a *What the hell?* expression as he takes in the police tape.

His face changes again, and this time he's pissed.

Which means I'd better hurry.

"What are you doing?" he demands. He breaks the tape and throws it on the ground. "This is crime scene tape. It's for the police."

"You will tie that back," I snap.

"I will not." He gestures toward the trucks driving off. "Did you tell my men to leave? You have no right!"

He storms over as I finish securing tape to the last beam. "I have every right!" I shout. "You're going to ruin this town. I'm filing paperwork today. By tomorrow, you'll be served with papers that say unless you comply, you may not build on this land."

"Unless I *comply*?" He shakes his head. "Lady, you cannot shut this down. You have no authority. You're supposed to show up, tick some boxes, and leave. End of story. That's all there is to it."

The nerve of this man! "You know what?"

"What?" he shouts, his face inches from mine.

"You don't deserve that lambicorn."

His expression pinches in confusion. "What?"

I point behind him, to the creature who has followed him outside. The poor baby bleats pathetically. "The lambicorn. You know, the small, innocent being who thinks you're its mother? Well, you would make the worst mother in the world."

His face changes then, shifting from its slow-boiling fury to a cold, icy mask.

When he speaks next, his tone makes me feel like I'm being erased. "Get off my site. Take your police tape and leave."

"Fine by me."

"Good!"

I grab the roll of tape, and even though I'm doing everything to calm my inner turmoil, power builds, ley lines throb red, and the tape bursts into flames.

I screech and drop it to the ground. I stomp on the flames until they're out, hoping Stone didn't see.

"Are you an arsonist, too?" he accuses.

"No, I am not an arsonist." I snatch the tape from the ground.

"Then why was it on fire?"

"The sun . . . did something." The tips of my fingers are singed, and I blow on them.

"It's cloudy," he corrects.

"It spontaneously combusted!"

As I walk away, he shouts, "Don't ever show your face here again, or I'll make sure you're fired!"

My stomach plummets. This is the job I was meant for. No one else can do it, and I've completely screwed up.

I want to burst into tears.

No. I will not cry. I won't be overlooked.

There's only one thing that can make this better, and that's where I'm headed now.

Chapter 5

COCO

"So this is your office," Cristina says.

I rise from my desk and make a grand gesture with my arm. "Please, enter my domain."

My friend laughs as she walks in, her gaze brushing over the room.

"I know what you're thinking: How could a country girl like me wind up with such an elegant space?"

"It *is* nice." She playfully punches my arm. "You did good, kid."

The office *is* nice, with big windows overlooking Main Street. When I arrived yesterday, the desk was butted up to said windows, but that felt a bit too open, so I moved it into a corner.

Cristina crosses to the bookshelves on the wall. "Wow. You've moved in fast."

"No, those were left by Dot, the woman who had this office before me. I guess she passed away and no one ever took her books."

"Judging by the thickness of the dust on these shelves, looks like Dot came ages before you."

She lifts a dusty finger to prove her point, and I smirk. "It's nothing a little elbow grease can't fix."

"True. Not to mention she left quite the collection—we've got history of the town, crochet patterns, and then . . ." Cristina sucks in a breath. "Have you seen this?"

"What?"

I walk over as she pulls a black book halfway out from its slot, revealing just enough cover to expose the title: *Spells and Craft.*

I study the silver swirling script. "Is that real?"

"I don't know." Cristina pulls her blond hair over one shoulder and begins braiding it. "But who in town would have a book like that? Not after what happened."

"Maybe she was one of *them*."

"I doubt it. You know what people think about witches around here." She shivers, stares at the book for one more beat before saying, "You should get rid of it."

"It's harmless."

Worry thickens her voice. "I don't know."

"Besides, witches don't exist."

Right? That's not what I am. I'm not a witch. I'm a person with blue sparkles on her fingers who sometimes touches things that just so happen to spontaneously combust.

This does not make me a witch.

I tip my head and give my friend a teasing look. "Do we actually think an old lady who worked in Zoning for twenty years hid a real spell book in this office?"

Before Cristina can reply, I grab the book and open it. The air in the room shifts, and a breeze ticks up the back of my neck, lifting my hair so that it flutters over my shoulders.

The page I've opened to reveals a "spell" for removing skin moles. I tap the paper. "Come on. This isn't magic. It's an old lady's remedy book."

"I don't know," Cristina says uneasily.

I push the book back into its place on the shelf. "I'm not going to worry about it. Come on. I didn't ask you to lunch so we could stare at my boring office. Let's grab something to eat."

"I'm so glad you called." Cristina dabs her mouth with a napkin. "Gloria's never disappoints. This empanada is amazing."

I nibble my own golden-brown pastry. The inside is lovely—cumin-infused ground beef with a citrusy tang. The filling sings in my mouth as the buttery crust melts on my tongue.

I moan. "This is the only thing that could make me feel better today—a meal from Gloria's."

"Your wish was my command, milady," my friend jokes.

Gloria's sits near the end of Main Street, next door to Sparkle Bar, the local watering hole. Across the street is city hall, where only an hour ago I marched inside and dropped off the *kill* paperwork for the resort.

Then I called Cristina.

The streets of Mystic Meadows bustle with tourists. The unicorn statue in the middle of it all shines bright, its hooves high in the air like it's leading the town to victory.

"Okay, what's wrong?" my friend asks. "You never eat this many carbs for lunch. So I'm guessing either your mom called to announce Brittany's running for president and has a real shot of winning, or you've ended a relationship. Since you're not dating anyone, my bets are on the White House."

"I eat carbs," I argue.

"Not deep-fried ones—and not three at a time."

I eye the trio of empanadas sitting on my plate. "You have a point."

"So, what's up? Wait. Did they try to get you to come work in the family business again?"

"No. That ship sailed a long time ago. I did them a favor by taking a position in licenses."

Mainly I didn't join the family business because I'm not the star. I'm not some big influencer. Everything with me is so messy my mom doesn't even see me. If she did, she'd probably turn toward Brittany even more.

Cristina nods in understanding. "So, how is the new job going?"

I groan.

"Come on, it can't be that bad."

I steel myself and admit glumly, "When Rowe returns from her honeymoon, she's going to kill me, is how it's going."

"What are you talking about?"

I put this as delicately as possible, given the fact that one of my best friends doesn't know about my stupid fingers or that I can see ley lines. You saw how Cristina reacted to the book. What will she do if she finds out about my *curse*—I mean, gift?

"There are, um, certain zoning regulations that aren't in line with the Summit the Maddoxes are building. I told Stone very politely and he wouldn't listen, so I may have gotten some police tape, wrapped it around the building, and went to city hall, filing paperwork to suspend their construction permit."

As I speak, Cristina's eyes get wider and wider and wider. She finally blinks. "I'm sorry. Did you say you *killed* the Maddox resort?"

I cringe. "When you put it that way, it sounds awful. But believe me, there's a good reason for it."

"You told Stone Maddox— Have you seen him by the way? Pane is handsome, but there's something about Stone. He's not as polished as Pane, a little rough around the edges. In a good way. Here I thought you were going to tell me you met him and had wild sex on his desk. Not that you killed the project."

"Cristina . . ." I chastise.

"I know, you don't have wild sex. But I can't imagine Pane would allow construction to be wrong. He's built before. The family knows what they're doing."

"Yes," I reply slowly, "but Mystic Meadows is different. We have ley lines."

My friend puffs out her lips as she considers this. "But how does that matter when it comes to construction?"

"Well, um . . ."

"How is everything, my darlings?" Gloria appears beside our outdoor table. The restaurateur is in her sixties (probably) and emigrated from Cuba thirty years ago. Her dark hair is streaked with gray, and she wears a pink apron with the name of her shop scrolled across it. She's built like a grandmother and smells like spice and cinnamon. Her personality is warm, welcoming, and I feel like she's a second mother to me, even though I don't actually know her beyond the restaurant.

But you know, a person can dream.

"The food is great," I tell her.

"Wonderful." She pats my shoulder. "Enjoy, and let me know if you need anything."

"We will," Cristina says brightly, but as soon as Gloria's gone, she shoots me a pointed look. "So you're killing the project."

"Yes. *No.*" I drop my voice and lean forward, hoping to make her understand. "All Stone Maddox has to do is make some changes and everything will be fine."

"What kind of changes?"

"Just a few small ones," I lie.

The last thing I want to admit is that Stone needs to break all the concrete that's been poured and start over. The more I've sat with this, the more I've realized that if the resort hadn't been built directly on ley lines, none of this would probably matter.

But it was, and here we are.

She shrugs. "I know Pane, and he's pretty reasonable. Like, very reasonable. I don't know Stone at all, but if what you're saying is something that has to be done, I'm sure they'll fix it."

"Well, he was pretty angry."

Cristina's gaze scans the street. "Speak of the devil. Here he comes now."

"*What?*" I screech.

I turn and sure enough, a huge white SUV comes to a screeching halt outside city hall.

The door flings open and Stone Maddox steps out, slams the door, and yells, "Dammit!"

Then he opens the door again and pulls something out.

"What's that?" Cristina asks.

"A lambicorn. According to him, it showed up on the site today."

"Oh my gosh! It's so adorable! I want to pet it."

She rises and I yank her back down. "Don't. Do you see how mad he is?"

Stone charges into city hall with the lambicorn kicking the air playfully as it follows behind.

I slowly eat my empanada, watching the door with bated breath. A few minutes after he enters, Stone storms back out, his face even redder than before.

Oh no. This can only mean one thing: He tried to get my filing thrown out but it held, and now his construction is for sure delayed.

He's going to kill me.

Stone's gaze tracks across the road and finds me.

I duck down and my nose lands squarely in my lunch. My stomach is in knots, and now my nose drips with empanada juice.

"Did he see me?" I squeak.

"Yep."

"How does he look?"

Cristina pauses. "Can a person look angrier than a volcano?"

"Considering that volcanoes are filled with lava, I don't think so."

"Then he's officially hit world-obliterating anger level."

This is not good.

I peek through the slats in the small fence sectioning off part of the sidewalk for Gloria's diners, and spot Stone Maddox, looking bigger than life, being escorted by a kicking and bleating lambicorn that I think may have just passed gas and shot a rainbow from its butt.

I turn my face back to my plate.

A second later, a shadow falls over me. I squeeze my eyes shut. I do not want to look up. I do not want to look up.

Then comes Stone's casual voice. "Whatcha doing?"

I don't answer, thinking maybe he'll go away if I ignore him.

"Baaaaaaaa," the lambicorn bleats beside him.

I feel a tap on my shoulder. "You. Whatcha doing?"

It appears I don't have the power of invisibility, which to be honest, is really too bad. I would trade my blue sparky fingers for it in a snap.

I slowly unfold and look up. The jade of Stone's eyes has turned molten with fury and a shadow falls over his jaw, making his scowl look even gloomier, darker, more foreboding. And why, under all this fury, does his sharp gaze rattle me more than the fury does?

I wipe my nose with a napkin and play dumb. "Are you talking to me?"

He sneers in disgust. "Was I talking to you? Yeah, I was talking to you. You got my project shut down."

"It's not my fault," I argue. "The materials you're using—"

"Look at this town!" He throws his hands up. "It's fine. It's perfect! There's nothing wrong with it."

He's so loud people turn to look. At him. At me. At us. Arguing. I spot Mrs. Malfree walking her portly black pug, who wheezes with every step. Mrs. Malfree knows my mom, which means she'll be ratting on me within five minutes. A call from Mom will be incoming by the top of the hour.

I can just hear her now: *Brittany's never gotten into a street fight before. Does your sister need to have a talk with you?*

I want to scream.

Stone shoves his finger in my face. "You need to march over to that building"—he cocks his head toward city hall—"and un-file your paperwork. Then I never want to see your face again."

I grind out, "No."

He blinks. I guess he's not used to someone standing up to him. "What did you say?"

"I said, no. I won't do it. I stand by my filing."

"All right." He drums his fingers impatiently on the white fencing. "Then show me."

"Show you what?"

"Where my construction is ruining this town."

"What?"

He pushes away from the fence with very muscled forearms. Muscled fingers, too. "If you're so certain I'll destroy Mystic Meadows, prove it."

My stomach flips over. His building is weakening the lines, but there might not actually be *proof* of that yet. All I spotted was a brown patch of grass. What if there isn't anything else to shore up my case?

And what if there is?

I drop my napkin and say to Cristina, "This will only take a minute. Hold my empanadas."

She reaches for my plate. "Do you actually want me to—"

"No, I don't. It's a saying."

Stone wipes a hand down his tired-looking face. "She meant it like guys do when we say, *Hold my beer*. Little Miss Pretends-to-Be-Mayor is trying to be funny."

Our gazes latch and we glare at one another.

It is *on*. I will find proof his resort is destroying my town. I will find it right now, because if I'm wrong, I won't just embarrass myself. I'll prove that I *am* nothing more than what he says—a nobody playing mayor.

Just how much can one heart break in a day?

Chapter 6

STONE

"And there it was—a tiny patch of wilting flowers, right on the outskirts of town."

Clarice Sinclair sets a fresh mojito beside me. "Another?"

"Sure. What the hell. My project's destroyed. I might as well drown in sugar while I'm at it." The older woman glares at me, and I instantly regret what I said. "Sorry, Clarice. It's been a bad day."

Isaac shuffles the cards and deals them around the table. One to Ron, one to McCauley, and one to me. "Texas Hold'em, okay?"

"It's fine," we all reply, not in unison.

"So how bad was the spot of land?" McCauley asks as he shoves hair from his eyes. McCauley is the yard guy in Mystic Meadows, makes a fortune mowing and sculpting lawns.

Sounds like a cake walk, and right now, I wish my job was that easy.

Who am I kidding?

I'm a Maddox.

We do not do easy or convenient.

I sit up and stare at the cards. Three of spades and eight of diamonds—two unconnected cards, which means there's little chance of winning this round. Figures I'd be dealt a shit hand. Just one more strike against today.

To McCauley, I say, "The wilting flowers weren't bad. A couple of dandelions and brown grass that looked like Roundup had been dumped on it. But when I tried to point that out, oh no, the whole thing was proof enough to *that woman*—"

"Coco," Ron corrects lightly, as is his way.

"Whatever."

Coco Higginbotham. Of course I haven't forgotten her name, but the guys don't need to know that. They might act like fourth graders and think I'm sweet on her. For the record, I am *not*—nor was I at any point—*sweet* on that woman.

That might be a lie.

The point is, I don't do sweet. I don't do feelings. I don't do anything but frustration, and even that's been rising today, bubbling under my skin. I push it down in an attempt to remain neutral.

Feelings lead to things like . . . *feeling*.

And I've had enough of it.

"The grass was proof enough that the materials we're using—which she said are somehow not allowed—are destroying the ley lines."

The lambicorn presses its head to my leg and I pull away. Let someone else take care of it. I'm done.

Done.

"And then what happened?" Isaac asks.

"She marched to city hall with pictures she took, like it was a crime scene, and insisted the whole town will suffer if construction doesn't remain shut down until I change the building materials. It wasn't enough that she'd already revoked the permit. She added the pictures on top to strengthen her case."

What a nightmare.

This is the first signature project my brother and I have taken on without our mother's money underneath us—and my entire future hinges on it being successful.

When I worked with the Maddox Group, there was always a cushion. Failure was never a possibility. And when we began building the Summit, failure wasn't even a flicker in my mind because of support from the community and my cousin Rhett coming on board. But now . . . it feels like I've been tossed into the ocean with a life raft just out of reach. Oh, and I'm surrounded by sharks.

Sharks that all look like Coco Higginbotham.

With silky, dark hair and big doe eyes.

Shut it down, Stone. She is the enemy.

If I have to tell Pane and my cousin we've got to start over because of some ley lines? Good grief. Not only will we be behind schedule, but we'll also be over budget.

Well, I could always go back to working with Sylvia.

Hell no.

Not after what she did.

"What are you doing about the building?" Isaac asks.

"I put a call in to my attorney. Hopefully, we'll have this cleared up by tomorrow. It needs to be fixed tomorrow because my cousin is set to arrive soon, and if he sees us stalled, Rhett will have my ass. So will Pane. Hell, I'll have my own ass."

"Can your lambicorn have milk?" Clarice shouts from the bar.

"Goat's milk," I shout back. "Do you have any?"

"There's some in the fridge," Isaac tells her. When the three of us throw him questioning looks, he shrugs. "What? I got some today in case you showed up for poker tonight."

Ron pats the baby sheep, which still sits at my feet. Damn thing hasn't left my side all day.

So Ron, Isaac, and McCauley are actually Pane's friends, but I inherited them when I began work on the project.

It's been good to have friends in this town.

"Have you fed the lambi yet?" Ron asks, stroking its thick coat. "It looks hungry."

"No, I haven't fed it," I snap. "I've been busy trying to save the resort from a small woman who thinks she runs this town."

"Who, Coco?" Isaac laughs. "She's just trying to do what she thinks is right."

"Well, she's a real pain."

Even if she was adorable at first, with the whole pencil-in-her-hair thing and the joke about a cat poster in my trailer, those thoughts are now gone. I've erased from my body all semblance of anything that remotely hints at fledgling affection for her.

But Coco's still under my skin and she's not even here. I'm wound up. My chest is in knots, and feelings pulse through me in a manner I don't like.

I deal with it the only way I know how—by biting back.

"We've got a deadline," I growl. "No matter what, I'll get this project finished, and I won't be breaking concrete." The guys are silent as they study their hands. "And another thing," I add. "Who dropped that pile of bricks on the wrong side of the site? They left a mess."

Without looking up, Isaac answers with, "That was Antoine. New guy."

"Fire him."

Ron stops organizing the cards in his hand. "I thought you said, 'Fire him.' Must be hearing things."

"You're not. Fire. Him."

"The guy's got kids, a family. Trying to make a fresh start," Isaac tells me, like I'm supposed to be someone who cares.

"Not my problem."

The table goes silent except for Clarice, who gives a low whistle. "You're not like your brother, are you?"

"What's that supposed to mean?" I snap.

"Means whatever you think it does." She sets the bowl of milk beside the lambicorn. The sheep laps it up like its life depends on it. "Poor thing's thirsty."

"I didn't ask to be its mom," I grouch. "Would you like to have it? You can own a magical creature for free. People would pay millions for such an adorable thing. It might even have magic, though I don't know what that is yet, other than the gift to follow me everywhere."

"Better a creature than a human," Isaac mumbles.

"What's that?" I ask.

Isaac rearranges the cards in his hand and doesn't look up when he replies, "People and magic don't mix well in Mystic Meadows."

"You said that before. What's it about?"

He hitches a shoulder to his ear. "There are stories."

"What kind?"

McCauley pipes up when Isaac doesn't answer. "There's one about a garden. But what I remember is about a guy who lived outside town—named Tom. This was when the magic was really strong, so over twenty years ago. Folks said he could light candles without touching them, among other things. Then one day he vanished. No note. Just a burned-down house and a lot of rumors."

"But that doesn't mean someone hurt him," I challenge.

"Doesn't *not* mean it," Ron says darkly.

"All you need to know is that magic and animals, good," Isaac explains. "People and magic, bad. But I wouldn't worry about it. That lambicorn looks partial to you."

"That's what everyone keeps telling me, but I'm not interested. I don't even know why I care so much about *not* caring."

That's not true. I know, and I don't like it. Frustration bunches up my muscles, and I exhale a sigh so hard my lungs deflate. Everything in me shifts, coils, like I've got to explain it.

Before I can stop myself, I grumble, "When you grew up believing your dad didn't give a shit about you—a lie concocted by your own mother—the last thing a person's interested in is being responsible for something that can be hurt."

There's a long stretch of quiet at the table. My insides feel raw, jagged, the edges razor sharp.

Good God. Why don't I just open my mouth and vomit all my secrets? It's that woman. First my mom called, and then Coco spun me out of control.

"It was all Sylvia Maddox being Sylvia Maddox," I add bitterly. "Besides, do I look like a mother to any of you?"

McCauley eyes me. "Get rid of that scruff on your face and maybe you could pass for female."

"Ha ha. Hysterical. I can see why my brother likes hanging out with the three of you."

Ron talks around a mouthful of potato chips. "Before all that stuff came up with Coco, it looked like the two of y'all were getting along."

The men stare at me, waiting for an answer. Are they serious? "Are you talking to me? You think Coco and I were getting along?"

"You did give her a hard hat," Isaac points out.

"Yeah, so she wouldn't die from a freak accident. It would be just my luck an inspector gets killed. And so we're clear, Ron, that woman and I were *not* getting along."

We were *totally* getting along, and it pisses me the hell off.

The lambicorn finishes lapping the milk and then curls up beside my chair. For a flicker, I note how cute it is.

Cute for someone else.

I study my hand. Two pair. Nothing that'll win. "Fold."

I drop my cards on the table and plow my fingers through my hair. There's got to be a way to keep the resort on schedule.

Clearly, demanding Coco change her mind won't budge her. The whole thing makes no sense. There weren't any restrictions on materials that I know of, yet she's saying there are.

She's also saying the ley lines are affected.

Wait a minute . . .

The ley lines.

The police tape. It didn't burn. It was ignited.

There wasn't a lighter in her hand, and no one, for the weeks that we've been working, has said one damn thing about ley lines.

Except *her*.

Because maybe she can somehow sense them.

Maybe she can even *see* them.

Shit.

That's it.

Coco can see ley lines. She has magic—magic she doesn't want anyone to discover.

Wait. Before I jump to conclusions, I need to go back and think.

So I replay the entire exchange in my mind, and when I'm finished, only one answer seems possible. My stomach flips. My fingers flex on the table. This is it. This is how I'll save everything.

Coco Higginbotham, the tables have just turned on you.

Though this feels like victory, another part of me hedges. If what the guys say is true, this could be bad for her.

Don't worry. Nothing bad will happen to Coco.

Not that I'll make sure of it. I just don't think it will.

"Do any of you know where Coco lives?"

Ron eyes me suspiciously. "You're not going to do anything dumb, are you?"

"No, of course not."

I'm definitely going to do something dumb. But this isn't for me. It's for the project. It's for my future. I'm protecting what needs to be protected—the resort, which will bring millions in revenue to Mystic Meadows. I'm building, but Coco wants to rip the future apart. Two can play that game.

"Just thought I'd talk to her, see if we can come to an agreement."

The guys tell me she lives within walking distance. I rise, slide on my jacket, and head out of Sparkle Bar.

Coco Higginbotham has no idea what's about to hit her.

Chapter 7

COCO

"What's this about a man yelling at you on the street?" Mom asks over the phone.

Turns out, Mrs. Malfree and her wheezing pug didn't disappoint. Mom called five minutes after Stone confronted me, and I put off phoning her back until late—long after I'd inspected the earth with Stone, and well past when I'd dropped my grandmother's ring off at the jeweler's.

My gaze floats over the tiny cottage I rent at the edge of town. The payment is cheap and the roof leaks often (okay, every time it rains), but it's my own space and it's painted yellow, my favorite color. Plus, the old woman who lived here before left all the furniture. Which means doilies protect the surfaces.

"Sorry I didn't phone earlier. I've been busy."

"It's fine, sweetheart. I was worried the man did something to you. Your father asked if we should head over and make sure you're still alive."

"I'm good. Tell Dad thanks, though."

I plop onto the velveteen couch. The material is great during the winter—soft and snug—but awful in summer. In August, I can't even look at the thing because the idea of peeling my body off it makes me want to break into hives. But in early spring, the cushions are cozy enough to curl up on.

So I do.

"So, this man?" she prods again.

"It was nothing. Just something to do with work."

"Did his license expire?"

My chest wobbles like it's about to burst into tears. I inhale sharply and instantly stop the sensation.

"Yeah, something about his license. We got it worked out, though."

What's the point of correcting her? She won't remember—not on purpose, but because Brittany takes up all her headspace.

"Well, since it's nothing big, I'll let you go. Oh wait—do you have camo you can wear on Saturday?"

No, I don't, but instead I fib. "I'll check."

"Great. Brittany wants to tape our annual hide-and-seek."

Awesome with a heavy dose of sarcasm. "Can't wait. See you then."

"Love you, hon."

"Love you."

As the call goes dead, there's a knock at my front door, which is about ten feet from where I'm sitting.

What now?

Through the window cut into the door, I spot a figure.

Who in the world knocks at eight o'clock at night? For goodness' sake, I'm wearing French poodle–themed pajamas. I'm not fit to receive visitors.

The knock comes again. "I can see you. I know you're in there."

The voice is low, gravelly, and bears a strong resemble to Stone Maddox's.

No way.

Stone Maddox cannot be here.

On my doorstep.

At night.

Wanting to come in.

My stomach twists, and just to accentuate it, blue sparks pop on my fingers.

"Ouch," I hiss, shoving my fingers in my mouth.

"It's Stone," he confirms.

What does he want?

The power surge fades, so I get up and flip the lock, but keep the chain latched. Then I open the door two inches.

"Hey." It sounds like a nice greeting, but his jade eyes are cold as liquid stone.

At his feet, the lambicorn also greets me. *"Baaaaaaa."*

I refuse to melt just because a small, adorable creature has attached itself to the devil. "Yes?"

"I was wondering if we could talk."

"About what?"

"The resort."

"There's nothing to talk about." I throw my hands up. "I've filed my report and the recommendation has been accepted."

"I know," he explodes. Then stops. Taps his fingers on his hips and tries again, this time in a calmer voice. "I know. It's just, I realize *we*—you and I—got off on the wrong foot, and I was wondering if we could maybe change that."

"How will we change it?"

"Let me in and I'll tell you." His jaw works overtime before he whispers, *"Please."*

I want to say no, I really do, but there's an earnestness in his voice that suggests he's telling the truth. "You smell like mojitos."

"I may have had one at Sparkle Bar. It was poker night."

"And they serve mojitos?"

"Clarice Sinclair's running the bar tonight. Do you know her?"

I burst into laughter. "Of course. Everyone in town knows Clarice. She has a habit of wiggling into my private life."

"Just yours?" he says, his voice teasing. "I think she likes to be in everyone's."

We stare at each other for a moment and I soften. It couldn't hurt to hear him out, right? I shut the door and unlatch the chain.

I open it and gesture for Stone to enter. The lambicorn steps inside, looks up at me, and bleats as if it longs for connection. I pick up the baby sheep and hug it, reveling in its warmth and melting at how soft its fleece coat feels against my neck. I rub my chin over the back of its head.

I just love this little guy.

Stone surveys the tiny house. "I never pegged you for someone who decorated like my great-grandmother."

"I never pegged you for someone who liked lambicorns."

"I don't," he says wryly.

"Me neither."

The tension is back as we stare at one another. My hackles rise, but I quickly remind myself that he's here to be nice.

So he says.

"Would you like some water?"

"Sure."

"Please. Make yourself at home."

As he sits in one of three options in the cramped space, I pour him a glass from the filtered pitcher.

"*Spells and Craft*," he murmurs.

Shoot. I hadn't realized the book was out. I'd brought it home from work wondering if it could offer insight into my blue sparks and the ley-line-seeing thing. But I haven't had a chance to read it. My stomach has been too tied up in knots over everything that happened today.

I hand Stone a glass of water and take the book from where it sits on the coffee table. Then I shove it in a small bookcase.

"It's just a bunch of folklore," I tell him dismissively.

His gaze remains glued on the book for several beats before it drops to his glass. "Thank you."

"You're welcome." I set my own water on the coffee table doily and sit on the couch, tucking my legs underneath me. "I would ask how you found out where I live, but this is a small town."

"It sure is." He takes a long sip of water, watching me so closely over the rim of the glass that a shiver squirms down my spine. "You know, for a small town, there sure are a lot of secrets."

Why's he looking at me like that? "Really? I've never noticed."

"I bet you haven't."

The lilt in his voice suggests the opposite. "That's funny. It sounds like you're suggesting I might know some of those secrets."

"Don't you?"

"Don't I, *what*?"

"Have some of your own?"

"Secrets," I deadpan.

"Yes."

I run my fingers through my long hair. "I'm sorry, I'm not sure what you're talking about."

"I think you do."

Trying to kill some of the tension in the room, I glance down at the lamb, who sits by his feet. "Your dadda has gone crazy. He's suggesting I have secrets."

I bring the glass to my mouth and sip the water just as Stone says, "I know about the ley lines."

"You know about the ley lines? That's great! When will you start fixing what's broken?"

"You don't understand." He leans back and stretches his legs in front of him lazily, as if he suddenly holds all the cards. Then he levels a gaze on me that spears straight through my throat. "I know you can see them."

The room goes so quiet you could hear a feather fall.

The second his words slam into me, blood pounds in my ears. Under me, my legs lock. I wrestle down a lump in my throat. "What are you talking about?"

He tucks his arms behind his head. "I figured you'd try to play this off, but here's the thing: No one mentioned a word about ley lines until you showed up. Then you appear, the ley lines are a problem, and somehow a roll of police tape ignites in your hand."

"I told you, the sun."

"There was no sun," he snaps, so hard that I clamp my lips shut. Stone drops his hands and says in a low, dangerous voice, "I know what you are, Coco. And I know what will happen if people find out. Some things don't go over well in small towns, do they?"

They don't. People get kicked out. Shunned. Worse.

Much, much worse.

I lift my nose. "You know what I think?"

"I can't wait to hear this."

"You're delusional. You've hit a roadblock and can't accept that maybe you have to change something in order to fix the resort. Instead of doing what you need to, you'd rather railroad, threaten, and destroy me."

"Destroy you?" He laughs. Darkness flashes over his eyes when he adds, "How can I destroy someone who doesn't even matter?"

His words slice me in half. He must see my reaction, because he flinches, and for half a second his gaze flicks to the lambicorn. The creature whimpers softly, brushing against his boot like it felt the wound, too.

Stone shifts in his chair like the floor beneath him has tilted. But then he blinks, shakes it off, and turns back. It makes me wonder whether his words were so harsh that they hurt him as well.

"You can see the lines and you don't want anyone to know. But I know because you can't hide from me."

Beneath my feet, the earth pulses, shudders. I reel my emotions back in and shake my head. "You don't see anything about me." I rise. "You've had your fun. You've shown up. You've drunk some water. Time to go."

His jade eyes sparkle with victory. The emotion is so thick it makes a knot clog up my throat. It takes every ounce of willpower I have to tamp down the fear churning like a tide in my gut.

Stone rises. He towers over me, signaling a reminder of exactly how small I am. I don't feel physically threatened. I'm not worried for my safety. But he is big, powerful, and rich.

And I'm a shadow in his path.

He slides his hands into his pockets. "If you don't pull the paperwork and tell city hall you made a mistake," he warns, "then I will make sure everyone in town knows what you are."

I fold my arms, trying to muster every ounce of false bravado bouncing around in my body. Trust me, there isn't much. "It's not true."

"Right. And that's why you don't have that spell book over there."

"That's just a . . . that's a . . ."

I can't find an excuse because *all the words* have disappeared from my head.

He nods. "That's what I thought."

Stone moves past me to head out, but before he reaches the door, he turns. "You have until tomorrow morning. Thanks for the water."

He pulls a dollar from his pocket and drops it on the bookcase. His jaw flickers briefly as if he's weighing this choice. But then he leaves with the lambicorn following close behind.

I flip the lock and slide the chain back in place before collapsing into the chair and dropping my head in my hands.

What am I going to do? If he tells, I'll be a . . . No, I can't think about it.

But of course I have to think about it. That's what we do, consider all the terrible consequences, tell ourselves somehow it makes things better to know the worst in any situation.

So what I'll be is a freak, a social outcast, a spawn of Satan.

Stone Maddox can't say a word. I can't let him reveal my secret.

But how can I stop him?

Just as I give up hope, a quiet hum fills the room. It's not coming from the fridge or any other appliance. I rise, searching it out.

Is Stone still outside, humming to destroy my sanity?

Totally possible, but the sound originates from inside the cottage, and it grows as I approach the bookcase.

My gaze drops to the spines lined up in a tidy row. They look normal, but *something* is vibrating.

Curious, I run my fingers across the leather-bound books, wondering whether I'm going batty. But when my fingers brush the spell book, it *throbs*.

I shriek and jerk my hand away.

The spell book.

Its humming intensifies as if it's not just calling—it's waiting.

For me.

It wants me to open it. No, that can't be. Or can it?

Ever so slowly, I reach for it, my hands quaking as they slide the tome from the shelf.

I've almost got it out when I change my mind. "No."

I push the book back in place, but it continues humming. I hug my arms and stare at it. It seems to stare back.

"I won't use you."

But what if it could help? What if the book could solve this problem? What if it could save me from Stone Maddox? It probably can't, right?

But what else can I do? Wait for him to tell the town what I am? Wait for people to show up at my door with pitchforks?

The hum grows. It slides across my skin like goose bumps prickling my flesh.

It won't hurt to take a tiny peek, will it?

No, it won't.

Slowly, I slide the book from the shelf.

Ready or not, here I come.

Chapter 8

COCO

As soon as the book is in my hands, the humming stops. I place it on the coffee table and sit on the rug underneath, tugging on the frayed woven fabric as I blow out a gusty breath.

There probably isn't a spell inside that will help, and even if there is, more than likely I won't be able to cast it. I'm not really a witch.

At that thought, sparks fly from my fingers and set one of my romance novels on fire.

"Ah!"

I jump up, bang my knee on the table, hobble-run to the kitchen, wet a towel, and extinguish the fire, which is mostly out by the time I reach it anyway.

I was not about to let one of my romance novels go down in a blaze.

Adrenaline rushes in my veins as I sit back down. "That wasn't good," I murmur, unfolding my legs and staring at the book. It feels like my bones are rattling inside my skin. My breath is too big to be held.

"It's all okay," I tell myself. "I'm going to open this book and see if there's a spell that will do what I need. There probably isn't, but it doesn't hurt to look, right?"

Of course it doesn't hurt, just like it doesn't hurt to window-shop. This is practically the same thing.

Besides, Stone won't listen to me. So maybe there's something in here that will help him see what I do.

I've tried reason. I've tried explaining. I've even had him shut down—but Stone Maddox refuses to bend.

He doesn't see *me*.

And I don't need him to.

But I do need him to see the truth.

I peel the cover back slowly, and a wind rips through the room, blowing my hair across my face. The lights flicker. The windows shudder.

I drop the cover and sit back. That's a coincidence, right?

Sure. A coincidence.

The windows are old. The electrical is ancient. The air conditioner kicked on.

A shaky breath slips from my mouth, and I decide to try again. The moment my fingers touch the book, it buzzes. I flinch, but swallow down my worry and open it. The same thing happens—wind slices, windows rattle, lights quiver.

I scoot back. "It's time for reinforcements."

Cristina yawns as she opens the door. She tugs at the bathrobe she wears over a pair of silky pajamas. At her feet sits a piggycorn. A rumble comes from inside the house and suddenly five more of the little creatures appear. They race down the hallway toward the door, sliding to a stop on their rumps, each bumping into the one in front of it, and pushing the first piggy onto the porch.

They're adorable, with tufts of pink fur atop heads from which a delicate golden horn protrudes. They are the cutest.

Almost, if not cuter than a lambicorn.

"Come in," Cristina says tiredly. "The piggies came to greet you."

I run my fingers atop silky heads of hair as I follow Cristina into the old farmhouse. It smells like baked bread and patchouli—yeasty and welcoming.

"When do Rowe and Pane return?" I ask as we enter the kitchen.

Cristina pulls out a pan and a carton of milk. "I can't remember. In a few weeks? From the pictures, it looks like they're having a great time in Fiji."

"I bet." I scan the counter and spot pictures of Rowe and Pane dotting the surface. "And her mom? Doesn't she live here, too?"

"Moved in with her boyfriend, Bill. But I think they're traveling in his RV."

"Oh, right. I knew that." Rowe and I are friends, but not besties. "And so you're watching the farm while they're gone?"

"Someone's gotta keep this place running," she says with a sly smirk. "Besides, with the spa, we're open five days a week."

Months ago, Rowe's farm was in foreclosure. But Pane turned it into a day spa as his entry in the competition to win the Maddox Group. Now it's a thriving establishment.

Cristina pulls her blond hair over one shoulder. "So tell me, what's all this about?"

"Well." I inhale a deep breath, hoping to find some courage. "Stone Maddox came by."

Her eyes widen. "Your house?"

I slide onto a stool at the breakfast bar. "He told me unless I find a way to make all this disappear, he's going to . . . ruin my life."

"Let me call Rowe."

Cristina reaches for her phone on the counter, but I grab it before she can wrap her fingers around it. "No. We're not calling Rowe on her honeymoon. I can handle this and I have a way—*maybe*."

"How's that?"

I unzip the fabric bag I sewed in high school when I was really into making my own clothes, and pull out the spell book.

Cristina takes one look and shakes her head. "No, Coco."

"Cristina—"

"No. I can't believe you even brought that here. Are you crazy? If something happens . . ." Her voice fades, but her pointed look does not.

"All that's in it are wart-removal recipes."

"Then why is it here?"

I stammer. "I—I just thought—"

"No." Cristina nods to the book. "No. That thing spells trouble, and I'm not trying to make a pun."

My entire body deflates. "I know this isn't what you expected when I asked to come over, but Stone Maddox is . . . what he's doing with the resort is wrong."

"How?"

"He needs to fix things but refuses to. If I can make Stone see the materials he's using are bad for Mystic Meadows"—yes, I thought this up on the way over—"then maybe he'll change them."

"'Change them'?"

"It's better than nothing."

She studies the book warily. "But, Coco . . ."

"I know what you're thinking—this is wrong. This is evil, this is all the bad stuff. But magic is back in our land, and no one's ever said a piggycorn is evil. Besides, it's all just stupid fun." I let that sink in and then add softly, "You don't think this will really work, do you?"

"Well, maybe . . ."

"Come on. It'll make me feel better."

My friend stares at the book for a long moment until she finally says, "Okay. Let's see what we've got."

I slowly open the spell book, and this time, a full-on gale rips through the room, rattling the rooster-painted dishes that hang on the walls.

The piggycorns scurry to the back of the kitchen, where they bunch into a huddle, glancing around the room nervously.

Cristina takes a step back and whispers, "I think we're going to need something stronger than hot chocolate."

Chapter 9

COCO

Ten minutes later, a frozen margarita sits to my left and Cristina is on my right.

I run my fingers down the book. "Ready?"

She lifts her glass. "More than ready."

I turn the first page, only to discover a message printed on the white-marbled vellum. It's written in loopy script that honestly makes me a touch envious.

But even though the script is pretty, the message is not.

WARNING. THE USE OF MAGIC ON THOSE AGAINST THEIR PERMISSION WILL HAVE DEVASTATING RESULTS—AND COULD LEAD TO DEATH.

"Um . . ." Cristina grimaces. "Do you think that's real?"

"It's an old spell book and is probably just a bunch of nonsense."

Even I don't quite believe that.

Cristina taps her fingers against the rim of her margarita glass. Indecision is written all over her face. She's seconds away from backing out.

"In our defense, we're not using this spell to hurt Stone. Besides, it's probably not going to work anyway."

I laugh weakly, but Cristina doesn't. "I don't know. It feels like we're dabbling in something we shouldn't."

My stomach twists into a pretzel. It does *feel* like that, and my inner compass, the one that generally points north, is spinning into a death spiral.

I can turn back now or I can move forward.

"Come on. Let's just have some fun. It's no big deal."

I offer Cristina an encouraging grin and she slowly nods. "Sure. No big deal. What's the worst that could happen?"

"We're not going to kill him."

"Right." She sounds more convinced now. "Let's do it."

I dive into the book, flipping pages. The spells are written in English, which is a blessing, but some have Latin-looking names.

I sip the mango margarita Cristina made. It's sweet with a touch of sour—just tart enough to make me keep sipping.

"What are we looking for?" she asks.

"I have no idea. But I'll know the spell when I see it."

"Okay." She peers over my shoulder. "Here's one to get rid of chin hair. I don't think you want that."

"Nope."

I flip the page and discover remedies for increasing beauty and teeth-whitening. This book is for sure old, since both of those things can now be done with surgery and toothpaste.

We keep scanning but only find entries for reheating your tea and soup.

It's not until we reach the middle of the book that the spells suddenly shift, and everything changes. The pages become more brittle. The ink, darker.

"Here's one for making dandelions bloom prematurely," my friend says. "Though be warned, bees might swarm."

"Good to know . . . Oh, here's a spell for a light hex lift. Temporarily removes minor curses."

"What about major ones?"

"I guess you're screwed."

She laughs and sips more of her drink. We turn the page, and both of us suck air.

"'To See Light,'" we say in unison.

Behind us, a picture frame clatters onto the counter. We jump.

Cristina and I exchange a worrisome glance before turning back to the book. I read the description: "A spell for someone to open their eyes."

Cristina continues where I left off: "To grant the recipient clarity of perception, allowing them to see that which lies beneath, beyond, or within. Often used to perceive magical auras, ley lines, or truth-bound illusions."

This is it! If I can get Stone to see the ley lines, then my problem is solved! He'll realize I'm right, he's wrong, and he'll fix the materials.

All will be well in the world!

Cristina's eyes sparkle with delight. "Co, this is full blown, like an orgasmic-level bomb that just dropped in our laps."

It is. It's like the book knew I needed someone to see ley lines and it delivered the goods. But I will temper my excitement. "Let's read the rest."

She keeps going. "Pierces all mental veils—internal and external—to reveal hidden truths. Ingredients: garlic, eggs, vinegar."

"Apple cider or white?"

She shrugs. "Doesn't say, but I'd go with apple cider and make sure you put some of the cloudy mother in it. Oh, wait. There's also glow grass."

"What's that?"

"I think it's what Rowe has. She can make her grass glow by lying in it and moving her arms up and down."

I clap cheerfully. "Yes! I've heard of that."

"It's in the backyard." She hunches over the book, still reading. "We also need something of the person who you're casting the spell on."

I pull a dollar bill from my bag. "This was his."

"How'd you get that?"

I wave her off. "Never mind."

My blood is zinging. This is real. This is happening. All we have to do is get the ingredients and cast the spell.

"Wait," she says, and my hopes crash and burn to the ground. "There's a warning."

"Another one?"

Cristina points to small script at the bottom of the page, and I read aloud: "Spell should not be used on individuals not possessing magical signatures. Ingestion of glow grass may result in identity instability, temporal disorientation, or full cognitive reset."

"Hmm. That is a problem," I muse. "So maybe we just use a pinch of glow grass?"

She nods. "Agreed. Hell, we don't even know if this spell's going to work. The book is old, and neither of us are witches."

I laugh uneasily. "Exactly. Okay, let's gather the ingredients and do some casting."

Twenty minutes later, we're eagerly watching a pot atop the stove bubble happily with water, garlic, egg whites, and vinegar. The kitchen smells like we're brewing up a mean all-purpose cleaner.

"Now we need a drop of your blood," Cristina says.

I frown. "Is this blood magic? I don't think that's good. Isn't that, like, frowned on in every witchy movie ever?"

"It's just one drop, and that's what the spell calls for."

"Okay." I get a knife from the drawer and position it over my finger. "Should I jab or slice? Wait. I might faint. I can't slice my own finger. Can you do it?"

Cristina eyes the knife. "Let me see if I can find a needle."

I exhale with relief. "Much better idea."

She leaves the room and returns with a small sewing kit. My friend digs out a needle and hands it to me. "Here you go."

I find a lighter and sterilize the tip. Then I poke my finger, watching as a bead of blood swells on my skin before it falls.

The pot hisses, and the lights flicker.

"Must be a storm on the way. Let me get some candles just in case we lose power," she mumbles.

Right. A storm.

She returns with the candles and lights them. I snip off a piece of the dollar bill and watch as it floats into the pot.

"I'm sure you could still spend the rest of that," she tells me.

"Oh yeah, there's a lot left over."

Cristina grabs the bundle of glow grass we harvested from outside. There's nothing magical looking about it now, but when we plucked it, it lit up like a Lite-Brite.

She drops a pinch in the pot. "Say the words."

"Why are you whispering?"

"I don't know," she still whispers. "This feels serious somehow."

I agree. My stomach is doing somersaults, while my skin buzzes with electricity.

I stir the ingredients and look back to the book, which lies open on a recipe stand. *"Lucem videre."*

The lights snap out, pitching us into darkness except for the warm glow of candlelight.

"Do you think that's bad?" Cristina asks.

"No, it's fine. Like you said—a storm must be passing through."

I'm sure she doesn't believe me, because I don't even believe myself.

There's a knot the size of a basketball in my throat. I swallow it down and say the next words. *"Veritatem videre."*

A wind howls through the kitchen, plastering my hair to my cheek. But I keep on.

"Veritatem videre. Lucem videre. Incantationem in noctem iacere."

The wind screams like the room is filled with the spirits of a thousand ghosts. The ingredients in the pot bubble turbulently.

Cristina grabs hold of my arm. "Coco, what have we gotten ourselves into?"

While she whips her head around like crazy, the chaos in the room—the howling wind, the bubbling and hissing ingredients—hits a crescendo.

It feels like a thousand strings shoot from my stomach, going in every direction. It isn't chaotic. This is in tune. I'm connected to the wind, the ingredients, the very earth. Underneath my feet, ley lines throb from miles away, strumming for me.

As the feeling intensifies, as the noises heighten, my stomach fills. It's a bubble growing inside my belly, rising with the intensity, putting pressure on my spine. And as it balloons, everything becomes louder, harder, deeper, and then all of a sudden—

The bubble pops.

The intense feeling falls away like a flower dropping petals in the breeze. The wind stops howling, and the pot gives one final death knell hiss. A line of steam rises, curls into a ball, and vanishes.

The lights flicker back on, and it feels like all the oxygen's been sucked from the room.

"That. Was. Wild," Cristina whispers.

The magic of the spell still lingers in the air, blanketing the atmosphere with energy.

Then it dissipates, too, just like the steam that vanished from the pot.

I exhale a shaky breath and respond to my friend. "Yeah, that *was* wild. What do we do now?"

She scans the text. "Now you bottle up some of the substance— Ew, that is gross."

I peek over the rim of the steel pot and agree. The mixture has taken on the appearance of dark-green slime.

Cristina pats my shoulder and says teasingly, "Now you get to feed it to him. According to the book, it won't take much. But he's got to eat it. I guess make sure whatever you put it in is delicious."

She blows out the candles and slides off the stool. "Do you have a plan for how you're going to get Stone Maddox to ingest that?"

It takes a moment for one to form, but once it does, it's solid.

A slow grin unwinds across my face, though inside, my stomach flutters. "Oh yes, he'll take it. And once he does? He'll see everything."

Cristina shoots me a worried look, but I wave her off.

"Maybe. It's just a joke, right? Nothing's going to happen."

Chapter 10

COCO

"What do you want?" comes Stone's grumpy voice from inside the trailer.

No one said this would be easy.

"I'd like to talk," I reply cheerfully.

A moment later the door swings open and Stone Maddox appears, scowling like a broody pirate hero in a romance novel. It wouldn't surprise me if he said, *Argh, walk the plank, missy.*

But he does not. Instead, he snaps, "If you've decided to accept my offer, you don't need to be here. You need to be at city hall, pulling the paperwork that's screwing me over!"

He shouts the last part with such force his breath blows my bangs from my eyes.

As much as I would like to say his breath smells awful, it doesn't. It carries notes of coffee and hazelnut.

Two things I love.

I lift the pastry box and sleeved to-go cup I'm holding. "I've come with a peace offering."

His gaze briefly flickers to the box before settling back on me. His eyes smolder—not in a good way. Instead of looking like he wants to strip off my clothes one piece at a time, Stone looks like he wants to tear me limb from limb.

I would much rather be stripped.

Wait a minute.

What am I thinking? I hate this man. Despise him. Detest him. Even if he does have molten-jade eyes.

He scoffs, yanking me from those strange thoughts about him, which I will now light on fire and forget ever existed.

Stone folds his arms. "I've already explained how you can bridge the peace between us. Or are you here to talk me out of telling your little secret?"

"Peace offering first? Then we discuss?"

"There's no discussion."

I shake the box. "I have breakfast."

At the doorway, the lambicorn appears, blinks up at me, and opens its mouth. *"Baaaaaaa."*

"Hey there, little cutie." As I pet the creature, I say to Stone, "I see you still have it."

"Can't get rid of the damn thing."

"Have you fed it?"

He shrugs. "It eats grass."

He is so *not* worthy. "Lambi, I was going to ask if your *mama* is being good to you, but looks like I have my answer."

"I should kick you out just for that."

"You should." I grin. "But don't you want to hear what I have to say?"

"You hold no cards here."

"No. But I *am* holding pastry—the best in town."

He eyes the box with lust. "Fine. Come in. But make it fast. I don't need more problems from you . . . in your skirt and your hair and your . . ." He gestures toward me, shakes his head. "Never mind."

My jaw unhinges. "My skirt? What are you talking about? It's a pencil ski—"

"I know what it is," he snaps.

"Well, I'm sorry my looks offend you." Fury bubbles and boils inside my veins. One of the ley lines flashes. I exhale. I didn't come here for a fight. Must rewind and start over. "Look, I'm sorry my appearance makes you feel . . . *however* you do."

His gaze turns so icy cold a shiver winds around my spine and practically lifts me off the ground. "Lady, I don't make it a habit of *feeling* anything."

His words are a sucker punch to the throat. I can barely breathe as I wrap my mind around what he just said. Stone doesn't feel? What does that even mean?

How can someone not feel? *Why* would someone not feel? Why would anyone do that? The best part of life is feeling.

"Then I'm very sorry for you," I reply quietly.

He eyes me like he's inspecting a crate of bananas straight from the Caribbean, waiting for the giant spider hiding inside to leap out onto his face.

After a long moment he finally says, "Come inside."

I squeeze through the doorway, as Stone doesn't bother moving to give me a wide berth.

He shuts the door, and I squirrel over to one side of the trailer as he storms past. The lambicorn follows. Stone plops into his chair, leans back, and props his red clay–caked boots on top of his desk.

Despite everything else about him, Stone Maddox is rugged and rough. I've seen Pane, his brother, and he's refined. Like an ironed napkin—smooth, no wrinkles, all perfection.

Where Pane is that, Stone is his crumpled-up-paper-napkin brother. One etched in gold, obviously. There's no telling how much those two are worth.

I timidly place the box and coffee on the desk. "Is it okay if I sit?"

"Let me see first." He opens the box, eyes the Danish, and nods. "You may sit."

"The coffee's black. Creature Comforts has a great cup. The beans are custom roasted."

"I know. I like their coffee."

"It's good, right?"

"Oh yeah, it's one of the things I like best about this town," he says, his eyes shining as they land on me.

For a split second our gazes lock and all the anger between us dissolves.

For a split second, that is. Next thing I know, he's scowling again like a petulant child.

Stone pulls the Danish from the box, and I hold my breath. "I didn't eat this morning," he confesses.

I cross my fingers as he takes the first bite.

After I bought the pastry and coffee, I returned to my car and pulled out a small mason jar I'd stored the potion in. I unscrewed the lid, dipped in a spoon, and slathered what I hope is enough of the green goo onto the bottom of the Danish. It was thick and goopy. It also smelled slightly of vinegar.

Maybe Stone won't notice.

I then dropped a small spoonful in the coffee, too, stirred, and capped the lid.

My thinking was that if he didn't eat the Danish, maybe he'd drink the coffee.

Stone takes a big bite, frowns for half a second, and then keeps chewing. I exhale the breath I've been holding.

So far, so good.

"Now." He wipes his hands on a napkin I brought. "What did you want to talk about?"

"I was hoping we could walk outside."

"Why?"

There wasn't any information in the book about how long the spell will take to work, so I'm hoping it'll activate quickly and Stone will see the ley lines.

He watches me carefully. Oh no. I doubt one bite will be enough, so I pick up the coffee.

"You should wash your breakfast down."

I start to hand it to him, but my fingers slip and the cup tips over.

I watch in slow-motion horror as the rim hits the top of his desk and the lid pops off. Coffee spills everywhere, spraying onto his lap and sliding over the blotter on his desk, staining his papers.

Stone jumps up. "Son of a—"

"I'm so sorry!" My gaze skims the office, and I hope to find a paper towel dispenser nearby, but no such luck. My cheeks burn with humiliation. My hands shake.

This is going all wrong. All, all wrong.

Grabbing the few napkins I brought, I blot Stone's shirt. "I'm so, so sorry! I can't believe I've done this. I'm such a klutz."

"I've got it," he snarls. When I try to blot him again, he takes both of my hands in his. An electric shock jolts down my body, and I jump back. He releases me and says darkly, "Was your plan to melt my skin?"

"No, it wasn't." I curl my hands into balls to stop them from shaking. It doesn't help, so I just stash them behind my back. "I really did come here to give you this peace offering."

"Well, good job. The Danish sucked and now I'm covered in coffee."

So he *could* taste the potion. Well, that answers my question about the flavor.

He unbuttons his shirt and yanks it off. "If there's nothing else, you may leave. Unless you're about to make a phone call."

Stone crosses to a closet and opens it, taking a shirt off a hanger. My jaw opens slightly at how muscled he is. His arms have ridges and hills that flex with every movement.

I should not be staring at him, but I can't help it.

He keeps talking, and I force myself to look away from his muscles and concentrate on his face as he puts on the shirt. A thought occurs to me: Is this how guys feel about boobs? Are they as entranced by them as I am with man muscles?

"One call," he explains. "That's all it'll take to clear up this mess. You can do that, or I can tell the mayor's office about his newest magical land coordinator."

This. Is. Humiliating. There's no way one bite of the Danish worked, and of course I've destroyed the coffee, and fat chance Stone will take food or drink from me again.

I've lost.

I'll lose my job, my family will know my secret, and instead of thinking I'm awesome like Brittany, they'll shun me for being weird and different—even more different than I already am.

Stone stares at me, no doubt wondering why I'm not answering. If he only knew that I'm contemplating all my life's horrible choices and how each failure led me to this one moment, the moment where I break in half.

I mop up the last puddle of coffee from his desk and murmur, "I was trying to make things better, but I've only made them worse."

What do I do now? Let the magic be destroyed, or allow him to reveal my secret?

There's really no choice, is there? My decision is made.

"Wait," he says, but his voice is garbled.

I glance up as Stone reels back. He claws at his neck, his face turning bright red. Worry sifts through me.

Is the potion working? What is it doing?

Is it . . . hurting him?

His eyes meet mine, and they're wide with fear. Stone opens his mouth. Reaches toward me—

His knees buckle.

"Stone!"

I lunge forward as he crumples, face-first, onto the floor.

I don't think he's breathing.

A crack echoes through me as if my own bones are breaking. My lungs seize. A cold, slithering wave of nausea coils in my gut.

Oh my God.

I just killed Stone Maddox.

Chapter 11

COCO

I tuck my hands underneath Stone and try to flip him over. My God, he must weigh two hundred pounds. It takes all my strength to get him on his back.

I collapse against him and press an ear to his chest. Nothing. Oh, God. He's really dead. I've actually killed him.

The taste of metal fills my mouth, bile claws up the back of my throat, and all I can think to do is bargain with God. *Please, God, if he lives I will never touch magic again. I'll do whatever you want. I'll be nicer to people. Smell more roses. Anything, if Stone Maddox just lives.*

I never should have opened that spell book. I should have listened to Cristina.

My gaze falls to Stone's collar, where a triangle of white peeks out from underneath his button-down.

Of course I can't hear his heartbeat—the man has two shirts on.

With that one thought, the small promise of relief makes me inhale, dims the pulsing worry that heats my body.

I must find another way to check his pulse.

Think, Coco. Remember every CPR class you've ever had. I had to take it every year when I was a summer lifeguard.

I slide two fingers to his neck, searching for a beating artery. My face has gone completely hot. Sweat sprouts under my arms and my palms are drenched.

The lambicorn rushes over and butts Stone's head gently, trying to wake him.

"It's okay," I tell the lambi.

The sheep takes one look at me, lifts its nose, and returns to pushing against Stone.

Did the creature just throw shade?

The lambicorn bleats again, and a faint beat drums beneath my fingers.

Oh, thank God! He's not dead!

Oxygen swooshes through my lungs and tears prick my eyes. What a relief. It feels like the world has color again and I can breathe.

"Stone! Wake up! Wake up!"

Though it's *more than* tempting to slap him awake—let's face it, he would most certainly deserve it—I shake him instead.

"Wake up!"

His eyelids flutter before slowly opening, and the jade is clear and bright.

The darkness I'm used to seeing when he's angry at me—which is literally every single encounter we've had—isn't there.

"Are you okay?" I prod.

He sees me, nods, scans the office.

"Can you sit up?"

"Yeah."

I move aside, pushing down the hem of my pencil skirt—you know, the ones he hates. "How do you feel?"

"Okay." He nods again. "What happened?" he asks in a gentle voice.

I've never heard this tone from him.

"Do you feel okay?"

He stretches his arms, blinks. "Yeah. I feel great."

He starts to get up, but his eyes widen and he sits back down.

"You sure you're okay?"

"Oh yeah." He dismisses me with a wave. "There's just one thing."

"What's that?"

He scratches his head. "Can you tell me who I am? I can't seem to remember."

Chapter 12

COCO

Is Stone joking? He's joking, right? Got to be. I search his face for signs that he's pulling my leg, or arm, or entire body.

"You . . . don't know who you are?"

He scratches the scruff on his cheek. "It's the strangest thing. One moment I was—well, I can't remember what I was doing. And the next . . ." He shakes his head. "Did I hit my head?"

Quick, Coco, lie. Ugh, how far I've fallen. Since I can't exactly reveal that I spelled him, it's the next best explanation. "Yes, you hit your head."

He looks around. "On what?"

My gaze lands on the thing closest to me. "A hard hat. Yep. You hit your head on a hard hat. Wow. They are making those things way too . . . *hard* nowadays."

I grab his hat from off the desk and knock my fist against the top of it to demonstrate.

He scrunches his face in curiosity. "How did I do that?"

"It fell. From the ceiling. I don't know how it got up there. But it dropped right on your head." I reach for Stone, but stop short of actually touching him. "Does it hurt?"

He rubs his head and frowns. "It's fine. I probably needed to shake something loose anyway. Man. Must be a really hard hat. I mean, I can't remember *a thing*."

Wow. He bought it. He bought my lie.

Part of me regrets saying it, but another part of me knows this is called self-preservation, and I need to be preserving as much of myself as possible.

Stone shoots me a lopsided grin that highlights how handsome he is. My stomach flips, traitorous and ridiculous, because now is not the time for that. "My memory'll come back soon. I'm not a quitter. At least, I don't think so."

God, please don't let him ask me if he's a quitter. And he's right: Maybe his memory will launch right on back into his brain in a few minutes.

He starts to rise and I push him down so hard he shoots me a shocked look. "Maybe you should stay put for a second."

"I'm fine. Don't make a big deal about it. What're you going to have me do next, take a nap?"

Maybe?

His eyes suddenly flare in surprise, and I think, *He's remembered who he is and will have me arrested for trying to poison him.*

But this isn't what he says. Instead, awe fills his voice. "Is that a *lambicorn*?"

I blink. It's worse than poisoning. I've completely wrecked his brain.

"It *is* a lambicorn." Stone frowns in distaste, which makes rows of lines cut across his forehead. "What's it doing?"

I rub my forehead as the lambicorn sniffs the floor. "It's checking out the carpet."

"It looks hungry."

"Yeah, it probably is." *Because you haven't fed it.*

Stone opens his arms and says tenderly, "Come here, little guy."

What's happening?

Isn't he supposed to kick the lambicorn? Ignore it? Attempt to give it to me?

But this is not what Stone does. He rises, crosses over to the creature, and pets it.

My knees go weak, but I straighten, locking them tight. This isn't sweet. This is terrifying. He's not acting like Stone—he's acting like someone who cares about things.

This is not the Stone Maddox of five minutes ago. That Stone Maddox would rather shoot out his own eye than pet that lambicorn.

"If you'll excuse me, I need to make a quick phone call." I poke the air for emphasis. "Don't go anywhere."

He picks up the lambi and nuzzles his face against it like it's his favorite stuffed teddy from childhood. "How could I go anywhere when this cutie is here?"

This is all wrong. I dash from the trailer so fast my shoe nearly pops off. Outside, I dial Cristina's number. My stomach is in knots. I'm sweating. Pressure builds in my fingers.

In front of me, a ley line flashes red. I exhale slowly.

Calm down, Coco.

Cristina answers five rings after my near cardiac arrest. "So, how'd it go? Nothing, right? That's what I was afraid of. Well, we tried."

"No," I whisper-shriek. "It's much worse than nothing happening."

"What do you mean?"

My insides curl up and die, just like I want to. "I'm in deep trouble."

"Why?"

"He's lost his memory."

She gasps. "What?" I hear the sound of a car honking, and Cristina yells, "Sorry!"

"Don't have an accident," I tell her, cringing.

"How can I not? Let me pull over." When her voice comes back on the line, it's crisp, and the background muffle of being on Bluetooth is gone. "He has amnesia?"

"Yes. No. I don't know." I ball up a fist and press it to my eye, inhaling and exhaling deeply, trying to calm my electrified nerve endings. "Yes. I think so. He can't remember who he is."

"We're in deep shit."

"I know! What do we do?"

"Don't panic."

"It's too late for that."

The trailer door opens and Stone appears with the lambicorn tucked under one arm. "Hey, I think this little guy's starving. Should we get it some milk?"

"Yes, we will," I say, forcing brightness in my voice. "Let me just finish this call."

"Okay." He pauses and surveys the empty construction site. "Where are we?"

I sway on my feet but catch myself from falling. "I'll tell you all about it. Give me just a minute."

"Hey, I ate some of that pastry on the desk."

"No! Don't eat that!"

"Too late. It's gone. Had a weird aftertaste."

It feels like my body is collapsing in on itself. "I'll be inside in just a minute and we'll get all of this sorted out."

"Yeah, that would be great. Because I still don't know who I am."

"Your name is Stone Maddox."

A divot appears between his brows as he considers this. "Nope. Doesn't ring a bell."

"Of course it doesn't," I mumble. After eating the entire Danish of Amnesia, it wouldn't.

"Maybe I should go to a hospital."

"One minute." I lift a finger. "Give me just one."

"Sure, this little lambi and I will hang out until you're done."

"Great."

I give him a tight smile, impatiently waiting for him to disappear so I can figure out how to extract myself from this mess before I'm sentenced to death by firing squad in front of the entire town—or something even more archaic, like *stoning*.

After he finally disappears inside the trailer, I collapse against the side of the building.

Cristina's voice breaks the silence. "Holy shit, Co."

"I know. That's what I'm trying to tell you."

"Can you come to the farm? I'll turn around and go back. Bring Stone and the book. Let's see if there's a way out of this."

"I'll be there in ten minutes."

It's lucky I still have the book with me, having left it in my car, as by the time I got home from Wadley Farms last night, I was exhausted.

So that's the one good thing about right now. The one bad thing, however, is Stone.

Amnesia Stone gets distracted by many things.

"Whose office is this?" he asks when I enter the trailer.

"Yours," I say, beaming while trying not to die on the inside.

"Really? There's no personality to it. It doesn't seem like me."

I grab the empty Danish box and toss it in the trash. "That's probably because it's temporary. Come on. I've got an idea on how to get your memory back."

"Thank goodness, because I'm going out of my mind." He stares at the blank walls, scours the desk surface. "If it wasn't for that lambicorn, I'd probably be tearing my hair out."

"Well, we don't want you doing that. Let's go."

He starts to follow me and stops. "Wait."

I turn around. "Yes?"

"How do I know if you're a good witch or a bad witch?"

My breath hitches. "What?"

"That line just came to me. It's from a movie, isn't it?"

My stiff shoulders loosen in relief. It's just a line he remembers. He's not accusing me of anything. But maybe he should be. "Yes, it's from *The Wizard of Oz*. It's very famous. See? You've got some of your memory in there."

"Yeah." He smirks, and those jade eyes of his are warm, welcoming. They flicker down my body, lingering on my legs before they climb back up, settling on my face. "I know you're a good witch."

"Sorry?"

"I mean, good." He shakes his head. "Not a witch. Just good."

It feels like a thousand eels are slithering inside in my stomach. "Let's see if we can get you fixed up."

"What are those little cuties?" Stone asks as we pull up to Wadley Farms and a dozen piggycorns rush to the fence to greet us. "Are those *piggycorns*?"

"They are, indeed."

Stone lifts the lambicorn's front hoof and waves it. "Look, your little cousins are coming to meet you."

I have really got to get his memory back. I almost like the old Stone better.

Almost.

Don't hold me to that.

Cristina greets us at the door. "Stone, meet my friend Cristina."

"How are you?" he asks. "I'd take your hand, but I'm holding this little guy."

"He's very cute," Cristina admires.

"Isn't he? Or she?" Stone frowns at me. "Does it have a name?"

"I don't believe so."

Is this really what we're worried about right now when you have amnesia?

"Do you have any milk?" Stone asks as we step inside. Then he stops and gazes around the foyer. It's a gorgeous space. The walls are painted a welcoming green with clean white trim. There's a cozy waiting room and a mahogany reception desk constructed of old doors. The place smells like wisteria and cotton.

Stone whistles. "Nice. I love the design—it's so sleek. Very posh. And the smell." He snaps his head in Cristina's direction. "This is a spa, right?" Before she can answer he adds, "I've been here before. The design feels familiar."

"That's because you know the designer."

"I do?"

"Yes, you do," I say, tugging his arm.

I'm not interested in explaining more—like, you know, telling Stone he has a brother. Once that can of worms opens, he'll call Pane.

I'll be immediately implicated. I'll be fired. My life will implode. But hey, my mom will finally notice what I'm doing, because I'll be front page news.

Stone nods in understanding, but his eyes are vacant. "Right. I know the designer."

Cristina grimaces, and I shrug like, *Yes, this is the level of amnesia we're dealing with. We'd better fix him, and fast.*

She points to the kitchen. "You'll find milk in the fridge. Feel free to give that little fella whatever you need."

The lambicorn bleats as Stone walks off.

"We're going to prison," she whispers once he can't hear us. "Or worse—someone will disappear us."

"I know." I cringe. "This is so bad."

She stares at me like, *Duh.* "So?"

"So . . . what?"

"What's his amnesia like?"

"What does that mean? It's amnesia. I don't know specifics." I drop my voice to a whisper. "This is *magically* induced. I don't know if there are *rules* to how it's supposed to go. And if there are, I didn't see them on the page with the spell."

She shakes her head. "We are so screwed. But! Let's be positive. You did *bring* the book."

I hold it up. "Here it is."

"Let's see if we can find a reversal spell."

We rush into the office and open the book. This time, the breeze that flicks through my hair doesn't faze me. We turn to the spell we used, looking for—hell, I don't know what, an antidote to jump off the page.

Cristina points to a black smudge. "What's that?"

"What's what?"

"This. I think it's words."

"It's so tiny. It looks like dirt."

She pulls open desk drawers, frantically searching. "There's got to be a magnifying glass in here somewhere."

I frown at the book. "You think *those* are words?"

"Pretty sure."

Then I need to schedule an appointment with the eye doctor, 'cause I don't see it.

"Found one!"

She crouches above the page, holding the lens. "Yes! It's words. See?"

I huddle beside her and gasp as text comes into view. "If things go awry and the spell-caster needs an antidote, it can be found on page 462." I raise my brows. "Wow. That's very specific—and I don't remember seeing numbers on the pages, do you?"

As soon as the words leave my mouth, numbers float to the top of one corner, like seagrass surfacing on a lake.

She straightens. "Did you see that?"

"I saw it," I squeak. "Maybe we imagined it."

"Nope. Not imagined. I'm going to scoot on over to page 462."

"Good idea."

My voice is no louder than the sound of a mouse scrabbling across a floor. I shove down the mix of worry and fear that's pooling in my belly and wait until Cristina finds the page.

"Here. There's a spell." She scans it and flaps her hands in excitement. "This is doable. You could absolutely do this. Yes! Okay. Oh, wait."

Her expression falls and so does my hope. "What? What's wrong?"

"This one ingredient, lunaria bloom. What it that?"

I'm about to look it up on my phone when the sound of someone clearing their throat comes from the doorway. Stone stands at the threshold, holding the lambicorn in one hand and an apple in the other. He talks between bites.

"Good news."

"You got your memory back?" I ask.

"No. The lambicorn is a *he* and I've named him Hercules."

It's the cutest. Name. Ever.

My stomach lurches. Oh Lord, I'm going to be sick.

Stone continues, "There's also another lambicorn outside. I saw it with the piggycorns."

"Oh. That's great."

"Thanks." His gaze flicks to the book. "So. Whatcha doing?"

I slam the book shut. "Just some research on amnesia."

"Any luck so far?" he asks.

"Still working on it." *And no, this isn't a spell book in case he asks.*

"Okay," he says sharply. His eyes darken like they usually do when he and I are in the same room. I knew this niceness wouldn't last forever. It was too good to be true. "There's just one thing."

"What's that?" I ask.

Stone's eyes narrow to slitty wedges of death. "Exactly *who* are you?"

An even better question is, how much of the truth and how much of a lie do I tell him?

Chapter 13

COCO

"Sorry," I say, dismissing him with a friendly wave. "In all the commotion, I forgot that *you* forgot."

Stone swallows a bite of apple. "Yeah, nothing's come back yet."

He levels a steely gaze on me. Or *is* it steely? It feels steely. Like, soul-stripping, the kind of gaze that peels back layers and instantly spots the truth.

It makes me feel like he'll say at any moment, *You poisoned me and I lost my memory! You're going to jail, where a woman named Bertha will make you her girlfriend and you'll do anything for a cigarette.*

Anything.

The first rule of lying is to keep the lie in the same hemisphere as the truth—not that I'm an expert. I don't generally lie. However, this situation is an exception to the rule. To be clear, *my* rule about *not* lying.

"You and I? We work together."

"How?"

"On the project."

"What project?"

"The resort."

"*What* resort?"

I sigh. This is harder than it should be. "You are building a resort in Mystic Meadows."

The lambicorn bleats and he puts it down. Stone takes a bite of the apple, leans against the doorframe, and watches me with a gaze that makes me want to disappear even more than I normally do. "Why am I doing that? Building a resort?"

Beside me, Cristina holds her breath. I'm not sure if it's because she's waiting to see whether, at any point, Stone will recover his memory, or I'm going to lie about every question he asks.

I clasp my hands tightly. "You're building a resort because you see the potential to make a lot of money. Mystic Meadows, my town, recently had some cool things happen."

"Like what?"

"Like, well, the lambicorn."

His gaze falls to Hercules, who looks up at him, too. Stone's expression softens. "I gotta say, this little guy is super cute. I bet when I recover my memory, I'll discover I have an entire farm filled with creatures like this one."

"I doubt it," I mutter.

Cristina elbows me. "Maybe you can take Stone back to the site and see if it jogs anything. Meanwhile, I'll look into this." She taps the book. "Between the two of us, we'll help get your memory back."

"Let's hope so," Stone murmurs.

"Whatever this is, it's temporary. I'll fix it. I always do." He considers this. "At least, I think so."

On our drive back to the construction site, Stone pulls out his wallet and checks his ID. "It says I live in New York. That doesn't feel right." He turns to me. "Why doesn't that feel right?"

"I think a lot of things aren't going to feel right." *Like how nice you're being to me.* "Once your memory returns, you'll get everything sorted out."

"But I'm not a big-city guy. I'm like a tropical island, piña colada kind of guy who uses a machete to clear a rainforest. Does that sound right?"

"Well, uh—"

"Tell me about this project we're working on."

Relieved he didn't force me to answer the machete-rainforest-tropical-drink-with-an-umbrella question, I happily divert. "You're building a world-class resort right here called the Summit at Mystic Meadows."

He folds his arms. "And how are you involved?" There's a noise in the back and Stone peeks between the seats. "Hercules," he says in a gentle but firm voice, "don't eat the seat."

"It's fine." *It's the least I can do for ruining your life.* "He's not going to harm anything."

Stone turns back around. "What were we talking about? Yes! I remember! Whew. Thank goodness I remember one thing. The resort. How are we working together?"

"I'm what's called a magical land coordinator. My job is to make sure the project works alongside the magic in Mystic Meadows."

"And is it? Is the project doing that?"

"Oh, look, we're here. Right back at the trailer."

"Yeah, where I got my memory knocked out. But that's okay, I feel it coming back. Just gotta make sure I don't bang my head on any more hard hats. Come on, Hercules. You ready to get out?"

I park the car and we exit, heading toward the building.

Stone takes two steps and stops. "Something's wrong."

Oh no, here it comes. He's remembered and recalls how much he hates me and how he was going to blackmail me, and what's worse is now he has even more blackmail material. *Want me to tell the police you nearly killed me? I will build this resort however I damn well please.*

He scans the site, brow furrowed, a dark shadow passing over his face. "Why isn't anyone working? If this is a construction site, where is everyone?"

"Well, uh, that's a good question . . ." As I flounder to tell him, an idea hits me. "Hey! Let's go inside."

"What? Why?"

"Because maybe if you look at the plans, it'll trigger your memory. Help you recover some of it."

He snaps his fingers. "Yes, that's a great idea!"

Before I can stop him, he rushes over and scoops me up, lifting me into the sky. "You are brilliant!"

His arms are strong, and he raises me like I weigh no more than a sheet of paper. I look down at him as he gazes up at me, and there's a beat—a stretched moment where my throat closes.

The warmth in his eyes. The heat of his touch. It all hits me hard, and I laugh, a small, startled sound, like someone who's never been picked first finally being seen.

Stone laughs, too, and the sound makes my lungs squeeze.

"Sorry. Got carried away," he explains, slowly lowering me to the ground. He stares down at me, and I find myself wanting to keep looking into his eyes. This strange man who I couldn't stand yesterday is someone new today.

A man who doesn't know who he is, I remind myself.

I clear my throat and step out of his arms. "It's okay."

"You know, I don't even know your name."

"It's Coco Higginbotham."

"Higginbotham. That's a mouthful."

I tuck a strand of hair behind my ear. "That's what you said when we first met."

"See? I'm in here. Somewhere." He winks playfully, and I nearly pass out from the utter and complete change in him. "Come on. Let's take a look at these plans and see if they jog my memory."

Stone taps the page. "Why would I design the resort like this? It makes no sense. It's all flow but no essence."

The blueprints are a series of lines with tiny writing. It's like trying to read a foreign language. I cock my head to see if a different angle will help.

Nope. Doesn't do a thing.

"Like right here." He runs a finger across the map-sized sheet of paper. "The finishes are sleek, but there's no personality. It's cold, sterile. This isn't something I did. This needs to be changed. Immediately. Where's my phone?"

My body goes numb. His phone? Stone's phone will have contacts. People who know him. People who will freak out about his amnesia.

Or they could help him remember.

I spot the phone on top of a filing cabinet. There's a brief tug in my core. Give it to him? Don't give it to him?

Coco, the imaginary angel sitting on my shoulder whispers, *he needs to remember who he is.*

"It's right here." I slide the phone from the surface and hold it like a peace offering. "Maybe you can get some answers."

He scowls. Here it comes. The old Stone is back. It was good knowing you, New Stone. I nearly mutter to Hercules, *Get ready to return to being hated.*

Stone takes the device and pauses briefly.

My stomach curls into a giant pretzel. He'll open his contacts. Call his brother. Discover I'm a horrible human being. The resort will be built. My town will be destroyed.

"I don't remember the passcode," he says after a beat.

"Maybe it's your face."

He shakes his head. "No. It would never be that simple. I need more security than a face or a thumbprint. Don't ask me how I know that, but I do."

"Well, see if any numbers come to mind." *Why am I signing my own death warrant?*

Very slowly, Stone enters a series of numbers. The screen quivers. It instantly locks him out.

My pretzeled stomach unknots a tiny bit. "It'll come to you. I'm sure it will."

"Yeah," he says uneasily. "I hope so." Then he levels a lopsided grin at me that's so warm it's disorienting. "I can't believe I signed off on this design. Whoever I need to talk to about changing it, I will."

"Here's a fun fact," I say, smoothing a hand over the blueprints. "You're the boss, so you don't actually have to talk to anyone. You can do whatever you want."

"That's right." Amazement laces his voice. "I am. I'm the boss. Maybe that's why all the guys aren't here—they also disagree with the plans and they're on strike."

"I don't think that's how it works."

He breezes past me, taking the blueprints with him.

"Where are you going?"

"To check out the building."

"Right behind you."

Hercules follows, kicking up his back legs with glee as we pick our way over the red clay–topped construction site.

Stone charges over the earth, striding so fast I can barely keep up. Gosh, but he is tall—and really built. And that's just the start. He's also got a broad chest, and thick, sandy hair. And those eyes— Okay, I've already talked about them. But today they're all warmth and not molten anger.

He's nice, this Stone.

I mean, you know, for right now. For someone who doesn't know who he is, he's nice.

He reaches the foundation and walks around the space, studying, nodding, shaking his head.

I keep a safe distance, ready to answer any and all questions. After a couple of minutes, he crosses back over to me with the rolled blueprints tucked under one arm.

"How could I do this?"

Curiosity piqued, I ask, "Do what?"

He points. "You see those lines over there? They run under the resort."

My knees buckle, and my voice comes out hoarse when I ask. "What did you say?"

"They're ley lines. Right?"

My nerve endings ignite. It feels like I've been stabbed with a thousand tiny needles in every sensitive spot on my body.

I nod absently.

His gaze tracks the ley lines. "I see where they're coming in, under the foundation, but where they go out, they're weak. Look, they're headed straight for town. If I let construction stay this way, it'll be detrimental. At least, I think so." He turns to me. "Don't you think?"

I nod again.

Holy shit.

The spell worked. Stone Maddox sees the ley lines and now he wants to help. He wants to change the building!

For once, someone sees what I do. He sees what needs to be done and he's listening to me.

And then the worst thought possible takes root in my head: *I'll never let Stone return to who he was. Even if it kills me.*

Chapter 14

STONE

I've destroyed the ley lines. They're weak and it's all my fault.

It's difficult to explain what losing your memory is like. I feel certain things innately—like when I said I seemed like a tropical island kind of guy. That's me. For sure that's me.

But people? I have no idea who's important in my life. That's terrifying. No doubt I've got a best friend out there who could walk me through this. If he's out there, I'll find him.

Right now, I've got Coco, and she feels like an anchor, like a way to ground myself, and more than anything, I need grounding.

But back to the ley lines.

They're so obviously present. How could I have ignored them before? The glowing, milky-white streams run right under the site, and when they come out the other side, their pulse is nearly obliterated.

Coco said this is *my* construction. Well, what kind of man am I to see something so beautiful and pretend it doesn't matter? Minimize it, ignore it, walk all over it, even when it's staring me in the face?

My actions were on a path to destroy this town, and I feel awful about it, like I don't belong here.

Coco moves to pick up Hercules. The lambicorn scampers away, hiding behind my leg. "He's just shy," I explain.

I pick up the baby and hand him to her. Our fingers brush, and my lungs do this very strange tightening thing.

"Thank you," she says, her lips tipping up timidly.

"You are very welcome."

She coos in the lambi's ear, "Let's wave to the town." She lifts his hoof and the lambicorn bleats before it squirms, wanting down.

Watching her, I realize Coco belongs here. She didn't ruin anything. She didn't wreck ley lines. But I did.

Who *was* I this morning?

A feeling falls on me, dropping like a thousand gallons of water: Am I even likable?

I am now—*I think.* Maybe that's all that matters.

Coco puts Hercules down, brushes her hands on her skirt, and walks over. "Everything okay?"

"No. I don't recognize the man who okayed these plans." My gaze sweeps over her, and her presence feels familiar. Her smile is warm. Her eyes are, too. So it feels right to say, "But I recognize something about you."

Coco blinks. Her cheeks turn red.

"I mean, it's very easy to be around you. Must be because we work well together," I clarify.

She clears her throat and nods to the hideous monstrosity that's supposed to be the beginnings of a resort. "It's the materials."

She's so pretty. Yeah, I know. I'm supposed to focus on what she's saying, but I can't. Correction: I *will* focus in a moment.

For now, I drink her in. Coco's got really dark hair and hazel eyes—green and brown rimmed in gold. She's also got this adorable nose with a little bump on the bridge. And her curves are spectacular—she's round and soft in all the right places. Just looking at her makes my chest seize.

Not to mention what another body part of mine does.

Are we more than two people working together? Whatever we are, I can't mess this up like I nearly messed up the resort.

She nods to the foundation. "The materials," she tells me again.

"What was that?"

She sidles up beside me, and I get a whiff of her scent. She smells so good, like lavender and cedarwood. Like a scent I should remember.

"The foundation is hampering the lines. Limecrete would be a better choice than concrete, and other materials can be used instead of the steel beams." She wrinkles her nose. "What? Why are you looking at me like that?"

"Was I looking at you in some way?"

"Yeah."

I cock my chin. "How? Do I have resting dickface or something?"

She throws her head back and laughs. The sound warms me, and I can't help but smile. I may have screwed up the building, but I haven't screwed up things with her. Good.

At least I've done one thing right. I'm here to build a resort, but maybe I need to build something else first. Something I lost.

Right then, my stomach growls and I realize I'm famished. "You hungry?"

She wipes tears from her eyes with the back of her hand, still laughing. "Yeah. Are you?"

"Starving. Let's find someplace to eat." I scan the site and see a white SUV. "Is that mine?"

"It is."

"Great. I'll drive. That, I can remember how to do. I *think*. We'll find out. Come on." I walk off but turn around, stepping backward. "And don't think you're getting off the hook from answering my question. I know I've got resting dickface. Be honest."

She laughs again and a fissure of happiness spreads through me.

I do remember how to drive—and no, I don't hit anyone or anything on the way to the restaurant. It's really strange. I can't grasp anything solid about myself—no names, no faces, no history. Just skills. I know how to drive but not who taught me. Can quote movies but can't picture watching them. It's like someone deleted my life but left the operating manual. That's about the best description I can come up with to explain what this feels like.

All those thoughts are set aside when I get my first glimpse of town. I do a double take, in a good way. White buildings sparkle like sugar under the sun. Painted rainbows dance on nearly every windowpane. A unicorn statue stands tall in the square like a guardian of joy. It's ridiculous. And perfect.

It seems like I've arrived in a place that only exists in dreams.

Or maybe a movie.

"I've been missing this place my entire life," I murmur as we drive down Main Street.

Coco laughs again and my stomach does this whole constricting thing. It's so easy to be around her. Plus, she *was* at the trailer bright and early this morning.

Did she stay over last night?

Oh my God. I have no idea where I sleep.

"Mystic Meadows is pretty special," she says, sounding genuinely proud. "For a long time the ley lines were latent, but in the past few months they renewed, and we want to keep things that way."

"And the unicorn?"

"There are unicorns here."

I nearly slam on the brakes. "Get out."

This shouldn't take me by surprise since Hercules is a lambicorn, but you know, amnesia and all.

"No." She drums her fingers on the door. "We really have them. Do you want to meet one?"

"Hell yes, I want to meet one. Who doesn't want to meet a unicorn?"

"I'll see what I can do."

"Will it have magical powers? Will it look into my soul and tell me if I'm a good witch or a bad witch?"

Coco's face changes and her expression becomes worried. I grab her arm and lightly shake it. Her gaze darts up to meet mine and my pulse quickens. "I'm just kidding. I know that I'm a bad witch and you're a good witch."

She smirks and points for me to pull over.

"Where will we be dining today?" I ask, parking.

"At the best barbecue in town: Unicorn Tails."

"Well, with a name like that, it's got to be excellent."

Do I like barbecue? I have no idea, but I'm about to find out.

Inside, the place looks like a herd of unicorns battled an army of cowboys and somehow they both won. Small statues of unicorns dressed in Western saddles and bridles are sprinkled throughout the place. There are even six-foot paintings of them. No lie.

I might buy one. Add it to my collcction.

Wait. Do I have an art collection?

It seems like something I would have.

Dear God, I'm going crazy. This temporary forgetfulness should be over by now, but it isn't. It's staying with me.

Okay, Stone. Don't panic. You are calm. You are cool. You are in control.

But I'm not, am I? There are no workers at the site. I'm destroying ley lines. The last thing I am is in control.

My heart shudders, and I breathe through it. No, I may not be in control, but that's okay. Sometimes you gotta wing it.

"So what's good here?" I ask as we sit.

"The barbecue."

"I figured that." I say it with a smirk and her lips slowly tip upward. "I mean, what should I order? Tell you what: You order for me. Get whatever you think I'll love. You know me."

She laughs nervously. "Sure. I'll order."

When the waitress walks up, Coco asks for two of the Unicorn Samplers and iced tea. Then I settle back in the booth and inhale the hickory smoke smell that permeates the place.

"I could never work here. I'd be hungry all day," I confess.

"You think?" she asks, twisting her straw wrapper around her finger.

"I do." I ball up my wrapper and drop it on the table. "All right, so the site. I've ruined the ley lines. What happened? Whoever I am . . . why did I do that? And do I have to move the resort? I feel like that's a bad idea. I'm not using my own money, am I?"

She takes a long sip of her tea, drinking for so long that she empties the glass and starts sucking in air. "I need more tea. Do you want some? Let me call the waitress back."

She lifts her hand to call the waitress, and I grab it gently and tug her arm down. "Why do I get the feeling you're not answering me on purpose?"

I'm still touching her. Her gaze falls to her arm, and I slowly unhook myself. As soon as my hand leaves her flesh, it feels like I've lost something.

Yeah, you've lost your memory, you big moron.

Coco rakes her bangs from her face. "Well, you didn't know."

I frown. "What do you mean, I didn't know?"

She pulls out her phone. "About the materials. I've mentioned the limecrete, and steel beams can be replaced with cross-laminated timber. It's called CLT for short. It's already been used successfully in high-rises. See?"

She taps her phone, and a moment later she's flashing a picture of a sleek, glass-front building. "This is in Milwaukee. You can use CLT to build the resort and it won't harm the ley lines."

"How do you know this?"

"Because it's more naturally friendly, which is what the ley lines need."

"Huh. And your research?"

"I've done some. I don't have all the answers, but I know a little."

"A little? Don't diminish yourself. You know a hell of a lot more than me. I'm just the guy ruining everything. You're the one fixing it."

She drags her teeth over her bottom lip in this absolutely adorable yet vulnerable gesture that makes my body harden.

She takes her phone back and taps again. "I can show you more. There are ley lines in a few other places in the world, and this is what they use to build, too."

I hitch a brow. "Do they have unicorns?"

"No, they don't. But they have ley lines."

Coco gives me a pointed look. She's earnest about this. I get the feeling, even though I've only just met her, that she wouldn't lie.

"So what you're saying is, I have to start over."

"If you want to keep the ley lines healthy, then yeah. Look, I know it's a big task, but it's what the land needs if it's to maintain and stay strong. Mystic Meadows just got its magic back, Stone. We can't lose it again."

No pressure.

But it's not even a debate. As I mull over how to do this, our food arrives. My plate is gigantic, and food fills every square inch.

"Thank you," I tell the waitress as she leaves to refill Coco's glass. "Okay. You have to tell me what all of this is."

"The yellow block is corn bread that they cook and then put on the griddle for a minute before serving. It's amazing. Those are baked beans—they're sweet, with bits of pork in them. Then there's the actual pulled pork. There's also macaroni and cheese, coleslaw, and for dessert, banana pudding."

"It's a feast, and I'm starving."

I take one bite of the corn bread and moan. "Oh my God. It's so buttery and—"

A coughing fit overtakes me, and I swallow several gulps of tea to wash down the corn bread.

Coco grimaces. "I forgot to warn you. You've got to be careful with corn bread. It's sometimes dry, which makes it easy to choke on."

I tap a fist to my sternum. "Better late than never."

For the next few minutes, I do nothing but eat gloriously amazing food and try to figure out a way to restart construction without killing the deadline, which I can't remember but know exists.

Screw it, I decide. Protecting this land is more important than a deadline. I'll take whatever heat someone throws at me. In the meantime, I've got to figure out how to get workers. Fingers crossed my memory returns by tomorrow.

As I dig into my second bite of pork, my phone rings. I pull it from my pocket and do a double take at the name flashing across the screen.

My stomach falls, but at the same time hope lifts within me.

"Do you know who it is?" Coco asks, peeking over to take a look.

"Yeah." A slow smile spreads across my face. "It's my brother." I toss back my head and laugh. "I have a brother! I'm not alone!"

Chapter 15

COCO

My stomach plummets to the floor and explodes into a million pieces.

Pane has called Stone.

Stone knows he has a brother.

My ass is so cooked.

Lines etch across Stone's brow as he studies the phone. His finger hovers over the screen briefly before he finally swipes and puts the device to his ear.

"Hey." He shoots me a worried look that asks, *Is* hey *something I say to answer calls?*

I don't answer, obviously. Instead, my gaze falls to my plate and the food I no longer have an appetite for. This is it. Stone will tell Pane he can't remember who he is. Pane will listen, probably panic a little, and realize there's no way in hell a hard hat fell from the ceiling, slapped Stone's noggin, and caused him to forget his entire life.

I deflate because the hammer is about to drop—right on me.

"Excuse me."

I head to the bathroom, as I can't bear to be present for my own undoing. And I was just beginning to like this version of Stone, too. But let's face it: When he told me to order for him because I "know" him, I died a little inside.

I don't know him.

He doesn't know me.

We don't even like each other.

It's clear now that my ask was too big. Fixing the resort while protecting the ley lines was too large a dream. I'm not a big dreamer. I'm a small person living a small life.

As if to confirm my own opinion of myself, blue sparks dance on my fingers. They smart, and I squeeze my hands closed.

"Go away," I snap.

They fizzle and die.

For once.

I finish up in the bathroom, splash cold water on my face, and text Cristina to see if she's discovered anything about the flower. What was it called again?

She doesn't answer, which probably means she's giving a massage. So there's nothing to do but face my demise. Oh well, it was fun saving my town the whole five seconds it lasted.

As I head back out, my stomach performs an Olympic gymnastics floor routine. Stone is now off the phone, and the heaviness of doom blankets me.

It might be better to grab my purse and make a break for it rather than take the verbal beating that's coming.

Stone sees me.

And smiles.

With genuine warmth.

A cozy feeling slowly bleeds over my chest. A feeling I quickly shake off.

There's no time for that here.

"Hey," he murmurs in a way you welcome someone who's cherished, not hated with an ever-loving passion.

"Hey," I squeak as I slide into the booth.

"How do they get it so gooey?"

"Sorry?"

He lifts a fork piled high with macaroni and cheese. Strings of cheddar stretch from his plate to the utensil. "The macaroni. How is it so gooey? And I mean that in the best way possible, of course."

I'm thrown off-kilter. My world is supposed to be imploding and he's talking about food? One thing I'll say about this new Stone Maddox: He certainly keeps me on my toes.

"Extra cheese, maybe?" I inhale a deep breath and decide to go for it. It's better to hear the truth from him now rather than wait until later. "So . . ."

He takes a bite of macaroni and moans. When he finishes chewing, he replies, "So . . . what?"

Is he serious? He's really going to make me say it? "You have a brother! It's amazing you remembered. What did he say when you told him?"

Stone sets his fork down. Emotions war in his eyes when he answers, "I didn't tell him."

My brain short-circuits. "What?"

"I have a brother named Pane. A sister named Natalie. But that's all the pieces I have. The blanks aren't filled in more than that," he growls. Scratches his cheek. "Sorry. Pane asked how the construction's going. I said great and kept it short. I don't *remember* how much he had to do with picking the building materials, and I didn't want to get into it."

"Why not?"

His brows lift in surprise. "Because I'm changing it. All of it. And I didn't want to tell him I can't remember anything, because I assume he won't let me touch the plans if he knows I can't recall who I am. Besides, I don't need him trusting my judgment."

"You don't?" The words slip out before I can stop them. "I mean, I can understand that. You'll probably remember any minute now, anyway."

"Yeah," he mumbles, jaw working. "The plans as they are now don't feel right. And for the sake of this town, I need to make them perfect."

My mouth drops. I have no idea what to say other than, "Oh, okay."

He stabs the macaroni with his fork. "I don't even know who I'm working with on the site. Who's the construction manager?"

A slow smile spreads across my face. "I know who your construction manager is."

"Great. Because we're gonna need him to start breaking up concrete. First thing tomorrow."

I shouldn't be happy about this. I should be worried, terrified, feeling that all this is wrong. But I don't.

This is macaroni-and-cheese goodness, not the fallout I expected.

Which means today is the *best day ever*.

"I have bad news," Cristina says when she calls me later.

After lunch, Stone and I returned to the construction site. He tried to get into his computer, but no luck. So instead, he made lists of building materials with the intention of heading to Mystic Meadows Hardware to order everything.

He's finished the list and is now playing fetch with Hercules, who is a quick learner.

"Go long!" Stone yells as he tosses the tennis ball we found in the office.

"Baaaaaaa!"

The lambicorn barrels toward the ball. Stone glances over at me and grins. "He's just getting down the basics right now. Don't worry, in a few days he'll be a pro."

I nearly die laughing.

"Co, are you here?" Cristina says, sounding impatient.

"Yes. Sorry. I'm here. You were saying something about bad news?"

"Well"—the sound muffles as if she's moving the phone from one ear to the other—"that lunaria bloom? I can't find anything about it."

"Maybe we don't need it."

"Great! His memory's returned?"

"Not exactly."

"Coco," she warns.

I ignore her foreboding tone of voice. "You remember how I had such a hard time with Stone? How he was so awful?"

"Remember? I saw it firsthand when he yelled at you."

"Right. Well, that seems to have disappeared and he's still kind of nice, like he was this morning."

There's a beat before she says, "It won't last."

My insides collapse as if she's right, but part of me wants to think maybe this *will* last—at least a little longer.

"Coco." Cristina's voice is stern. "He needs the antidote. What if he never remembers? Ever? Even if no one finds out what we did, this is still bad." She sighs. "I'm not even sure how it happened."

I am. I'm sure how and why. Because the same power that's stoking the land somehow stoked something inside me. So if my secret gets out—which, once Stone remembers who he is, it will because he'll keep his promise and tell everyone about me—I'm done for.

"He has remembered some. Pane called."

"No! What happened?"

"Stone didn't tell him about his memory. He doesn't want anyone to know."

There's a long pause as my friend considers this new information. "All this does is buy us time. It doesn't change anything. We still need the flower. I mean, how would you sleep at night if he never got his memory back?"

"And I got to keep this version of him?"

"I'm serious."

"I know you are. Yeah, I'd feel awful. I couldn't do that."

And I can't. Even though I love that he wants to change the resort, Stone Maddox needs his memory. With any luck, it'll return when he's so far into the new construction there's no way to back out. He'll be a hero. Once he sees how people love that he respected the ley lines and the town, how could he be angry with me?

He'll be pleased. In fact, I bet he'll wind up thanking me for giving him temporary amnesia.

And maybe piggycorns will learn to fly.

Yeah, it's pretty much a long shot.

"Run, Hercules," Stone calls to the lambicorn, who kicks his body sideways as he leaps toward the tennis ball.

"I've got to go," I tell my friend. "But I'll see if I can find out anything about the flower, too. What's it called again?"

Cristina tells me and I make a mental note about the spelling. Then we hang up and I turn to Stone. He's scooped Hercules under one arm and is making his way over to me.

"Little Hercules is picking up fetch quickly." I scratch the lambi behind the ear, but he leans away from my touch, clearly annoyed that I'm petting him. Could he be mad at me?

Don't be ridiculous, Coco. He's a baby. He's not mad that you hurt his daddy.

Probably.

"Looks like you're gonna have a wide receiver on your hands in no time."

Stone laughs and then snaps his fingers. "Football. I like football."

He beams, focusing on me in a way that suggests I'm the most important thing in this moment. Instead of the attention making me feel big, it does the reverse and makes me feel small.

I look off as he says, "I know what a wide receiver is."

"Just like you know how to read blueprints. Everything about you is trapped in here." I tap my temple. "We've just got to get it out."

Hercules squirms and Stone puts him down. The lambicorn runs off, finds a patch of grass, and begins munching on it.

Stone's gaze flicks to the trailer. "I guess that's where I sleep. There's a shower in the bathroom, and I'm thinking the couch folds out into a bed."

He sounds uneasy. The man just lost his memory. Should he be alone? No, probably not.

Here is where I jump into a situation that I shouldn't. My mouth leaps before the rest of me, guilt and more guilt racking my body because, really, all of this is my fault.

But before I can stop my stupid brain, I spit out, "You can stay at my place—if you want. You probably shouldn't be by yourself in case . . . you remember something."

He looks over my shoulder, and emotions flash across his face. Worry. Uncertainty. Then he looks back at me and says, "Yeah, it's probably best you keep an eye on me. I'm trusting you to keep me out of jail. Besides"—he touches his cheeks—"I'm really not crazy about this."

"Your scruff?"

"Yeah. I'd like to shave it off. See what I look like underneath, because there's no way I'm keeping this beautiful face from the world."

It's so surprising—*he's* so surprising—that I laugh, a full-force, stomach-muscles-hurting kind of laugh. After a minute, I manage, "Yeah, you can't starve the world of that beauty."

"I know."

Our gazes hold for several beats before I glance down, rubbing my arm. "I've got a pretty comfortable couch. If you can handle lace doilies and old-lady furniture."

Stone grins again. "For some reason, I think lace doilies and old-lady furniture might be my favorite things on earth."

"Except for Hercules."

"Obviously. How can you even *think* I'd leave him out of the equation?"

I chuckle and walk toward my car. "You can follow me over. I'm sure you'll want to leave early in the morning to get here and get started."

"Yeah. I need the names of the guys and their numbers. I also need a different phone, one I can make calls from."

"We'll pick it up on the way."

"Fantastic."

As we load up in our respective vehicles and are about to head out, Stone rolls down his window and motions for me to do the same.

"Everything okay?"

He drapes an arm over the steering wheel. "I just wanted to thank you. If you hadn't been here this morning to help me, I don't know what I would've done. I'm really grateful to you."

I nod and grin tightly, pretending my stomach isn't burning as if fire ants were biting me from the inside.

I wonder how grateful Stone will be when he discovers the truth.

Chapter 16

COCO

We're still full from lunch by the time we reach my house, and I figure dinner will be nothing more than cereal. I put down newspapers for the lambicorn to potty on (fingers crossed it works) and tell Stone the couch pulls out into a bed.

We're just about to yank that sucker out when the doorbell rings.

When I answer, a small army of old ladies, as well as Cristina, who's holding a bottle of wine, is standing on my porch, which is no bigger than a postage stamp.

My stomach bottoms out because I've completely forgotten what night it is. "Hey, y'all. I've . . . been expecting you."

"Expecting who?" Stone comes over and peeks out the door. "Hey, ladies."

"Why, hello, handsome," Clarice says. "I didn't know you'd be joining us for book club."

Stone quirks a brow my way. "Book club?"

"Uh, yeah." The words *I forgot about it* nearly leave my mouth, but that would insult the women who genuinely read the monthly assigned books and want to discuss.

So not only did I forget it's book club night—more importantly, I forgot it's my night to host.

I gesture for them to enter, and a small stampede of seventy-year-old women charges into my tiny living room.

The septuagenarians are followed by Cristina. "I tried to call you," she says as the women pull Stone aside and pepper him with questions.

Clarice interrogates him first. "What'd you think of the book?"

He plows his fingers through his hair. "Well, I—"

Another says, "Did you know who the killer was? Did you guess it?"

"Um, I wasn't—"

"Do you want to be our dead body?" Clarice asks.

The women gasp with excitement.

Stone hears this and his brows pump with mischief. He bows with a flourish. "It would be my honor to be your dead body."

The women cheer with delight and Stone laughs. His eyes shine bright and a lopsided smile smears across his face.

He looks genuinely happy, genuinely delighted. Genuinely pleased.

All these genuine emotions wafting off him confuse the hell out of me.

My mind spins as something inside me shifts.

There isn't time to poke and prod the feeling, because the ladies begin bossing Stone around, asking him to push the furniture against the walls and move lamps.

Clarice calls over her shoulder to me, "Where's the police tape?"

"In my car."

"Well, it ain't doing no good out there. Bring it in here."

"Yes, ma'am."

Cristina follows me outside. Daffodils sprinkle both sides of the garden walkway. The yellow blooms inside the white petals make me swell with happiness.

"So," my friend says after I pull the slightly melted tape from the trunk of my car.

"So, what?"

She shakes her head in disbelief. "What is he doing here?"

"I couldn't just leave him in his trailer all by himself."

"So you brought him to your house."

"What else was I supposed to do?"

"I don't know." She leans her hand against the car. "I guess he shouldn't be alone."

"My thought exactly."

"Have you found the flower?"

"I haven't had a chance to search."

Cristina nods in understanding. "Maybe you'll have better luck than me."

"I hope so." I nibble my bottom lip in thought. "In the meantime, I'll watch Stone—and don't worry. Everything's going to be okay."

Her gaze flicks to the street. "Famous last words."

"Hey," Stone calls from the house.

I cock my head. "Yes?"

"You two found that tape yet? The ladies are getting impatient. For some reason, they really want me to be this dead body. I'm not sure if I should be scared or excited."

Cristina laughs. "Maybe both."

"Great. Can't wait."

"We'll be right in," I tell him.

"He's certainly different," she mumbles as we make our way inside.

He sure is.

What initially began as a group chat to gossip about old men—a chat Cristina started because the ladies couldn't figure out how to create one themselves—eventually became a book club that I somehow got roped into.

Every month we pick a different novel. Many of them are *very* spicy. These ladies love their steamy sex scenes. But every once in a while, we hit a mystery for variety—and because the ladies like to reenact the actual murder as if this is some sort of private murder-mystery party.

Which is what's happening now.

"Walk in like Blake did," Clarice directs Stone. "Act like a real jerk, and then Coco will stab you in the back."

Stone enters the room, hunching over like a villain in a kids' cartoon. He rubs his hands together and says in a thick European accent, a mixture of German and Count Chocula, "I am so evil. Look at how evil I am."

"He was Canadian," Betty, another local, corrects.

"Eh, I'm so bad, eh," Stone says, which makes everyone laugh. I grab my sides to keep from falling over in a fit.

"Now, Coco," Clarice directs.

I step behind Stone and say in a fiendish voice, "This is for all the people you've hurt," then mime knifing him in the back.

Stone whispers over his shoulder at me, "Did you do it?"

"She did it!" Clarice shouts.

He doubles over. "I've been stabbed. Someone got revenge on me for being evil. I'm dying! I'm dying!"

He gives one last croak and collapses on the floor. Hercules trots over and licks his face.

Clarice hands me the police tape. "About time someone killed that evil Blake. Let's clear the crime scene."

Quickly as I can, I press the tape around Stone. He opens one eye. "How long do I have to stay like this?"

"How long would you like to?" I ask, smoothing a line of tape next to his arm.

"If I stay here, will they stop asking if I have a girlfriend?"

I frown. "They've asked that?"

"About twenty times." His gaze flicks to me, softer now. "I think they want me to say it's you."

Something catches in my breath. "Oh."

"Hurry up over there, lovebirds," Clarice snaps. "Mabel brought strawberry pretzel salad, and I can't wait to dig in."

Stone's expression shifts to intrigue. "Strawberry pretzel salad? That will either be amazing or make me vomit."

I laugh and finish taping around his legs. "It's pretty amazing. As long as you like cream cheese, Jell-O, strawberries, and pretzels, you'll love it."

"I could dig it."

I finish taping around Stone and he gets up. "Ladies, you've successfully killed me. Thank you for your cooperation."

"Let's give him a hand," Clarice says, and they clap, congratulating Stone on his performance.

The rest of book club dissolves into a light sprinkling of conversation about the novel, people gushing over Mabel's strawberry pretzel salad (which is amazing, as always), and the ladies thanking Stone for coming and telling him they hope he visits again, though next time it would help if he read the book.

They also ask about the resort—how it's going, et cetera. Stone keeps his answers generic.

As the women clean up and book club winds down, Clarice makes a point to approach Stone. "I gotta admit, I had you pegged all wrong."

Even though I'm picking up paper cups and plates, I pause to listen.

"How's that?" he asks.

"When I overheard you tell Isaac to fire that guy because he left some bricks in the wrong place, I thought you were one of the coldest-hearted sons of bitches I'd ever encountered. To be honest, when I saw you were here, I thought, *Oh, great, which one of us will he try to fire from book club?* But you didn't. You were a good sport, and for that, I thank you."

Stone looks dumbfounded for a beat, but then he smiles and recovers. "Yeah, that was quite a moment I had about those bricks."

Clarice claps his shoulder. "Stick with Coco. She's good for you."

Soon as Clarice steps toward the door, the women surround Stone to say their goodbyes.

He says all the right things: "I had a great time at book club . . . Yes, I loved being the dead body . . . Hit me up next time you need someone to act it out."

I catch him looking at me as he says goodbye to Mabel. He quickly glances away, and my stomach tightens.

I pick up several more cups and drop them in the kitchen trash before scurrying outside.

"Clarice?"

"Yes?" She slowly turns. I scan the street and don't see any sign of her tractor, which means she caught a ride with someone—probably Cristina.

"I have a question for you."

"Shoot."

I suck in a deep breath. Here goes nothing. "Back when there was first magic in town . . . I've heard the stories of people with abilities."

"What about it?"

"Well"—I twist my fingers—"is there any truth to what happened, like people disappearing and all that?"

Her eyes narrow. "Why do you ask?"

"I don't know, just wondering."

"This is God's country. Back when the magic happened, it was one thing for the unicorns to appear, but magic in people?" She shakes her head. "They were seen as working for the wrong team. Do I agree with that? Do I think unicorns are devil-worshippers? 'Course not. But you can't change what people think."

"But what if that person couldn't help it?"

Clarice takes a slow step toward me. "I wouldn't care, like I said. But the others? *They* would care. They would care a lot. So if someone has abilities in that vein, they need to keep them very, very quiet."

"Good thing I don't know anyone like that," I reply glumly, doing my best to ignore my wobbling stomach.

This wasn't the news I wanted, but it's not unexpected. Hearing that showing my abilities will only lead to pain stings in a way that's impossible to ignore.

Clarice pulls her purse strap higher on her shoulder. "Why're you asking about all this?"

"No reason." I rub my arm nervously. "Just curious."

"If there's nothing else, I got a belly full of strawberry pretzel salad, and all that sugar's making me sleepy. This old gal needs to hit the hay."

I squeeze her arm. "Good night."

"Night."

I say goodbye to the rest of the group, sharing a long knowing look with Cristina, before I head into the house, where Stone is tossing trash in a garbage bag.

"Well, *that* was fun," he says with a smirk and a mischievous glint in his eyes.

"Highlight of your day—fending off old ladies?"

He gives a mock bow. "Even if I *could* remember the past year, I would still say this was one of the best nights in it."

He says it lightly, but his words land hard and make my stomach do this weird swooping thing.

Stone holds the bag open and I toss dirty plates inside. "Not to mention," he continues, "I will now learn how to make strawberry pretzel salad and eat it every. Single. Day."

A real laugh escapes me and I look up to see him smiling down. Light dances in his eyes, and one corner of his mouth tips up slightly higher than the other.

He watches me openly, studying me, and I feel completely exposed, as if there's no secret he can't see.

Which is really bad seeing as how . . . well, you know.

"So how did you wind up in a book club with all those ladies?"

"Oh, that started as a group chat to find eligible bachelors."

His brows lift. "For you?"

"No." I chuckle. "For ladies of a certain age. And somehow it wound up becoming that."

"Do you like it?"

"Yeah, I do," I tell him as affection spreads through me. "I love those ladies, and they don't mind that I'm me."

He frowns. "What's that supposed to mean?"

"Oh, you know."

"No, I don't."

He watches me carefully and I shake my head. It's too much to explain. "They just accept me for who I am."

"Don't most people? Don't you accept *you* for who you are?"

"Sure. I mean, yeah." *I guess.* How did this conversation get so deep, so fast? "I mean, what I'm saying is that sometimes when people see the messy, they don't . . ."

"Stick around?"

"Yeah. Or they don't hear you. See you."

"You get ignored."

"Right."

Our gazes lock and my neck heats. I didn't mean to say so much.

His voice becomes low, gravelly. "You don't seem messy to me. In fact, you're really good at this."

"At tossing cups in the trash?"

"No." He rolls his eyes. "Smart-ass. I'm talking about people. Those women. You've got a great group of friends, even if they do go in for their curler sets once a week."

I double over laughing at that and say, delighted, "You know about curler sets!"

Stone scrubs a hand up the back of his head. "A thing I wish I didn't remember."

We both laugh and step forward as if we're falling into each other's orbit.

He looks down at me. I look up at him, and there's no denying the tension in the air, the pull of him. He handled the book club ladies with all this golden retriever energy, and it has disarmed me.

He's unexpectedly charming and warm, like a cozy blanket in front of a fire. He's this wonderful surprise, and my body hums at the nearness, at the pull of him.

How can you go from hating someone one day to being drawn to them the next?

It's ridiculous.

Impossible.

Stupid.

Spellbound.

And a thought occurs to me: Maybe I've been so busy keeping people out that I forgot how to let anyone in.

"The ladies asked more than once if you were my girlfriend."

My stomach jumps, but I tamp the feeling back down. My voice comes out soft. "Did they?"

He nods, tipping my answer over, seeming to study it, like he's inspecting me right now.

"Mmm," is all he says.

He shifts closer, lips directly in my trajectory. My own act like they're just along for the ride, tilting up toward him.

His gaze flicks to my mouth.

My eyes land on his. Stone has soft lips, piercing eyes, strong features—all of which draw me in.

No.

This is wrong. Stone doesn't know who he is. I can't kiss him. I can't even entertain the thought.

I clear my throat, step back, and search for another cup. Oh, there's one!

He opens the bag for me to drop it in, but his smile fades, as if there's a rain cloud hanging above his head.

"What's wrong?"

"It's just that . . ." He cinches the bag. "Did I really fire a worker because they left bricks in the wrong spot?"

The earnest look on his face makes my stomach quake. "I can't say for sure because I wasn't there. But . . ."

I let the rest of the sentence hang in the air. Stone's gaze latches on to mine, and it feels like there's a line of strings running from my ribs to my stomach, and they're all being plucked at different times.

"But it sounds like something I would do. You were going to say that," he notes.

"Yeah," I admit glumly. "It does."

This sinks in and he stares at the floor in thought. "Coco?"

"Yeah?"

His eyes lift, and the look of worry and longing in them makes my throat shrivel to the size of a hazelnut. "Would I *like* me?"

Why does this small question make me wince? "I'm not . . . sure."

He nods and yawns. "I'm pretty tired."

I pull out a new bag and put it in the trash can. "Me too. Let's get your bed set up."

As I grab blankets and pillows, I'm unsure what tomorrow will bring, or who Stone will be when it comes.

Will he be the man who ignores the ley lines, or the other man—the one who surprises me minute by minute?

Chapter 17

STONE

We spend the next day going over building ideas. Blueprints are spread across the table like a puzzle I'm trying to solve. Coco hovers nearby, offering suggestions that are brilliant, by the way. Her ideas for materials knock me off-kilter. She knows her stuff.

But the real surprise is, she doesn't feel like a stranger. Even though I can't remember her, there's something familiar about her, like I've known her forever.

When she leans in to point at the plans, her hand brushes my shoulder. It's warm. Intimate. Like this isn't the first time we've touched.

Like we've done this before.

A hundred times before.

"All right, guys, we're changing the plan."

Ron and Isaac stare at me blankly.

"You got the go-ahead from the city?" Isaac asks.

My head swivels until my gaze lands on Coco, who stands a few feet away in a patch of grass with Hercules. The lambicorn ignores the grass completely and nibbles on Coco's skirt.

Can't say I blame him. That woman's got legs that go on for days.

Cool it, Stone. You don't even know if there's anything going on between you.

If there isn't, someone needs to tell the undercurrent of electricity that flows whenever I look at her. It feels like we're both light switches dying to be flipped.

On. Not off. Don't misunderstand me.

But our relationship is professional. I mean, isn't it? Coco hasn't said otherwise, and I can't remember what I had for dinner a week ago, much less pick apart the past details of my life.

Plus, I still can't get into my phone or computer. I tried again this morning, but the passwords didn't come to me.

And what's weird is, I don't care. It feels like I should, but I don't.

Which makes me wonder—what if I used to be the guy who got it all wrong because he didn't stop to look, to think? What if I was the guy who hurt people and didn't care?

What if I'm good at this now—plans, execution, details—because I have a clean slate I didn't ask for?

And it's an ache. Knowing I'm missing part of myself and acknowledging that it hurts. It feels like there's a hole in me that can never be filled. But at the same time that hole gnaws away at me, there's also an indescribable freedom, like I've been given a second chance and I better not screw it up.

Living. It feels like I'm really living.

Which begs the question: What was I doing before?

"Boss?"

Isaac blinks at me expectantly.

I drag my gaze from the clipboard I'm holding. "Yeah?"

"The city," he reminds me. "You get the go-ahead?"

"Right, about that."

Coco steps up, Hercules attached to her skirt. She bends to shoo him off, but the lamb jumps away before she can touch him.

"The city's given the all clear, Isaac," she explains.

He scrunches his face in confusion. "But I thought things were on hold."

"We're going with new plans, new supplies. I ordered the concrete to be busted up," I explain. "We're starting over with different materials."

Ron and Isaac exchange a charged look. It's Ron who speaks. "New plans?"

"Well, mostly the same plans with tweaks, but we're changing materials. The others were, um, affecting the health of the town."

Coco suggested not mentioning that I can see ley lines. With everything else that's happened, keeping one more secret doesn't seem like that big of a deal.

"So we're to bust all this up?" Isaac asks, sounding worried.

"Yep. The sooner we start, the sooner we finish and can get the new structure in place. I've got shipments arriving starting tomorrow."

Ron stares at the bones of the resort like a man facing death. "It's a lot of work."

I clap his shoulder. Is that something I would do? Feels right. I'm going with it. "That's why we're gonna need more men, more bodies capable of doing this right. You know some workers?"

When they stall, I say, "What about the guy I asked you to let go?" I snap my fingers, trying to appear as if his name is on the tip of my tongue. "Who was that, again?"

Isaac's eyes nearly pop out of his head. "You mean Antoine? The one with the bricks?"

"That's the one. Why don't you see if he can come back? Tell him I made a mistake."

Ron and Isaac exchange another look. Isaac peers at me quizzically. "You feeling okay?"

"Never better."

The guys look from me to Coco and then back to me. Realization washes over their faces. They're wrong in their thinking, obviously. I'm not sleeping with Coco.

Right?

We're not, are we?

Should we be?

"All right." I clap my hands—discussion over. "Let's get back to work. Today, we bulldoze. Tomorrow, we start fresh, when the limecrete crew arrives. Got it?"

Isaac gives a little salute. "Got it."

"Yeah, I got it," Ron says.

Their spirits seem low, so I add, "Guys, I know this looks crazy, but trust me. The end result will be better all around. Okay?"

"Sure thing." Isaac rubs his chin. "And I'll call Antoine."

"Thanks, man." Do I say that? Call other men *man*? Again, I'm going with it.

Once the guys walk off, I ask Coco, "What was all that about the city signing off on the building?"

She absently twirls a strand of hair around her finger. "Just some red tape I had to defuse."

I'm about to ask her what kind of red tape when my phone buzzes in my back pocket. I pull it out and my jaw tightens.

"It's my brother," I tell her. "I need to take it."

She gives me an encouraging nod, even though her eyes are full of worry.

"It's okay," I tell her. "Maybe this will help jog my memory."

Coco cocks her head. "Let's hope so."

I shoot her a grin before stepping away to take the call.

Okay, Stone.

You can do this. You can talk to your brother and convince him you *have* a clue as to who he is *and* how the two of you interact.

Easy peasy.

I exhale a deep breath and swipe the screen. "Hey, man. How's it going?"

"Couldn't be better," he says, sounding happy. This is good. I can work with this. "The drinks are iced, the beaches are beautiful, and we're having a great time."

Major clue. My brother is not alone.

"That's great."

There's background static for half a second as it sounds like he's adjusting the phone. "How're things there? We on schedule?"

"We are on fire."

"Hey, Stone," pops in a female voice. "How's my town holding up?"

"Hey . . ." I have no idea who I'm talking to. "The town is doing great. I haven't burned it to the ground yet."

She laughs. "Good to know. Here's your other half back. I just wanted to say hi."

My other half? What does she mean by that. Wait.

We're twins! Pane is my twin! It's coming back to me. *Thank God.*

Pane returns to the line. "Rowe wanted to break in."

Her name is Rowe.

"Tell you what, getting married is worth it for the honeymoon alone."

He's on his honeymoon. I'm so glad I didn't say anything stupid. "When are you coming back, again?"

"Not for another month. We're taking our time. Might as well enjoy it, right?"

"Absolutely. If I was on my honeymoon, I wouldn't work for an entire year."

Pane laughs. "Right."

Which suggests I'm a workaholic. Got it.

"Anyway, don't get too comfortable. Rhett'll be visiting soon."

"Rhett," I murmur, hoping the name rings at least one bell. It doesn't. There's not even a hum purring in the back of my mind.

Pane continues, "You know how our cousin is—wants to make sure he's getting his money's worth."

"Oh yeah. *Rhett.*" Understood. Rhett is checking on his investment. Which means I should convince my brother everything is in line. "We're looking good here."

"You sure about that?"

"Yeah, why wouldn't I be?"

"Because you don't sound like yourself."

I scoff. "Maybe because I've been busy overseeing a resort."

"I take it back. You sound exactly like yourself."

I exhale the breath I've been holding. I'm still not telling him about the amnesia. Why do that when it'll be gone soon anyway?

The longer this drags on, the more questions I'll have—about my life, who's important to me, who isn't.

My gaze lands on Coco.

Her. She's the only person allowed to know the truth, because for some reason it doesn't feel like a weakness around her.

It feels like I'm opening up, like I'm sharing part of myself.

Which suggests I don't do this often. I've tucked myself away, and *that* feels more wrong than having lost my memory.

"As long as you've got everything under control, I'll let you go," Pane tells me.

I ache to ask him more. To find out about other things—like our sister. And our mom!

Our mom.

We have a mom.

Once again, that subtle hole widens inside me—a gap desperately needing to be filled, but one I want to fill naturally, without pushing, without begging for someone to explain my life to me.

"So, um"—*Keep it cool, Stone, don't raise any red flags*—"how's, um, Mom?"

There's a long pause, which makes me think he's hung up.

"Pane? You there?"

"Yeah, I'm here—but nothing's changed on my end. Why? Has it changed for you?"

"No, of course not."

He sighs in a way that sounds weighted. "What she did to us, I'll never forgive her for." My mind works to unpack the mystery, but all I draw is a blank slate. "But," Pane continues, "she did let Natalie move close by for school."

Natalie, our sister.

"Which reminds me, you need to pick her up on my usual weekend."

"Of . . . course. I'll be there. There's just one thing: I can't remember where it is. Can you text me the directions? But not to this phone. I got another one that's for personal use."

He pauses. "You sure you're okay?"

"Yeah, just really busy. There's so much going on. Oh no. I think someone cut off their arm. Here's the number."

"Can't I text it to this one—"

"No time!"

I rattle off the digits, ensure he's got it, and make muffled screaming sounds in the background. "It's worse than I thought. Gotta go!"

Then I hang up and exhale.

Holy shit.

I forgot to find out the day.

Later. I'll find out later. I take a moment and rake my hair from my eyes, recapping everything I know. My cousin will visit soon. I've got to pick up my sister from school?

I'm overloaded.

The project is weeks behind schedule, but if I hire extra labor, maybe we can pull this off before Rhett shows up.

My gaze tracks the ley lines where they throb slowly, quietly, undulating like they're struggling for breath.

Ron approaches. "You okay, boss?"

"Let me ask you a question."

"Sure thing."

Maybe one tiny little mention won't hurt. "Do you see some strange lines running on the ground?"

"What?"

I point. "Out there, something maybe sort of milky. Do you see them?"

He shoots me a worried look. "No, and if you see them, keep it to yourself."

"Why's that?"

He drops his voice. "We talked about this."

We did? "Maybe you could remind me."

Ron looks around as if to make sure no one can hear. He has a pretty jovial face—round, friendly, open. I like him immediately. Not sure if old me liked him, but *new me* does. "Once again—and don't forget this time, boss—there are some things this town will tolerate: unicorns, piggycorns, even lambicorns."

"Hercules," I correct.

"It's a fitting name," he corroborates. "But people with magic are trouble. *I'm* not saying they are. But if I were you, I'd keep the whole thing to myself."

With that, he walks off, and for a moment, I'm knocked back. Ron didn't seem to judge me, but—

Coco.

She's with Hercules, throwing the ball for him to fetch. Hercules runs past the ball and begins chewing grass. Coco sees me and waves. I wave back.

She can see ley lines, which means she may have ma— *Wait.* If she has the *M* word, then she's not safe.

From out of nowhere, a protective instinct uncoils in my gut, taking over my body. The thought of people turning their backs on her, hurting her, angers me.

There's no way I'll let that happen to Coco.

I know. I know I've got amnesia and that I don't remember our history.

But we *have* a history. I feel it. Every bone in my body tells me so.

She's a good person, someone who cares about others, who wouldn't harm anyone.

I'm not sure what this is—instinct, memory, fate—but I won't let anyone hurt her.

A chill skates down my spine. If she is magic and they find out, would they treat her like a unicorn?

Or like a monster?

Chapter 18

COCO

I split my time between the office and the construction site, guiding Stone on the best material choices—researching whether they're strong enough, tensile enough, and if they'll work with ley lines.

Stone hired a dozen more men, and construction is at full speed to make up for the time lost from having to start again from scratch.

It's all going great. Almost *too* great.

When Stone's not helping the guys and deciding what to do next on the site, he's playing with Hercules.

I have to admit, seeing those two warms my body all the way to my toes. As if to counter that warmth, Cristina asks daily if I've figured out what the lunaria bloom is.

I haven't.

And to be honest, I haven't tried.

Is that bad? It feels like it should be bad, like I should be thrown into some kind of purgatory, but every time even a twinge of guilt pinches me, I see Stone do something like pick up Hercules and laugh, and I remember how fragile this is.

How important it is.

Days slide by quickly, and Stone, Hercules, and I get into a rhythm in my tiny cottage. Stone makes breakfast. I make dinner, which is usually sandwiches or some kind of chicken dish, which is all I know how to make. He crashes on the couch and I sleep in my bedroom, relishing how quickly the project is taking shape.

The new limecrete set quickly, as if the earth itself helped us play catch-up.

Hopefully, the resort will be finished close to schedule. Fingers crossed. By the time Saturday rolls around, I'm exhausted. From intercepting the questioning looks the guys throw at Stone to tiptoeing around the fact that he has amnesia, there's been a lot to stay on top of.

What do you mean Stone's different? He seems the same to me. Oh? Why are we getting along now? We found a compromise. That's all. Of course he seems like the same Stone.

So when my mom calls bright and early, I'm not thinking about anything other than sleeping in.

"Good morning," she says cheerfully.

"Good morning," I reply through a yawn.

"Is the potato salad ready?"

"What potato salad?"

"The one for the get-together today." She now sounds terse. "You *are* bringing it, aren't you?"

"Oh, crap. I mean, yes, I'm absolutely bringing it. The potatoes just finished boiling." Do I even have potatoes? A quick mental check of all kitchen supplies confirms I do not. "What time do I need to be there?"

"By lunch. Brittany will be filming," she says proudly.

I groan. Not filming. If Brittany's doing that, it means she'll wrangle us into some kind of stupid survival game. *Great.*

"What's wrong with her filming?"

"Nothing," I chirp. "It's fabulous."

"Of course it is. Do you know how many views her videos get?"

"Not offhand."

"Hundreds of thousands. When you make videos with that many hits, then you can call the shots, Coco."

And that makes me slink back into my shell and want to disappear. "I'll see you soon," is all I can muster.

"See you then."

We hang up and I collapse back onto my bed. A knock comes from the door. "Come in."

Stone peeks his head in. He's just shaved and his face, without all that scruff, is shockingly handsome. Don't get me wrong, he was handsome before he shaved, but he looked rugged. Now Stone looks like the CEO of a company—all chiseled jaw.

I realize I'm staring, so I pull my covers to my chin.

"I shaved," he says proudly.

Behind him, Hercules bleats.

Stone glances back over his shoulder. "Just a minute, buddy. I said I was going to feed you. You've got to learn patience."

"Baaaaaaaa."

Hercules slides past him and heads toward my bed. The lambicorn jumps onto the mattress, and I grab hold of him, pulling him down to cuddle. In the past few days, I've learned Hercules is a *great* cuddler—when he lets me hold him for more than two seconds. There's nothing better than rubbing my chin against his baby-soft coat.

Hercules lets me hug him for a moment before he squirms out of my grasp and nibbles on the duvet. My eyes lift and I catch Stone watching me—his gaze unreadable but sharp, like he's taking in more than just my bedhead and pajamas.

A weird little flutter jumps in my stomach. I pretend not to notice the way his eyes linger.

"You look good," I say.

More handsome.

Stop it, Coco.

"You like?"

I close one of my eyes, pretending to inspect him. "Not sure. Where's the Stone Maddox I know?"

He lifts his brows and nods solemnly. "Still hiding inside me somewhere."

I cringe. "Sorry. That came out wrong."

"It's okay. I've had almost an entire week to get used to *not* remembering, and surprisingly, it offers a clarity that most people never have."

"Does it?"

"I have no idea, but it sounds good."

We laugh and our gazes catch for a breath. I look away first.

"However," he continues, "if I don't get into my computer soon, I'll have to pay someone to break in. I'm sure it's full of emails. But at the moment, they can wait."

We eye each other for a second before he cocks his head toward the lambicorn. "Hercules is hungry, and I figured you might be, too. I made eggs and smoked salmon. Not together."

"That sounds amazing, but I've got about ten pounds of potato salad to make and I'm out of potatoes."

He pulls a face. "Ten pounds? Are you secretly a squirrel? Where can you hide that much potato salad in your tiny body?"

I toss a pillow at him and he catches it to his stomach. "It's not all for me, dummy. There's this thing at my parents' house. A get-together for my sister. She's been out of town for a while."

He cocks a brow. "A get-together for your sister?"

"Yeah." I pick at a loose thread in my duvet.

Silence engulfs us and I know he's reading my disinterest.

"And does your family realize how amazing *you* are?"

My breath staggers. "That's very nice of you to say."

"It's not nice at all. It's the truth. Without you, I would've been lost this week."

Also without me, none of this would have happened and you would have your memory and blackmail me.

I nod slowly.

"Say it," he coaxes.

"I am amazing."

"There. How did that feel?"

Dishonest, because he doesn't know the deep parts of me, the truths I hide. "Pretty good," I lie.

"*Pretty* good?" Stone scoffs. "You can do better than that, but I won't push. Unless I also work part-time as a self-help coach, which is completely possible."

I laugh. "I don't think so."

"Me neither." Hercules jumps off the bed and trots toward Stone, who bends down and scratches the lambicorn behind the ear. Hercules closes his eyes and leans in to the scratch. For a second, this feels so easy.

So normal.

Too normal.

A tiny flicker of worry nudges the back of my mind, but I push it aside.

"So this get-together with your family," he says, "is it big?"

Oh, God. He wants to come. Stone wants to meet my family. I've never gone to one of these things with a guy before, and definitely not with one who might remember he hates me at any moment.

"It is big. There are lots of cousins. But just so you know, my family is different."

He crosses his arms and leans casually against the doorframe. "They've got three eyes? Tentacles? Don't worry, unless they've got two heads, these people have nothing on me."

I can't help but laugh and fall back onto the bed. When I glance up, his eyes shine with mischief. "Physically, they're normal. It's just, they have this one tiny hobby—well, not a hobby. My parents have made a business from it."

"And that is? It's bowling, isn't it? We'll show up and everyone in your family will be wearing matching bowling shirts."

"Stop it! I only have one pillow left to throw at you, and I need it for the back of my head."

"And I was hoping to catch another one. Here. Take this one." He tosses the other pillow onto the bed, where it lands at my feet. "Better?"

"Better." I sigh. "If you help me make potato salad, you're invited to come."

"And here I thought I'd be spending a Saturday at the park, just me and Hercules."

"After today, you might wish you had made that choice."

He rolls his eyes. "My eggs are getting cold. You coming or not?"

"Yeah. Let me get dressed."

I make a motion for him to shoo, and he grabs the doorknob and begins to close it. Before he completely disappears, Stone pops his head back through the crack.

"But seriously, your family can't be that bad."

I quirk a brow. "Just wait and see."

Chapter 19

COCO

"I was not expecting this," Stone says when we arrive at my parents' house.

"I told you," I reply, adjusting the huge tub of potato salad on my lap.

Stone watches my family through the windshield. "Are they military?"

"Worse. They're preppers."

"Oh, that explains all the camo."

"Does it?"

"No, not at all."

I laugh. "That's what I thought. Come on. Let me introduce you, then the men can drag you away and test your manhood by making you shoot targets."

His entire face brightens. "They'll let me shoot a gun?"

"If you *don't* shoot, they'll think less of you. It's a rite of passage at these things."

Stone watches the scene. There are a lot of people roaming around: kids, men, women—my cousins, aunts, and uncles.

"Sometimes I get feelings about people. Like right now, I feel like Natalie would love this," he murmurs.

"Natalie?"

"My sister." He frowns, thinking. Then his eyes pop wide with excitement. "She's an excellent poker player and has whipped my ass so many times it's embarrassing. So let's keep that between us. She also loves my brother, Pane, more than me, but that's okay. It's not a competition."

He smiles victoriously, and a quiver of happiness vibrates inside me even though it's laced with sadness.

I wish I had that kind of easy affection with my own sister. But there is, without a doubt, a competition between us, and Brittany's star has always shone brighter than mine. So bright that our relationship feels like a test I didn't study for.

Stone leans back and exhales with satisfaction. "Like I said, sometimes I get feelings about people." He eyes me. "About relationships."

He's not talking about me. He's not talking about me.

But my heart does a stupid skip thing, as if it hasn't read the room.

I squeeze his arm and an electric shock jolts me. This would be the perfect time to pull away, but I don't. Not when his skin is warm, solid, tethering me to this strange little bubble of a moment.

I drop my hand and he rubs the back of his head. "I feel underdressed."

He's wearing jeans, a casual button-down, and dark boots.

"You look great. It's not camo, but it'll do," I joke. "Want to meet my family?"

"Absolutely."

"Dad, this is Stone Maddox. Stone, this is my dad, Harold."

Dad steps away from a spot of earth that's smoking hot. Yes, actual smoke wafts up from underground. Several of my uncles and cousins stand around it, drinking bottles of water, discussing the underground firepit.

Stone extends his hand. "Nice to meet you, sir."

My dad takes the hand and surprise flits across his face. He appraises Stone and gives a classic dad nod. "Maddox, huh? Aren't you the one building that resort?"

"Yes, sir. That's me."

"Hotels are your business, huh?"

"Sure are."

My younger cousins run past us, screaming. One of the boys chases his sister while holding out a salamander.

"It's going to touch you!" he yells as she shrieks with fright.

Mom comes up, holding out her hands. "Coco, you brought the potato salad. Thank you!" Her gaze lands on Stone, and she does a double take. "And you brought a guest."

"Coco brought a date."

I turn as my sister Brittany stalks toward us wearing bedazzled camo pants, a black sequin-covered short-sleeved T-shirt, and a camo baseball cap with her name spelled out in more sequins: BRITTANY BLAZE.

That's her YouTube handle.

"Hey, Brittany."

Instead of going in for a hug, Brittany high-fives me—hard enough to make me wince. My hands stings as I lower it, but no way will I shake it out.

"Mom, Brittany, this is Stone Maddox. Stone, this is my mom, Dana, and my sister."

"Pleased to meet you," Stone says to both of them.

"So Coco brought us some fresh meat, huh?" Brittany folds her arms and leans back, giving Stone a good once-over. "You know how to shoot?"

Of course he doesn't! I grab Stone's arm. "Maybe we can go easy on—"

"I do," he replies to my surprise.

"You do?"

He nods. I can't tell whether he's bluffing or not.

"Well," Mom says, "Coco, let the boys and Brittany go shoot. While they're doing that, can you please help me in the kitchen?"

"Um—"

"Great. And did you put the pickles in the potato salad?"

Crap. With everything that's happened this week, the pickles slipped my mind.

My shoulders slump. "No, I forgot."

Her face says it's not okay. "That's fine. I have some we can add. Brittany got them this morning from the store."

"Yep," my sister says, stretching out her arms, "I was afraid you'd forget like last time."

And let the emotional digs begin. "Good thing you saved the day."

"Yeah, and we're gonna have some fun later. We're gonna play Hide from Brittany."

"Fantastic," I say without enthusiasm.

This is classic Brittany. She hunts us like a sixth grader, filming for her YouTube channel the whole time. But you can't say anything negative about it because she makes a ton of money, and my parents think it's great she's teaching survival techniques to a new generation, even if she's doing it in pink camo.

"I'll help in the kitchen," I confirm to my mom.

Stone frowns as if he doesn't approve. I itch to tell him I'm more than a girl who forgets pickles and is only useful to her family when it comes to making potato salad, but I don't.

The moment slips away.

Stone leans over and whispers in my ear, "Do I smell corn bread?"

"Yeah. It's probably baking in the kitchen."

He pulls back and winks. "Save me a slice."

My insides melt as my dad claps him on the shoulder. "You ever been to a pig roast where they cook the hog underground?"

Confusion scrolls over Stone's face for a moment before one side of his mouth tips up. "Can't say I have."

"Come on, let me introduce you to everyone. Would you like a water? You can have beer after we shoot."

"Sure. Thanks."

With that, my dad, sister, and Stone walk off to do manly survivalist things like shoot guns while I get stuffed in the kitchen slicing pickles for potato salad.

We go inside and the kitchen smells amazing: Beans bake in the oven and cabbage simmers on the stovetop, with corn bread cooling beside it.

"Mom, you've outdone yourself."

"It wasn't just me—it was your aunts, too."

And as if on cue, the side door opens and in storms a handful of aunts. They see me and exclaim in happiness, charging over to pull me into hugs, see if I've lost/gained weight. Do I have any wrinkles? Not yet, but I need to be careful. Aunt Susan knows a face cream that will keep my twentysomething skin looking young and full of collagen. Aunt Whitney says if that doesn't work, she knows a great plastic surgeon.

They are a gaggle of fun and laughter, charging in and taking over everything, pouring canned margaritas into glasses, fussing over the salad, laughing at each other's jokes.

They're a mixed bag—a couple are my dad's sisters, a couple married in. They're all *over* prepping, but they love get-togethers.

A shot rings out from outside, and Whitney, wineglass full of canned margarita, crosses over to the window, peeks out, and says, "Who brought that guy? Who is that?"

She turns back to face us, her expression as pinched as the tight white jeans that hug her athletic frame.

My mom looks up from the bowl of egg whites she's whipped to stiff peaks. "That's Stone Maddox. Coco brought him."

Susan turns around from where she's rinsing dishes. "Shut the front door. Coco, you brought Stone Maddox?"

My cheeks immediately heat. "Yeah, I guess I kind of did."

"Stone Maddox from *the* Maddox family? They own hotels? Lots of them? They're filthy rich?" Whitney asks.

Every pair of eyes is on me, and it's not just my cheeks that are on fire now. It's my entire body.

That's when Mom says, "Don't be silly. It's not the Stone Maddox from that family. Coco doesn't know them."

You can hear a pin drop. Susan and Whitney exchange a look. So do my other two aunts, Michelle and Margie.

The door opens again, and in steps my grandmother, pushing inside the house with her cane. "What's going on here? When's that pig going to be ready?"

I stifle a giggle as Margie and Michelle walk over to help my grandma Annabelle. We call her Nu-Nu because back when she was born, she was the youngest, and so she was nicknamed New. *New* eventually became *Nu-Nu*.

My grandmother has olive skin and a mass of hair dyed jet black. This old lady isn't going into that good night gently, or anytime soon.

She's from my dad's side of the family and is straight out of Louisiana Creole country. She even has the Creole accent. Some things just stick with you your whole life.

Margie and Michelle escort her to a chair by the window. She peeks out and says in her thick accent, "Who's that handsome man out there with the cute butt?"

Whitney swats her playfully. "That's Stone Maddox. He's Coco's date."

My eyes flare wide. "He's not my—"

Mom sighs. "Your daughters seem to think Coco knows a billionaire. I tried to tell them otherwise."

My grandmother slowly turns in her seat to me and says, "That's real nice. You can tell by the way he walks—got money hips."

Susan and Whitney roll their eyes in unison, and all gazes are on me again, waiting for an explanation. My mom shakes her head, tsking, mumbling about how that's the most ridiculous statement she's ever heard.

Part of me wants to shout that yes, I know the real Stone Maddox, and I'm worth more than potato salad and pickles, but the words die in my throat because I don't think she'd hear me.

My grandmother watches my mom for a minute, an unreadable expression on her face. Then she squints at me. "You didn't even give me no sugar."

I laugh and wipe my pickle-juice-covered fingers on a towel before crossing over and kissing her on the cheek. That is what *sugar* is to my grandmother—kisses, not an actual bowl of the sweetener. Though there's a funny story from when I was a kid, when she asked me for sugar and I brought her a sugar bowl. That of course just made her laugh and pull me into a hug.

"You got my ring sized yet?" she asks with happiness dancing in her eyes.

"You mean *my* ring?"

"Shoot." She dismisses me with a wave. "Already taking ownership. I like it."

"Yes, I'm getting it sized now."

She squeezes my hand as her eyes water from tears. "Your grandfather would've wanted you to have it."

I pat her hand. "Thank you for trusting me with it."

"Of course." Nu-Nu leans in. "Don't tell nobody, but you're my favorite granddaughter."

"And you're my favorite grandmother," I reply, wrapping an arm around her shoulders.

I peek out the window and see all the men and Brittany shooting at bull's-eye targets a ways out, facing the woods. One of my uncles shouts at the kids, no doubt reminding them to stay far away from the guns.

Stone turns toward the window. I wave, thinking he won't see me, but he does and waves back, smiling.

My insides do that strange fluttering thing, and I turn back into the room, ready to resume pickle slicing.

"That Brittany sure likes to hang out with the boys," Nu-Nu murmurs.

"Because no one makes her come to the kitchen," I mutter.

Nu-Nu lifts a brow.

Mom leaps in. "Her YouTube channel is successful because she's a girl doing what most girls don't. She's unique. Different. And people crave her content."

Mom sounds so proud. I wish for once she'd sound like that when she talked about me, instead of dismissing my license job—which I don't even have anymore.

"She's certainly something," my grandmother mumbles, making it sound more like an insult than a compliment. "You know what I think?"

"What's that?" Margie asks, sipping her drink.

"I think Coco did bring a date, and he's cute. I want to meet him. Coco, go tell him your grandmother wants to meet him."

Worry pools in my stomach. That's too much focus on me. If I get Stone, my mom will ask if he's really *the* Stone Maddox, and before he answers, she'll say, *See? He's not rich. I told every single one of y'all there was no way Coco could be friends with him.*

I quickly attempt to come up with an excuse as to *why* he shouldn't be accosted by these women. "I'm sure he's busy. There's plenty of time to meet him once the food's ready."

Aunt Whitney crosses to the window. "Is that a lambicorn? Coco, did y'all bring a lambicorn?"

"It's a lambicorn," Nu-Nu says from her perch. "Coco, go get that lambi. I want to see it, too."

"Yes, ma'am."

As I start for the door, Nu-Nu stops me by throwing her arm out. "You don't have to go now."

I pull my apron off. "Why's that?"

She gives my mom the side-eye. "Because that fella you brought is heading this way, and he's got the lambicorn in his arms."

Here he comes, and Nu-Nu's either going to approve or disapprove of him. Fingers crossed she likes him.

Because, I realize, I do.

I like Stone Maddox a lot.

Which means I'm in trouble.

Chapter 20

STONE

Soon as Harold slips the rifle in my hand, my body falls into muscle memory. The feel of the wood stock is familiar, the smell of gunpowder is reminiscent of a blurry memory, and the way the butt of the rifle feels against my shoulder is anchoring.

He gives me a stern fatherly look, the kind a dad gives before prom. It's an *If you even think about impregnating my daughter tonight, I will blow your nuts off* kind of look.

Yeah, and he's a prepper, which means not only does he have a thousand weapons that can kill me, but he also probably has a huge tub of rice to hide my body in.

Wait. How do I know that? Oh, right. That whole I-know-stuff-but-I-don't-know-how thing.

"You ever shot one of these, Stone?"

"Yes, sir. But it's been a while."

"Whereabouts are you Maddoxes from?"

"New York."

He nods. "What do you think about Mystic Meadows?"

"I like it. It's . . . magical."

"And how long have you been dating my daughter?"

Dating your daughter?

Coco and I aren't dating. Right? We're not dating. We're friends. She's my friend. She was there when the hard hat hit me on the head, which was very early in the morning.

Very early, as in before working hours.

What was she doing in my trailer that early?

Oh my God. What if we'd had a night of carnal pleasure? What kind of man makes love to a woman and then loses his memory?

I glance up at the house and my chest constricts. What if we're dating and it's killing her not to tell me? Maybe she wants me to remember on my own. Maybe she doesn't want to tell me because that would manipulate my memories.

"Dad, lay off," Brittany says, walking up to the weapons table and grabbing a rifle. "It's the first time Coco's brought a guy here since high school. Give him a chance. Let him shoot before you decide how you feel about him."

I'm about to give Brittany a look that says *Thank you for saving me* until she adds, "Besides, this will take about two seconds because we all know city boys can't shoot."

A couple of the uncles laugh, but Harold says, "What do you say, Maddox? You ready to prove you can do it?"

"Yes, sir."

"Let me give you a quick rundown of this here rifle." He points to a switch. "There's your safety. Call out *Fire in the hole* when you're ready to shoot."

Just then, Brittany yells beside me, "Fire in the hole!"

I cover my ear as she pulls the trigger. The sound is so thunderous I feel the echo of it.

After she shoots, she uses the binoculars to take a look at the target and then passes them to me. "Don't feel bad if you don't come close to me. I've been shooting for years."

Her bullet landed slightly to the right of the bull's-eye. It's close. Very impressive.

There are three targets set up in total, with uncles and cousins all taking turns shooting at them.

"You're up." Brittany smirks. "Don't disappoint us. The last guy Coco brought got scared off."

Harold sits behind the table and pats the seat beside him. "Take a seat, Maddox. It's easier to shoot."

I sit beside him and lightly venture, "Why'd he get scared off?"

Brittany shrugs. "Couldn't hang with the guys, I guess."

"The guys?"

"You know, them and me. 'Course, none of the dates I ever brought around were like that. They don't freeze. Right, honey?"

Out from the woods to the far right steps a man dressed in black. He looks ex-military. Like he could snap my neck with one hand while making a ham sandwich with the other.

"What's that?" he says.

"I said you don't freeze under pressure."

The man shakes his head. "Never."

Brittany points to me. "Jet, this is Stone Maddox. Stone, this is Jet, my husband and producer."

Jet shakes my hand a bit too hard, so I squeeze back. His eyes narrow before he gives a slight nod and looks away. "I was just checking the perimeter for the game later."

"We all good?" she asks.

"All good."

I'm in over my head. Coco's dad thinks I'm about to impregnate and ghost his daughter. Her sister has already labeled me soft.

Brittany points to a chair and Jet sits. "We were talking about how Coco never brings guys around."

Jet stretches his legs out in front of him. "Oh yeah. She doesn't date. Or maybe she does, but she keeps them away."

I can see why.

Harold nods to me. "Anytime you're ready, Stone, just call it."

I almost forgot I'm supposed to shoot. I pick up the rifle and press the butt to my shoulder. Then I drop my cheek and look through the scope, lining up the bull's-eye in the crosshairs.

Beside me, Brittany says, "Not everyone can be a natural like me."

A hammer hits me in the sternum—a tightening behind my ribs, like my body remembers something my brain can't reach, and it *hurts.*

That hole inside me just woke up, and it's full of pain. My God, so much pain I nearly fall over.

A voice rings out inside my head: feminine, low, older—my mother. Bright as day, I hear the phrase, *"Not everyone can be a natural . . . jerk like your father."*

It feels like I've been punched with a giant *Wreck-It Ralph*–sized fist. The memory is so sharp it stabs.

I'm not expecting the emotional fallout, and as quickly as it arrives, it morphs into something else.

Fury.

And I realize everything she told me about my father wasn't real. It was a lie that still rings in my heart.

A switch flips inside my head. The anger channels into my posture, my breathing. I slow it down, line up the crosshairs. "Fire in the hole!"

I pull the trigger and everything happens in slow motion: the sound of the rife exploding beside my ear, the kick of the butt against my shoulder, and the bullet launching toward the target.

Then it's over as quickly as it started.

I sit back and gently rest the rifle on the table.

Brittany smirks. "Don't feel bad for not hitting the bull's-eye."

She hands me the binoculars and I ease them to my eyes. "I hit it."

"What?" She shoots me a confused look before checking for herself. "Well, I'll be damned."

Harold rises. Soon as he does, all the rifles the uncles are holding go down. Coco's dad strides to the target. He pulls out a black marker and draws a circle around the hole I shot—a hole that's dead center.

"Bull's-eye," Harold calls out. "Good job, Stone."

I don't say anything. I can't say anything. Anger still courses through me.

I rise and turn toward the house as Hercules crashes into me like he's done a hundred times. I don't think, just scoop him up. Maybe I've done *that* a hundred times, too.

My gaze locks on Coco, who stands at the window, looking down at us. Her eyes catch mine—and everything inside me stills. Like she's the only thing that makes sense.

This is the first glimpse I've had of who I was—fury barely contained beneath the surface. And it is a bitter, rage-fueled monster.

I start to head toward the house when Harold stops me with, "You done shooting?"

"No, sir. I'm going to get Coco, see if she wants to join us."

"Shooting's not her thing." Brittany elbows her husband. "She hates all of this. Picks the same spot for hide-and-seek every time. She doesn't even try."

I'm not sure how long I've known Coco. A week? A year? But the way they talk about her, like she's invisible—it twists something in my gut. Like I've seen it before. Like I've felt it before. Maybe not with her. Maybe not here. But somewhere. And maybe that's why my hands shake from a memory I didn't know I had, and why I want to walk straight into that house and pull Coco out of it.

I reply quietly, calmly, emotions tamped down, "Maybe it *is* her thing. She just hasn't been given the chance to show you. Either that, or you never listened."

"Oh, we've listened," Brittany says, scoffing. "She prefers it up there."

I put Hercules down and give Brittany a pointed look. "Maybe someone should ask if that's where she wants to be instead of *assuming*."

Harold, Jet, and Brittany exchange looks that say either *Who is this serial killer that Coco brought home?* or *Maybe he has a point.*

I'd give it a fifty-fifty shot at either one.

Brittany lifts her eyebrows. "Okay, sure."

With that, I turn on my heel and head for the house to rescue Coco.

Chapter 21

COCO

When Stone enters the kitchen, all conversations stop. Nu-Nu speaks first. "Coco, introduce me to this handsome young man."

It was just a few nights ago when he wooed all the ladies at book club, and the same thing will probably happen here. "Everyone, this is Stone. Stone, these are my aunts: Margie, Michelle, Susan, and Whitney."

Whitney winks at him. "There'll be a test later. Don't forget."

He chuckles, but it sounds tense. "I'll try not to."

And that's it. No mention of food. No wondering if someone made strawberry pretzel salad and if he can just sneak a corner, no one will notice, he'll cover it with whipped cream.

None of that.

Something's wrong.

Margie steps forward. "Is that a lambicorn?"

Stone's eyebrows lift. "His name's Hercules. Would you like to pet him?"

"Abso-freaking-lutely."

As my aunts surround him, oohing and aahing, Stone puts Hercules on the floor and crosses over to me. I take him by the sleeve. "I want you to meet my grandmother, Annabelle. Nu-Nu, this is Stone Maddox."

She peers at him with stars in her eyes. "Aren't you a strapping young man? Say, you like gumbo?"

The look of surprise on Stone's face is priceless, like she's snapped him out of whatever funk he's been in. "I . . . Of course."

"I don't make it much anymore, but for you, I'll cook one up. I'll even put extra chicken feet in it."

I bite my bottom lip. No doubt the last thing Stone expected to hear was that there will be chicken feet in his gumbo, but that is my grandmother—full of surprises.

"Thank you," he says, his tone softening. "Extra chicken feet sounds great."

Nu-Nu folds her arms over her stomach and grins with satisfaction.

He turns to me. "Hey, I was coming to see if you wanted to do some shooting."

I pull the apron over my head. "Are they asking if I'll join them? Is Brittany?"

"No, I just thought you might want to."

He says it a bit darkly, and to be honest, I'm not sure if I want to go, but since shooting is a lot of fun, I peg the apron.

"I'm heading outside," I tell my mom.

"But you hate shooting."

"Well, I'll be back."

And then Stone escorts me outside to shoot.

Target practice goes great. I hit pretty close to the bull's-eye (not right on, but close enough for me). My sister doesn't say anything, and my dad congratulates me, saying that *the young man* I brought is also a great shot. He even did better than Brittany.

She must be burning up. No one does better than her—at anything.

Two hours later, we sit outside with my family, digging into roasted pig that's been dug up from underground.

My potato salad and lots of other dishes my aunts created grace the two long tables that are smooshed together just for this occasion.

Hercules has a bowl next to Stone, who brought some goat's milk so the little fella wouldn't be hungry.

"What do you think of your first pig roasted in the ground?" Dad asks Stone.

Stone takes a bite and moans. "If I've died, this must be heaven."

Everyone laughs.

"I tried filming one of these get-togethers a few years back," Brittany boasts. "But the aunts got mad when I put them on camera."

"You didn't tell us we were going to be on," Susan grumps. "I hadn't done my makeup."

"She wasn't the only one who hadn't contoured," Margie adds. "If you want us to be in one of your little videos, you've got to give us time to put our faces on. Like today. I'm ready for hide-and-seek."

"Little videos," Jet says with a snicker. "Brittany's *little videos* get tens of thousands of views in hours."

"That reminds me," Mom says. "Co, how's your job going? Is that where you two met?" She points her fork at Stone and me. "In the licensing department?"

Stone's head snaps in my mom's direction. "Coco doesn't work in licenses."

A low hush falls over the table. My aunts and uncles, cousins and grandmother, lean in to hear more.

My mom blinks. "What do you mean, she doesn't work at licenses? Of course she does. Don't you, Coco?" Before I can answer, she keeps going. "Why would Stone think you don't? You haven't lied to him, have you? I thought I raised you—"

Stone's fist hits the table—not loud, but sharp enough to freeze every fork in midair. There's something in his voice, fierce and raw, that knocks the air from my lungs. Not just protectiveness. Not just anger. Something older. Like this hit a nerve that isn't just about me. As if, for a second, my mother's words cracked something open in him, too.

"Coco is the new magical land use coordinator in the Department of Zoning and Development. That's her job. She doesn't work in licenses."

Mom swallows audibly and puts her fork down. Her gaze darts from Stone to me, and she says in a lightly accusatory voice, "Why didn't you tell us? We would have celebrated your new job."

The silence is deadly now. All ears, all eyes are zeroed in on the conversation going down over a roasted pig and some root veggies.

My eyes zip around the table and clock Brittany, who's waiting with amped-up interest to hear my answer. My dad merely looks confused. My aunts also have looks of curiosity smeared across their faces, and all of them are probably wondering why didn't I say anything. Why didn't I tell my family I'd started a brand-new position? How could I be such a terrible daughter?

All the focus, all the intensity, makes me want to curl into my roly-poly shell and disappear.

"Well, I just . . ."

Forgot, I was going to say. *I forgot. My bad. Sorry. Everyone stop looking at me and put all your attention on Brittany, because that's what you want to do anyway.*

But before any of that can slip past my lips, something happens.

A warm hand glides over my lower back and settles there as if that's where it lives. My gaze falls to Stone's arm, which has disappeared behind me.

He holds me like a comforting touchstone, pressing into me lightly, firmly, telling me—with no words, just a feeling—that it's okay to be seen.

Even when all I want to do is vanish.

I clear my throat. "Well, to be honest, I thought I did mention it, but you must've forgotten. I started this week."

My mom's face falls. My stomach twists because I know she feels bad now, and because of it, *I* feel awful. It seems disrespectful.

The desire to once again retreat zips through me.

Stone rubs my back, his hand slowly circling. Heat races through my body, zapping me right in my lady parts. My mouth goes dry, and I venture a glance at him.

He's looking at me. Inches away. His jade eyes project warmth and confidence, silently saying, *It's okay. You're not trying to hurt her. You're standing up for yourself.*

My insides become molten. That tingling in my girlie region winds its way back up and tightens in my core. Everything inside me wants to collapse onto Stone.

His salty and sun-warm scent that is distinctly him wraps around me. His lips look soft but firm, and his silky hair is just begging for me to wind my fingers around it.

His eyes fall to my lips and my nipples harden. I'm suddenly aware of how close we are, how easily he could lean in—how much I want him to.

Is it polite to make out in front of family?

"Coco?" Mom says loudly, snapping me back.

I drag my gaze from him and focus it on her. "Yes?"

"Well, how is your new job? Do you like it?"

"Yeah. It's been challenging, but it's a lot of fun." I sneak a look at Stone because he is the reason why I'm saying both of those things, and one corner of his mouth ticks up in way that makes butterflies lift from the launchpad of my stomach.

"Well, that's wonderful. I'm sorry I forgot," Mom confesses slowly, like praise is something she gives away in coupons and I just cashed mine in for the month.

A tiny bit of pride blooms in me, but a shadow falls at the same time.

It hurts on so many levels.

Brittany clears her throat. I'm not sure if she's pissed that the attention is off her or if she's being sincere when she says, "It's time, y'all. Who wants to play Hide from Brittany?"

Chapter 22

COCO

As soon as Brittany pulls out her phone and begins recording, the game is on.

Not everyone plays, but those of us who do scatter like cockroaches when the kitchen light's flipped on.

I grab Stone's hand and guide him to my dad's shop. He takes one step inside and whistles. "Is this a bomb shelter or the world's biggest chili cook-off?"

A throaty laugh slips from my mouth. "There's a lot, isn't there?"

"Not just a lot—enough to feed an army. Or *two*." He nods over his shoulder at me. "My bet's on two."

One wall is covered in shelves filled with clear tubs containing either beans or rice. Those are the *homemade* rations. There's also a shelf devoted to military MREs, one for store-bought freeze-dried food ranging from chicken spaghetti to peach cobbler to strawberry oatmeal, and another shelf for five-gallon jugs of water.

I've been looking at this stuff for so long it's hard to see it with fresh eyes, but I do my best and realize my family looks either completely well prepared or absolutely insane.

Might just be a mix of both.

"And look at those supplies." Stone exhales another low whistle, suggesting he's impressed. "I've never seen so much fire starter and steel thermoses."

"My family makes go bags and sells them," I explain.

He quirks a brow. "Go bags?"

"Yeah. You put them in your car, and if an emergency happens and you're stuck in the wilderness for a while, the contents of the bag will keep you alive—if you know how to start a fire, that is."

"That is so cool."

I slide up onto a counter and swing my feet. "I guess. I never really wanted to have anything to do with it."

He crosses over to me and places a hand on either side of my legs, pinning me in.

My pulse immediately rockets into outer space.

So many questions fill his jade eyes. "Why didn't you want to work in the family business?"

I shrug, look away. "They wanted me to. It was kind of a big deal that I didn't, because Brittany promotes the company on her channel and my family is busy. But I'm just not as passionate as they are about it. Also, I guess . . . Well, you saw how hard it is to compete with my sister."

"Hey—sorry about earlier. The whole table thing." He rubs the back of his neck like he's embarrassed. "But your mom, what she said—it didn't sit right with me. It felt like a personal slight to you."

My insides twitch. "No one's stood up for me like that in front of them before. It's not that I haven't tried to. Some days it feels like I could tell my mother a million times that I hate something as simple as broccoli and she still wouldn't hear me." I exhale, and my body deflates. "It's hard living in a shadow."

"I guess it would be."

He takes a step closer. His pupils are inky black. A strand of his hair is out of place. I slowly reach up and fix it. Stone closes his eyes and leans in to my touch. I can't breathe. It feels like my lungs have stopped working.

His lids flutter open again and he murmurs, "As far as I'm concerned, you don't stand in anyone's shadow."

My voice is barely above a whisper when I reply, "That means a lot."

There's a long pause before he says, "How long until Brittany finds us?"

It's so unexpected that I can't help but laugh, hiding my mouth behind the back of my hand. I lean back. "Well, this is my spot, so she should be here in about ten minutes or so."

Stone takes a step back. "Your spot?"

"Yeah." I slide off the counter and cross to the far wall, where there's an unlocked cabinet. "We all have our designated spots. We've been in the same ones since Brittany started doing these. It's part of the script. And this"—I tug open the cabinet—"is where I go. It might fit two of us."

It *might*. The space is small and dark. The only way we'll both squeeze in is if my knee locks between his legs and his hands rest on my breasts.

My fingers spark at the tantalizing thought. As if to answer them, the ground beneath my feet quivers slightly, like a weak signal trying to be heard. Through the window, I spot a blue flicker spill over the grass. It's quick, gone just as fast as it appeared.

I've got to stop thinking about Stone this way. His hand does not need to be on my breast. We can't get romantically involved.

He approaches, and a scary thought enters my mind: Did he see the magic? Did he witness the sparks on my fingers? Does he know?

Stone rubs his chin, humor sparkling in his eyes. "This cabinet looks like a great hiding spot for a first-timer. It's small, dark. Things could happen."

He wiggles his brows, and heat immediately blooms on my cheeks.

Stone leans one shoulder against the cabinet and knocks on the steel surface. "So you're just going to go in, be where you're supposed to be?"

I shrug. "I guess?"

"You'll do this for a sister who didn't congratulate you on a new job, and who would have let you suffer in the kitchen—the same kitchen I pulled you out of so you could come shoot? I'm just saying."

A jolt of electricity shoots down my arms as I recall target practice. It's the one thing I actually enjoy about these extended get-togethers—besides seeing my *extended* family—aunts and Nu-Nu. "Did you see the look on her face when I almost hit the bull's-eye?"

He beams, and it rocks me. Stone is so beautiful. I may have tried not to notice before, but it's impossible to ignore now, when the fear and anticipation of being caught fills every moment.

"I saw the look Brittany gave you. I don't think anyone else did." He shakes his head and his mood shifts, darkens. "You don't deserve that."

"Hey." I step closer. "Are you okay?"

He pushes off the cabinet. "I don't know. No, I *do* know. I had a memory. Nothing concrete, but it left a bitter taste in my mouth."

"Want to talk about it?"

"No. But you don't need to cater to them like this. This isn't the Coco *Chanel* I know."

I bust a gut at his nickname.

The lines around his eyes soften. "The Coco I know dives headfirst into a project and isn't afraid to take risks. But I get it—this is your family, and for family, sometimes we bite our tongues."

Sparks of worry and hope flare inside me. "Do you remember yours?"

"Not a thing." He laughs bitterly. "But I know you're not supposed to let anyone treat you like you're *less than*. You let them, and it makes me angry."

He takes a step forward and his shadow falls across me. A knot clogs my throat as he leans in and whispers, his breath tickling the curves and planes of my ear, "Do you know what I want to do?"

My breath hitches at the sound of his sultry voice. "No."

"I want to hide somewhere else. Somewhere no one's ever discovered you." He pulls back. "Now, where could that be?"

I think for a moment and then snap my fingers. "I've got it."

Stone takes my hand, and tingles walk up and down my spine. "Great. Take me there."

"You're not allowed to touch *anything*," I say in a mock-stern voice.

Stone stops in the doorway.

Stares.

Looks at me.

Blinks.

His voice brims with awe. "Do you even know what you're asking? That's like demanding a kid who's all alone in a candy shop not eat everything in sight." He rests his hands on his hips and sighs. "No way will I be able to do that. This—all of this—must be touched." His gaze flicks to me. "Did that sound inappropriate? Because *that's* what I was going for."

I giggle and tug him by the sleeve into the room. "Just get in here so I can close the door." From the woods, I hear Brittany whooping and shouting. "She's caught another one."

"Poor bastard," Stone says with a playfulness in his eyes that makes my lungs spasm.

I softly shut the door and turn around, pressing my back to it and taking in the room I haven't fully stood inside of in years.

"I never come here," I murmur.

"Why not?" Stone leaves me and wanders to the far wall, where hundreds of original LPs are shelved. Hundreds. Maybe thousands. I have no idea how many records my dad owns. "If this was mine, I'd sit in here all day listening to albums."

"You would?"

"Yes." He swings around as I step up beside him. "I would lock myself inside this place and never leave." His face brightens. "Music! I love music! Maybe there's a clue to who I am underneath all of this." He tempers his excitement, gesturing toward the wall. "That is, if *milady* would allow me to peruse the shelves."

My stomach flutters at the word *milady*, and a laugh bursts from me. "I was joking earlier. You can touch. Peruse all you like. If you find something you want to listen to, we'll put it on."

Fire dances in his eyes. "Where?"

I point to a standing stereo system that's at least thirty years old. "There."

"That has got to be the god of stereo systems."

"Well, you know, if the apocalypse occurs and society crumbles, you must have music."

Stone nods in reverence. "Truer words have never been spoken."

I laugh again and he drops his hand to squeeze mine and then gently pulls me toward the wall. "Search with me."

"For what?"

"Jazz."

"Oh no. You're joking, right?"

He shakes his head, his gaze never leaving the wall as he scans the titles. "I am for sure *not* joking."

"What are you searching for?"

"I'll know it when I find it."

I run my finger along the titles until I find something he might like. "Charles Mingus?"

"Not in the mood. Something else."

"Why something else?"

He tips his face toward me, and his expression is completely open. There's no filter or walls. Nothing separates us.

"Because I love jazz. There's something raw and true about it. No secrets, no lies, just honesty. Musicians keeping the core melody while playing around it, sustaining that truth while dropping in other ingredients. That's jazz. And sometimes"—he smirks—"you can dance to it."

A tingle cartwheels down my spine at the mention of dancing. "Is that so?"

"That is so. Ah! Here!" He pulls a record from the wall. "Holy shit. Is this the original *Saxophone Colossus*?"

"I have no idea."

He whistles as he spins it over to the back. "This is original. Holy shit, I tried to get this. *Maybe.* I think. I wanted this. Yes, I did! I wanted it, and for some reason I didn't get it. Come on."

"Want to play it?"

His jaw twitches as if he's mulling it over. "No. I want something else."

He slides the album back onto the wall and scans more titles until he finds another. "We'll put this on."

"What is it?"

He winks. "A surprise."

My insides flutter as he handles the record like it's more precious than Hercules. He slides the vinyl out from the cover and gently places it atop the turntable, and with precision, he lowers the needle to the surface.

The sound is scratchy, but when the trumpet begins, my insides immediately melt. "'La Vie en Rose.'"

"Nothing says jazz like Louis Armstrong," Stone agrees.

He has quite possibly picked the most romantic song on the entire wall, and my brain screams, *This is dangerous.* I need to shut the moment down, pull the record from the player, and find something else to listen to—Charles Mingus, for instance.

Stone extends his hand. "Dance with me?"

Heat pours over my body, spilling down my hands and feet. "To this?"

"Humor an amnesiac who's holding his life together with rope and a lambicorn."

A throb of guilt hits me. "Do you really feel that way?"

He gives me his best puppy-dog eyes. "If you dance with me, you'll find out."

"You, sir, drive a hard bargain."

"And you, madam, aren't driving at all."

"What's that supposed to mean?"

"I have no idea. It just came out. Dance. Please. Humor me."

"Okay."

I slide my hand over his and experience an entire line of small explosions dancing across my flesh and up my arm as he pulls me to him.

I keep a good two feet of distance between us.

"You're supposed to relax," he murmurs.

"I'm relaxed."

"Okay, sure. Listen, if I can relax and I can't even remember two weeks ago, then you can relax."

Guilt drills into me. "I'm so sorry about your memory."

"It's not your fault," he says, which feels like I've been punched in the throat. "Besides, I'm not sorry."

Wait. "What?"

He hitches one shoulder to his ear. "I'm not."

"Why?"

"In a second." Stone cocks his chin, and I expect him to say something about his amnesia. But what comes out is completely different. "You never wear your hair down."

Talk about conversation whiplash. "Yes, I do."

"Not often." His gaze scours my face, questioning, wondering. "Will you let it down?"

"Um . . ."

"Please?"

And it's the *please* that gets me.

"Okay."

I don't wear my hair down often. I guess it's like armor. If I keep it up, I stay safe. But it's just the two of us, and there's nothing to be afraid of with him. His presence grounds me.

So I grab hold of the band. But stop. I'm struck by how intimate this feels—the closeness of him, the way he quietly studies me. He's looking at me as if I'm a star in the night sky, shining only for him.

And that's what propels me forward.

My hand slowly works to pull out the band, and I let my hair cascade over my shoulders.

Stone's eyes flare with surprise, like he's been hit with a baseball, and I realize I've been hit, too, but by something different—pride and panic.

The panic burns hot and quick, but then peters out, leaving pride that lingers.

And then that same pride is reflected in his eyes. He reaches out slowly, and with a gentleness that sends shivers dancing across my skin, he pulls my hair over one shoulder.

"You're so beautiful."

My cheeks heat. "Stop it."

"I will not stop it, because it's true. You are. So beautiful. And . . ."

"What?" I ask.

He shakes his head. "Just . . . something. Like I've seen this before."

He stares at my face, my hair. There's a look in his eyes—I've never had someone look at me like this, as if I'm the answer to a question they didn't ask.

A blush forms on my cheeks and I look away.

"You are so beautiful, Coco."

I look up and his eyes smolder. "Thank you."

"I mean it, you really are—inside and out."

We're studying one another, and it feels like I'm the target now, the center of the bull's-eye. I clear my throat, hoping to put distance between us and this conversation.

"Tell me about your memory."

He tips his head back. "I'll only tell you if you dance with me like you actually want to. You're miles away."

"No, I'm not."

He motions at the distance between us.

"Fine."

I take a hesitant step into him. His hand tightens around my waist, holding me close, and his body warms every inch of me.

"So much better." Stone squeezes my hand before he adds, "Have you ever thought maybe who you are *now* is who you're supposed to be and the past doesn't matter?"

"No, I never have."

He pulls back and frowns. "Why not?"

"Maybe I don't understand the question."

I look down and he hooks a finger under my chin and tips my face up until our gazes lock. "You understand exactly what I'm saying. You're faced with the past here, every time you visit."

That truth strikes a tightly wound cord in me. I'm reminded of the pecking order whenever I talk to my parents or see my sister. And Stone understands.

He sighs. "Something was taken away from me—something very important, by someone I care about."

"You were betrayed?"

He nods, tugging me closer, and I let him. Our bodies are only inches apart, and when I look up, his lips are right in my trajectory.

"Betrayed by someone I love," he confirms, spinning me out and pulling me in so that I knock into him. His body is solid and warm, perfect for cozying up to. "I get the feeling betrayal seeded inside of me."

"'Seeded'?"

"You know, like it was planting a garden of rage and bitterness."

I frown, a crease forming between my eyes. "Your heart is a garden of rage and bitterness? Must be a lot of weeds."

"Okay, who's the smart-ass?" His hand rises to my stomach and he tickles me.

I struggle to get away, but Stone's got one arm wrapped around me, while the other tickles my side.

"Stop! Stop!"

He releases his hold, but I don't move. I stay exactly where I am, pressed against him. His heart drums under my palm. His very presence is a luxury, and it's melting me, bit by bit.

Here, I don't feel like a castaway fighting to be seen. For just a moment, I feel like a diamond, a glittering gem.

"Were you ever going to tell me about your powers?" he murmurs.

My body goes rigid. "What?"

"I saw the sparks tonight."

My insides crumble. "No, I wasn't going to tell you. I wasn't going to tell anyone."

"Why not?"

"Because . . ."

My voice trails off, but he picks up the thread. "Because of how this town sees people like you? Coco, look at me." I do as he asks. "You are special, more special than you know, and I will be damned before I let anyone hurt you. Not just because you've helped me so much, but because . . . I just won't."

I'm completely gone. Lost. No one has ever seen my weakness, my messiness, and told me it's okay. That *I'm* okay.

His lips drop toward mine. "I'd take fireworks on my fingers any day of the week if it would give me a hint of who I was. I can build a structure. I can swing a hammer. I can design a resort. I know jazz like it's part of my DNA. But I have no idea if I was kind. If I was good. If I was the kind of man you'd kiss. And that's who I want to be."

I'm dumbstruck, blown away by his admission.

Then he lowers his mouth to mine, softly, gently, and I let him. This kiss is a question: Will I allow it?

I kiss him back, opening my mouth as his tongue sweeps inside. All of me dissolves.

It's been ages since I've kissed anyone, and even when I did in the past, it was just kissing.

It wasn't like *this*.

Louis Armstrong croons a sweet love song in the background, asking the woman he loves to give her heart and soul to him, and I feel myself cracking open, breaking apart, giving more than I ever intended.

And still we kiss. We sway. A moan whispers from my throat, and Stone's grip on me tightens in the most exquisite manner.

This is real.

This is *so* real.

But Stone isn't. He doesn't know who he is, and it's wrong of me to allow this lie between us.

I pull back slightly, breaking the kiss. My lips are swollen and want more. All of me wants more.

Stone presses his head to mine. "What's wrong? Not enough tongue for you?"

I burst into laughter. "No, no." My chest cracks as we stare at one another. *My God.* Who is this man who can wreck me so easily?

"There's something I have to tell you."

"If it's anything other than *That was the best kiss of my life*, you can keep it."

A sad smile pushes through my face. "It was an amazing kiss. But it's something else."

Stone starts swaying again. "Whatever it is, lay it on me."

"The thing is . . ." I falter for a moment under his warm gaze, his soft touch. He's holding me now, but in a second, he'll drop me like I'm made of fire, and I will be. I will have burned straight through his skin. "The thing is—"

Just as I have the nerve to tell him the truth, the door bursts open and there's Brittany with Jet behind her, recording.

My sister points to us and shouts, "Found you!"

Chapter 23

STONE

I am lost. Completely, utterly lost for this woman. It makes no sense. It's not normal to fall for someone you've only known a week.

But something happened to me when I lost my memory. Something broke.

Or maybe something cracked open—and what poured out was the part of me I never let anyone see.

And I want Coco. She fills me in a way that's impossible to explain. How she moves. How she laughs. How she's always got her hair up—everything about her has worked a spell on me, and I've been blown apart.

It feels like I've always known her. Like she's always been part of me. It's unexplainable.

I'm falling for her, and I'm terrified the man I used to be would never have deserved her.

What's worse, I'm afraid the man I was before—the one drowning in his own pain—would've shoved her aside. A person can't carry around what I was without hurting those nearest to him, and I don't even know specifics, just what I felt when we visited her parents.

I never, ever want to hurt Coco.

I love her with everything that's inside me.

It's been over a week since the party at her parents' house. We haven't kissed since then, and I'm dying to. I want to slide my hands up her cheeks and drink her in—taste her, feel her, make her moan.

But I'm trying to play it cool. It's going about as well as a fire in a paper factory. I send her maybe twenty texts a day, asking how she's doing at work, showing her pictures of what the resort's got going on. It's moving quickly, as if the earth itself is helping us.

Hell, it probably is.

Today I've left the construction site early. Coco had some errands to run, and I want to surprise her with a nice dinner.

I get to the cottage (yes, I'm still staying here—no, I don't want to leave) by midafternoon, trusting the site to the guys.

Hercules runs in and goes straight for his bowl. I finally grabbed the poor guy some feed to supplement his diet. I drop the groceries on the table and spot a small velvet box.

That wasn't here this morning. It sits there quietly, like the twin girls from *The Shining*, waiting to either take me to hell or to heaven.

Calm down, Stone. It's just a box.

Coco mentioned running back to the house before leaving again, but she didn't mention jewelry.

What's inside, I wonder?

Curiosity gets the better of me and I open the lid to find a ring—an emerald surrounded by diamonds. It's an antique, and beautiful.

My gaze lands on it for all of five seconds before a memory stabs me.

It's blurry, like I'm looking through a filter. There's the ring. There's Coco. And there I am, offering it to her.

Holy shit.

A cold shock vibrates through me, and I drop the box.

It clatters to the table. I rock back on my heels.

I plow a hand through my hair, and I realize Coco's been trying to tell me, wanting to tell me, but she keeps being interrupted—by me.

No. It can't be.

But maybe this explains why I feel so close to her.

Maybe it explains everything. Maybe we already promised each other forever, and I just forgot.

Chapter 24

COCO

Stone acted weird last night. He kept looking at me like I had a confession tattooed on my forehead. Like at any second, I'd reveal a truth he was already braced to hear.

But he didn't say anything.

Then he acted even stranger this morning—burning the eggs, forgetting to feed Hercules until I pointed it out—and I haven't been able to shake this sinking feeling that he *knows*.

Which means it's time to fess up.

When I reach the construction site, work is in full swing. My eyes pop wide as I take in everything that's been accomplished in a short period of time. The limecrete has been repoured. Beams have been erected. The structure looks like an actual building and not a weird skeleton sitting in the middle of a plot of dirt.

Soon as I park, I see Stone talking with the guys, giving orders. Isaac and Ron nod before moving off. Stone spots me, and one side of his mouth curves in a way that makes my stomach quiver.

I kill the engine and climb out. "Hey!"

"Hey yourself," he says, crossing over. "Glad you could come."

"Of course. I love seeing how it's turning out."

"The ley lines look good, don't you think?"

They pulse with power. "They do."

Stone watches me. I watch back. My stomach jumps off a diving board.

"So, I . . ."

"About last night—" he says at the same time.

We each pause for the other.

"You go first," I say.

He cocks his chin. "Coco, you don't have to tell me. I figured it out. I mean, the kiss we shared the other night should have been a huge hint. Right, Hercules?"

What?

Beside him, Hercules bleats up at me with narrowed eyes, like I did something to piss him off.

Stone, on the other hand, squints like he's remembering the kiss, and my God, we haven't even discussed it. We should. It was mind-blowing.

"It was really great," I admit.

"Are you *blushing*?"

He leans in and I wave him off. "I'm not blushing."

"Yes, you are. You are absolutely red." He touches my cheek. "It's adorable. Keep doing it."

I shake my head and he runs a finger down my arm, sending shivers spiraling to the ends of my hands and feet.

The mood instantly shifts, becoming surprisingly intimate, given that there's loud construction equipment surrounding us. A vehicle reverses, its horn blaring as it backs up.

He shifts his weight back and forth as if contemplating what to say next. Finally, he decides on, "I don't remember the man I was, but I want to be the man you *need*."

My throat shrivels to the size of a pin. I'm not ready for that sentence. It feels like he reached straight through my ribs, wrapped his hand around my heart, and gave it a gentle squeeze.

"That kiss we shared . . ." He brushes a finger over my cheek. "There's a lot that's wrong in my life right now, a lot I'm trying to sort through. But you don't feel like one of those things, and I know why."

He takes my hands and studies them, like he's learning me, knuckle by knuckle.

Oh, God. I want to die. All of this is because of me, and he needs to know it. I've got to tell him. Now. Before he falls for me. Before I fall even harder for him.

Stop—*even*?

Is my inner monologue suggesting I've *already* fallen? Of course it is. Has it seen the way Stone holds Hercules? Even the lambicorn is in love with him. And I'm pretty sure I'm next.

He rubs his thumbs gently over the tops of my hands. "What is it you wanted to tell me?"

"Wait. You said that you know why I don't feel like one of the wrong things. Why is that?"

"Nah. Go ahead. We'll get to me."

I take a deep breath. I can do this. I can tell him. Just like ripping off a bandage—right?

But it's not like ripping off a bandage, because this one is covered in feelings. I can't have Stone kissing me, thinking I'm wonderful when I'm the cause of his grief. It's time for him to know the truth.

No matter how much he'll hate me because of it.

I try to open my mouth, and it feels like my lips are superglued shut. He'll hate me. He'll walk away. He'll never speak to me again.

It's a risk that's worth taking.

I clear my throat. "The other day, when you hit your head—"

A shiny black SUV rumbles onto the construction site, kicking up a storm of dirt behind it. The windows are tinted so dark it's impossible to see inside. Who could this be?

I pull away from Stone. He clocks the movement, his eyes dipping to my hand before he pushes on his hard hat and prepares to greet his guest.

My mind races. Is it Pane, back from his honeymoon? Is he going to see the site and blow a gasket?

The door opens and a driver in a black suit gets out and opens the rear door.

Out steps a man—he's tall, with broad shoulders and wavy brown hair. He scans the site and then fixes his gaze on Stone, his expression grim as death.

"Cousin," he says, shaking Stone's hand. "Good to see you."

Stone plays this so cool. If you didn't know he had amnesia, you'd never guess. He smiles, his eyes warm, whereas his cousin's gaze is as cold as a steel blade frozen inside an iceberg.

Once they shake, Stone turns to me. "This is Coco. Coco, this is my cousin."

"Rhett," he murmurs, taking my hand, knuckles up, and holding it briefly before releasing it.

Knuckles up? This man was taught how to shake a woman's hand. And his name is Rhett? It suddenly feels like I've wandered onto the set of *Gone with the Wind* and I'm the underdressed extra.

Talk about Southern gentility.

Trying to save Stone, I say, "I didn't know you had a Southern cousin."

"South Carolina," Rhett tells me. "There's a small smattering of us Maddoxes there." He turns back to Stone. "I've come to see how my investment's going. From the looks of it, I've only got one question."

"What's that?" Stone asks.

Rhett's face scrunches in anger. "What happened to the resort?"

Chapter 25

STONE

"What *is* all this?" Rhett demands when we enter my office. "I've gotten invoices for limecrete? For materials we didn't discuss? What's going on? And why aren't you answering your emails?"

I slide into a chair and stare at my cousin. His icy eyes and dark hair ring no bells.

Rhett unbuttons his suit jacket and sits in the chair across from me. His jaw is snapped tight. His eyes burn with anger.

Soon as I tell him about my memory issues, he'll call my brother and pull me from the job.

No way in hell will I let that happen.

Doing this—working with the guys, building this resort . . . This is what I was made for. I feel it in my bones.

No one will take it away.

"I've been busy."

"*You're* busy?" Rhett scoffs. "Busy playing with that woman, no doubt."

Anger coils inside me like a cobra about to strike. "Coco has nothing to do with the changes. This land is magical, and because of that, it needed different materials. I didn't know it until we started building. Soon as I realized it, I pivoted. Trust me, what we're using is climate friendly, eco-friendly, and magical-unicorn-land friendly."

Rhett stares at me blankly for a beat before he tips his head back and laughs. When he's done, he wipes tears from his eyes and levels a frigid gaze on me. "What the hell are you talking about? The Stone Maddox I know cares about bottom lines, making money. Did something happen after that competition with Pane? Did it break you or something, because you didn't win the company?"

A slight stinging sensation settles between my shoulder blades. "Nothing has broken me."

Rhett points to Hercules. "And what is that?"

"That is a lambicorn. His name is Hercules."

"Hercules," he sneers.

The hairs on the back of my neck soldier to attention. The way my cousin says the lambicorn's name with obvious distaste, his lack of respect for this land, this town—all of it settles into my bones like dust over water.

This feels familiar, like somewhere deep inside the shell I call a body, there lives a place where I would align with this—where distaste of lambicorns and indifference to the land make sense.

The lambicorn approaches Rhett, who ignores him. Hercules, obviously sensing this is someone who is not of the same ilk as *us*, lifts his nose and trots over to me to be stroked.

It's lambicorn versus my cousin—a toss-up on who will win this outcome.

"And what about that ragtag crew you've got out there?" Rhett adds. "Looks like you picked them up from a shelter."

My hackles lift. "Most of those people needed jobs and I gave them one. They're hard workers. They're not stealing or doing drugs on-site. They're making up for lost time."

"Who *are* you?" he asks honestly.

For that, I don't have an answer, because everything Rhett says suggests I'm not the man he knows—a cold, shallow person who doesn't care about lambicorns.

"And what about that chick? She's no blond bombshell. She looks brainy. Not your usual romp in the hay."

"Maybe it's more than a romp."

He scoffs.

My shoulders fall because Rhett has confirmed my biggest fear. I was shallow, self-centered. Someone I don't recognize now.

Which means, maybe . . . maybe I don't deserve the good things in my life.

"Listen." My cousin drums his fingers on the chair's arm. "We're over budget, behind schedule, and you're making changes that haven't been approved by me or Pane. What's gotten into you? The Stone Maddox I know would never jump ship like this for some bullshit eco-materials no one's heard of."

"Maybe I've changed," I snarl.

Rhett glares at me. "That's all I need to know."

He rises and turns to leave. I follow.

My cousin throws open the door and steps into the bright Georgia sunshine.

Coco is outside, pretending to study her phone. But the worry lines on her face reveal she heard everything.

Rhett turns to me. "When I tell your brother you need to be removed from this site, he'll listen. Unless you've got some great reason as to why you should remain here, you're done." He shakes his head in disgust. "In only a matter of weeks you've single-handedly destroyed our budget, killed our profit margin, and ruined this resort."

I curl my hands into fists. To hell with the profit margins. We might go over a little here, but we'll make up the difference on the back end, when business starts booming.

Rhett holds up a finger. "Just one good reason why I shouldn't pull you off this build today—that's all I'm asking for. Otherwise, your name won't be on this or any project after. You better hope there's enough money in your trust fund to keep you secure until you die."

There are a million reasons to give him, but only one matters. Not the resort. Not the money. Not even the man I used to be.

"Her," I say as Coco looks up. "I shouldn't be removed because of her."

"What?" my cousin asks.

"All of this—the changes, being behind schedule—I've done all of it for her."

Coco looks over, eyes bright as a doe's. "For me?"

"For you," I say, opening my arms wide.

Then I cross over to her and take her hand. In the distance, the ley lines thrum strongly.

They're not weak anymore—they're thriving. And when I squeeze Coco's hand, they glow even brighter.

"*Her?*" Rhett's face twists scornfully. "Why would you do any of this for her?"

"Because," I start, looking down at Coco. The pulse at her neck flutters. Her cheeks are red. This is her worst nightmare, being exposed.

My God, how do I know this?

Because I know *her*, better than even I remember. Coco tucks herself away and hides around her family, but she can't hide from me because I see her.

In this moment, I stop worrying about who I was and walk into the man I am now—the one who sees her, who sees this land, who sees everything.

Emotions war in her eyes. She's afraid of this moment. She didn't want me to know the truth, to protect me, but I don't need to be protected, because I know what's real.

This is real. This feeling. *This* right here, right now. This is me looking at the past I've lost and telling myself I will not let those agonizing feelings take over ever again.

I'm here with her.

I squeeze Coco's hand and then pin my gaze on Rhett, who's scowling. "We're engaged," I say, my voice steady. "Coco and I are getting married."

Then I smile, just for her.

"And part of this resort is my wedding gift."

Coco sways like she's going to faint. And I don't blame her. She thought I forgot our truth, that we'd made plans for the future, and she's right.

But I'm not worried. It's all about to come back to me.

Chapter 26

COCO

What is happening?

Am I living in a mirror world? Is a white rabbit about to run by claiming he's late?

Right on cue, Hercules prances past.

I suppose that's close enough.

Stone murmurs in my ear, "I found the ring. You should have told me."

His voice is low, intimate, like a caress light enough to coax and an iron hot enough to brand. My skin flames from the closeness of him. But before I get too cozy and wrapped up in him, a record scratches in the back of my mind, and the moment is obliterated.

A ring? He found a ring? *What* ring?

Oh, shit. Stone found my grandmother's ring—the one she gave me—and he thinks it's for our engagement?

My stomach falls into an open pit.

He presses my hand to his breast, right over his heart. It pounds, thumping so hard I wonder whether his body is lying, too—or it's just telling a different kind of truth.

"We're engaged," he confirms to Rhett, as casual as a summer breeze. Like this is just a totally normal Tuesday announcement. Then he jerks a thumb toward the plans. "And the flower garden? Not in the original blueprint. That one's all me."

Then he whispers in my ear, "Just so we're crystal clear, the garden is my wedding gift to you."

He's building a garden for me?

My knees go full spaghetti.

Is this what swooning feels like?

It has to be.

And I'm all in.

Rhett waits a beat before he tosses his head back and laughs. When his chin drops down, fury blooms in his eyes. "You're joking, right? As of yesterday, I'd never heard of *her*, you're *MIA*, and when I arrive, there are materials being used we didn't approve of. That *I*"—he points to his chest—"didn't sign off on. Have you lost your mind?"

Stone slowly shakes his head. His sandy hair catches the sun, and streaks of dark caramel and platinum glint in the light.

I hold my breath as he looks Rhett dead in the eyes. "I've never had more clarity in my life."

An explosion of air swooshes from my lungs, and new air rushes in. It feels like the world does the same, like it came to a full stop waiting to see how this would play out.

And it hasn't started spinning yet, because Rhett isn't finished.

When he speaks, it's a growl of warning. "If I pull my investment, there's no way you'll be able to complete the resort."

"Then pull it," Stone replies, accepting his challenge. "I won't be bullied, and I won't be intimidated. What I'm doing—what *we're* doing"—he looks at me, and that swoony, lightheaded rush fills my head again—"is creating something new, something different, something that matters and will, when it's done, be hailed as visionary. Trust me."

His cousin swipes a hand down his face. He looks like a mix between exhausted and furious, as if he doesn't know which problem to tackle first: this new version of Stone or the resort.

I'd say it's a toss-up.

"Does Pane know? What am I saying? Of course he doesn't, because *he*, unlike you, would have called me. Your brother's not going to like this, Stone. *This* is the sort of thing that destroys relationships, rips apart families. You'll see. You may think it's fun to play since you've been left to your own devices, and this may be your way of getting revenge on Pane for whipping your ass when it came to the company competition, but this is going too far."

I wait for Stone to back down, to turn and change his mind, but instead he simply lifts his shoulders and keeps a steady gaze on his cousin.

Rhett's eyes flick to mine. "Best wishes on your upcoming nuptials." To Stone, he says, "You're worth a lot, you know. So much that people like you get used for it."

"She's not after me for my money," Stone growls. Then frowns. Worry flicks in his eyes. I squeeze his hand to convey I am not after anything.

Rhett shakes his head in disgust. "You'll be hearing from my attorney."

And with that, Rhett Maddox turns on his heel and enters the SUV. Dust and pebbles kick up under the tires as the driver peels out of the construction site.

I wave away the cloud of dirt that envelops us. Stone does the same before the corners of his mouth tick up into a wry smirk. "That went well, don't you think?"

I laugh feebly, feeling both broken and filled at the same time. "Stone, I—"

I'm about to explain that of course we're not engaged, that he misunderstood the ring. But he interrupts with, "Why didn't you tell me we're getting married?"

Everything's knotted and tangled, from the way my body sings when I'm near him to the crushing guilt that's slowly ripping me apart.

I lock gazes with his warm eyes—so mossy, so honest. And I want to be honest, too. Like Stone. Living in my truth the way he does.

For a moment I simply drink in the way he looks at me with such care. No one's ever looked at me this way before. No one.

And I can't let it go.

As my brain scrambles to come up with an answer as to why I didn't tell him we're engaged (probably because we aren't), he waves his hand. "Never mind, I know why you didn't say anything."

Surprising even myself, I answer with, "You do?"

Stone looks at me so softly, with so much tenderness, that my insides melt like a snow cone on a hot sidewalk.

"You didn't want to hit me with too much chaos with everything that's going on." He puts on a teasing voice. *"You don't know who you are, Stone? Well, guess what, you're marrying me, a complete stranger! Giddyap, partner."*

And right then, I lie to myself and think I'm doing this for him. Because if I snatch it all away, everything will crumble.

His tone softens. "I completely understand, and at the same time, you could have told me. Because *of course* we're engaged."

Of course *we're engaged?* I just . . . I can't wrap my mind around this statement. It scares the hell out of me. Because it means he feels something real. This is more than just kissing in front of my dad's music shrine.

Stone frowns. "Why didn't your family say anything when we went to their house?"

My ribs squeeze so hard it feels like my lungs will burst. I can tell the truth right now and Stone will never look at me with tenderness again. He'll never hold my hand.

He'll never kiss me in a way that fills me to my toes and makes me feel seen. I'll never feel like I've been picked first ever again.

I'll be starved of light.

If Stone is the sun, then living without him is being banished to a life of shadows.

"Because . . ." Then, like with all lies, when the floodgates open, water bursts forth. "We wanted to keep things a secret for a while. Let it cool. Feel it out. We didn't want the world to know before we were ready to tell them."

He takes my hands and rubs his thumbs over my knuckles. His warmth is a luxury I never want to be without.

"How would you feel if we told them now?" Before I can protest, he adds, "From the first moment I met you, I knew there was something special between us, and now that I know what it is, I want the world to know. It's not fair to keep this secret to ourselves."

That secret sits on top of a trapdoor.

He continues, and I shake off the sinking feeling opening in my stomach. "This also means—and yes, I'm going out on a limb here, feel free to catch me if I fall—if you knew me before the amnesia, then I've been afraid of something that doesn't exist. I couldn't have been an awful person because you wouldn't have loved me."

Loved you?

He keeps going, oblivious to the deer-in-headlights look I know is plastered across my face. "Don't you see? I wasn't awful, because you wouldn't have been with me. Plus, we may not have spent a lot of time together *now*, but I feel like *I know you*."

"You know me?" I whisper.

He nods.

Stone desperately wants to *not* be the person he was before—the person who threatened to blackmail me, the person who rejected Hercules, the person who called me a small bureaucrat.

That's all he wants. Redemption. Reinvention. A future that isn't shackled to his past.

Who am I to starve him of that?

My throat jams up as if a roll of toilet paper has been crammed inside it. I can't *not* ask. "*What* do you know about me?"

He slides a hand over my cheek. "I know you put the needs of others before your own. I know you have taken care of me every step of the way. I see you, Coco Higginbotham, just like you see me."

No one—*no one*—has ever said anything like this to me. Not in my whole life. And I want to believe it. I want to bathe in every second of this moment, so all I manage to say is, "Yes."

I'm saying yes to him. To being swept away in this moment, to being caught in a lie that feels truer than it should.

Stone taps my nose playfully. "This calls for a celebration."

"It does?"

My mind barely works. Or maybe it's working on overdrive and I'm simply unable to keep up.

Stone slides an arm over my shoulders and turns to the guys. The construction site is loud, full of rumbling and beeping, but Stone puts two fingers in his mouth and whistles, getting Isaac's attention.

Isaac signals to the guys to stop what they're doing.

"What's up?" he calls out. "Everything okay?"

"Everything's great," Stone yells back. "After work, we're going to Sparkle Bar to celebrate."

"Celebrate what?"

Stone pulls me closer to him. "Our engagement!"

The guys look surprised, and then seem to quickly realize that surprise is not the correct response, because Isaac slowly claps and yells, "Congrats!"

Ron joins him.

And while they clap and shout their congratulations, Hercules trots up to me, lifts his leg, and aims to pee on my shoe.

I barely move out of the way before the full stream splashes to the ground. What the . . . ? Sheep don't lift their legs to pee.

Apparently, this one does, and he's not happy with me. Neither is my conscience, because what I've just done . . . this is a ticking time bomb, an explosion that, maybe, with a little luck, I can avoid.

But how?

Chapter 27

COCO

The chair creaks beneath me as I drop my head to the desk, relishing the cool wood against my flaming, guilt-soaked skin.

Cristina's voice blares through the phone. "You did *what*?"

"I agreed," I tell her, my voice strangled, "that we're engaged."

"Are you out of your mind?"

"Apparently."

"Well?"

"Well, what?"

"How in the name of sweet tea and bad decisions did Stone get *that* idea?"

Then I explain Nu-Nu's ring and how he somehow put the two completely unrelated things together. I end with, "I couldn't find it in myself to disagree. Please don't kill me."

"I can't make any promises, Coco Higginbotham. This is low. Very low. Like, I'm-surprised-you-haven't-sunk-into-a-pit-of-despair low."

That's what I'm afraid of.

Cristina's voice is laced with worry. "This is bad."

My bowels tighten so painfully it takes a second to breathe through it. "You don't understand. His cousin showed up and started saying the resort was terrible. He asked what had happened to Stone because he's not right—"

"Well, he isn't," she snaps. "We deleted his memory. It's gone, and frankly, I don't see you being very worried about this, not like you should be. This is potentially catastrophically bad, and you don't seem to realize it. In fact, I'm beginning to wonder if you've lost your memory, too."

"Stop it. You know I haven't."

"Haven't you? You've had chances to tell him."

"I know, but he's different now. He's kind, and he met my parents—"

"You took him to the preppers? Oh my God. Now I know you've lost your mind. Did they chew him up and spit him out?"

"No, he was great. He defended me in front of my family."

There's a short pause before she realizes. "You've fallen for him."

"No, no, of course not. I haven't . . ."

"Collette Michele Higginbotham," Cristina says sternly, "you have to fix this. Not tomorrow. Not in two days. But right now. You cannot let Stone Maddox believe y'all are engaged. You can't. If you don't figure this out, I'll tell him myself."

"Wait. Just wait. We still don't know what the lunaria bloom is. Can you imagine what will happen if we tell him the truth and we're not able to fix his amnesia? That's even worse. Don't you think?"

It's not that I'm afraid to tell him. Okay, I'm terrified of telling him for many reasons I've already pointed out—the resort, the ley lines, the way he looks at me.

And how I'm probably looking at him.

I know. It's so bad. This can't go on forever—but maybe it can go on just long enough to ensure the resort gets built with the ley line–friendly materials . . . or Rhett sues him. Whichever comes first.

"Okay." She clicks her tongue. "You're right. We can't tell him without the cure. So that's where we start. We find out what we can about the lunaria bloom."

A little knot of worry loosens inside me.

"And, Coco, the sooner you fix this, the better off you'll be and he will be, too."

A pool of dread doesn't simply open in my stomach—it swallows it whole. Cristina's right. "In the meantime, while we're still trying to figure out the flower, there's a party at Sparkle Bar."

"For what?" She shrieks so loudly I pull the phone away from my ear.

"To celebrate."

"Good Lord, Coco. Celebrate what? Your fake engagement?"

"Something like that."

"Wow. Just wow. I've already beat my drum, so I won't keep harping, but all I'll say is, this is spinning so far out of control it's heading straight into the black hole of another dimension."

It's finally time for her to understand what I've been holding in. "If I hadn't done this, Stone Maddox would've destroyed the magic in our town. His project was killing the ley lines, Cristina."

The silence on the other end of the line stretches for an ungodly amount of time.

Sweat sprouts on my palms. It leaks onto my forehead.

I blast myself for telling her. This was one bombshell that should've stayed locked away.

"And how do you know the resort was hurting the ley lines?" she asks, like, *And you can be sure of this, how?*

My throat shrivels. "Because I can see them."

"You can *what*? I didn't hear you."

I exhale so hard my bangs lift off my forehead. "I can see the ley lines."

"You're a—"

"I'm not a witch," I hiss. "But I can see them, and because of the potion we gave him, Stone can see them now, too, and before we did it, he couldn't. He was set to destroy our town and take all the magic with it."

"You don't know that. There are ley lines out by Wadley Farms."

"The ones the resort is built on lead directly into town. The damage would have been severe. Detrimental. I did what I had to for this town and I won't apologize for it."

Cristina says quietly, "Why didn't you tell me?"

"Why would I? You know how people act whenever anyone brings up the topic. I was afraid you'd—"

"Oh my God, Coco." She sounds hurt. "You thought I'd turn on you?"

Her words vibrate inside my ribs, rattling the bones. "I hope at least you can understand why I did it."

"I do." She goes quiet, as if she's thinking. "But now you've got to make it right. You've got to tell him, or better yet, cure him. If he finds out, if this blows up, it won't just break him—it'll blow up your life."

I close my eyes. "Do you think I'm toast?"

"I hope not. But the one thing we need is that flower."

I raise my head, stretching out my spine, and then I fall back against my chair. "And how do I do search for it?"

"See if you can find out anything about the woman who owned the spell book. Maybe she can shed some light on what the plant is."

I'm pretty sure she's dead. Why else would she have left all her things? But maybe one of my coworkers knows something—how I can track down her children, for instance. Maybe they can help.

"All right. I'll see what I can dig up. But tell me, will you be at—"

"Yes, I'll be at Sparkle Bar," she says, sounding defeated.

Cristina might not agree with any of this, but she's going along for the ride, and right now, I need to get out of the passenger seat and let someone else take the wheel—like her.

We hang up and I steel myself, preparing to find out everything I can about the woman who left the spell book. Maybe, just maybe, I'll find the answers I need.

But what if this dead woman took the answers to the grave—and I just doomed us all?

Chapter 28

COCO

One step inside Sparkle Bar and the breath spills from my lungs. Fairy lights sprint across the ceiling, and elegant black cloths drape the tables. The entire place glows.

It no longer feels like the town's dive bar. Now it shines like an *upscale* bar.

I turn to Stone, whose hand cradles my lower back. "Did you have something to do with this?"

Red dots his cheeks. "I may have asked the guys to spruce it up."

"Congratulations!" Isaac, Ron, and his wife Jennifer shout, as well as other folks from town like Clarice, Cristina, and the ladies from book club.

They're all here—all of them—for me. For *us*. To celebrate our engagement.

I'm going to be sick.

"Can I get you something to drink?" Stone asks.

"Wine would be great."

"Be right back." He gives me a warm smile that melts my insides before heading off toward the bar.

There is so much to admire about Stone Maddox—his goodness, his kindness. Not to mention his strong shoulders and pecs. His body is drool-worthy even *with* clothes.

Not that I know what he looks like *unclothed*. Stone keeps a T-shirt on when he putts around the cottage. But I can only imagine the smooth dips and mouthwatering valleys that sculpt his abs.

Pressure coils in my core just thinking about him.

Better stop daydreaming or else I'll wind up in more trouble than I'm already in.

"Hey, girl." I look over as Jennifer wraps me in a hug. "Congrats."

"Thank you."

She lifts a glass of wine. "I'd cheers with you, but you don't have a drink yet."

"Stone's getting me one."

"Stone Maddox," she says, flipping her long brown braid over one shoulder. "What are the chances two local girls would snatch up the Maddox brothers?"

My stomach turns queasy. "Yeah, what are the chances?"

"Mmm." She watches him before glancing back at me. "From what the guys say, Stone's changed in the past weeks. He's acting like a whole new man. If you ask me, it's like he's under some kind of—"

She laughs before finishing the word, but my spine locks anyway.

I laugh weakly. "You never know."

Stone talks with Isaac and Ron, who hasn't stopped chatting since Stone grabbed our drinks. He looks over and shoots me a tender look. The ice in my stomach is quickly replaced with butterflies that lift into the sky.

Jennifer pats my arm. "I'd better save your fiancé before Ron talks him to death. If you'll excuse me."

As soon as she enters the conversation, Isaac leaves and approaches me.

"I figure I've got about one minute to do this," he says, eyeing the crowd.

"Do what?"

"Find out what the hell is going on." He looks at me hard, suspicion spilling from his eyes. "Two weeks ago you and Stone couldn't stand each other. Now you're engaged, and he's acting funny—like, really funny. Changing plans, rebuilding a resort. So what's the deal, Coco?"

Wow. I really wish I had that drink right about now so I could bury my face in it. "Why don't you ask Stone?"

"Because I'm asking you." Isaac smooths a hand down his braids and his tone softens. "Look, we've known each other long time, and I trust you. But something strange is happening. What is it?"

I *have* known Isaac a long time, and if I attempt to say it's nothing, he won't believe me. Might as well fess up.

"The day I came to inspect the ley lines, I saw the resort was weakening them. I tried to tell Stone, but he wouldn't listen."

"Sounds about right."

I frown. This is the part when he's supposed to say, *You can see ley lines? You're a hideous beast! Leave our village before we destroy you.*

When he doesn't, I slowly continue. "So I did something to help him see them."

Isaac lifts an eyebrow. "You drugged him?"

"No! Kind of? Not like that. I gave him a potion." I drop my voice. "It was supposed to help, not reset his entire personality."

"And the engagement?"

"He found a ring I'd had sized. And before I could stop him, he told Rhett we were getting married. I didn't plan this, Isaac. I swear. I'm not trying to take advantage of a Maddox."

Isaac tips his head like he's contemplating either forgiving me or locking me in cell for the rest of my life. After a length of time so painful I'd rather endure a root canal than wait another second, he says, "I do like this Stone better."

My bones liquify into a happy pile of mush. "I like this Stone, too. That's the problem. I wasn't supposed to."

Soon as he changes back, I'll become enemy number one and the blackmail scenario will be on. I exhale a hard sigh just thinking about how callous he was before.

Isaac shoots me a sympathetic look. "Well, the guy has compassion. The other Stone, he was hurt by his family and he was sitting in it bad."

"What do you mean?"

"Apparently, his mother kept him away from his dad for most of his life, told him and Pane that the man didn't want to have anything to do with them."

My jaw falls. "What?"

"Crazy, right?"

"It's terrible."

I look back at Stone. He's smiling, but you would never know what he's suffered. Well, you would if you'd met him before the spell got ahold of him. But today, this is the best version of himself, and somehow, I want to become the best version of me because of him.

Isaac starts to move away but I hold out my hand to stop him. "Are you . . . will you tell him?"

He shakes his head. "The man's happy. You're happy. But secrets don't stay buried long in Mystic Meadows. Especially not the magical kind. Eventually, you'll have to choose who you're trying to protect—and why."

As Isaac leaves, Stone disentangles himself from Ron and Jennifer and makes his way back to me. Our gazes never leave one another as he approaches.

"I hope white wine is okay."

"It's perfect."

He clinks his beer bottle against my wineglass. "You know, it's weird."

"What is?" I take a sip. The wine is cold and fruity. Perfect. "I mean, other than we're having a party at Sparkle Bar."

He chuckles. "Nothing about that's weird. I always envisioned my engagement party would be housed in a place with deer heads."

"You really can't go wrong with a few mounted bass and a stuffed bobcat."

"I think the turkey is what makes the place. I wouldn't know what to do with myself if there wasn't a stuffed fowl sitting on that table back there."

He points, and sure enough, a turkey is mounted in a standing position atop a table. The fowl holds its head high like it's the guest of honor.

Stone winks as I chuckle. He gives me such a tender look my knees weaken. Who is this beautiful, wonderful man? If I could bottle this Stone forever, I would. I want to preserve him, this moment, all of it, forever. My body aches at the thought that this is fleeting.

"Listen, I realize this probably isn't how you want to do this," he says.

"Do what?"

He points his beer around the room. "Announce our engagement. But as soon as I knew, I couldn't *not* do this."

He's so sweet. It hurts my soul.

He sets his beer on a table and steps closer. His voice lowers, like we're in a world of our own. "I want to know everything."

My mouth goes dry from his closeness, from his sea breeze scent, from his very presence.

"You want to know everything?" I ask, my tongue like sandpaper. "What kind of everything?"

"What's your favorite ice cream flavor?"

Oh, *that* kind of everything. Not the tell-me-all-about-my-life-and-fake-answers-you-know-nothing-about kind of everything. "Butter pecan is my favorite flavor, but only if the ice cream actually tastes like butter. Otherwise it isn't worth it."

"Mine is strawberry," he says matter-of-factly. Then his eyes bulge. "Yes, it is. Strawberry. Wow. I know that. All right." Stone snaps his fingers. "Favorite food?"

"Indian."

He sucks air. "Chicken tikka masala!"

"Yes!" I throw up my arms. "I love it!"

"Me too. Wait. I remember the first time I tried it. I was at a hotel . . . It changed my life. I may have cried afterward." He frowns. "Hold up. It's not my absolute favorite. Nothing can replace a great cheeseburger on a toasted bun."

"Oh, I agree."

He takes a swig of his beer. "What about movies?"

"Hmm. I don't have a favorite, but *Stranger Things* is my all-time favorite show."

"It's like if *E. T.* and *Close Encounters* had a fourth-dimensional baby that's crawling with demons!"

"Yes," I screech.

"Yes!" Stone tosses his arms in the air. People glance over curiously. "Just, um, found out she's not pregnant."

I elbow him lightly in the stomach and shake my head, silently telling him, *Not pregnant.* He takes my arm, slides his hand down it, and entwines his warm fingers in mine.

He is so lusciously warm.

This, I think. This is what real relationships are forged from—likes, dislikes, dreams, hopes, goals. Your heart tugging when you share something in common, and theirs doing the same.

But this is different because every piece of himself that Stone remembers shortens the ticking time bomb of *us.*

When people shoot us more curious looks, I add, "He's joking. No babies."

Then everyone returns to their conversations.

I look up to see Stone gazing down at me. My throat shrinks.

He squeezes my hand. "I love *Stranger Things.* Just like I know that I . . ." He swallows, and part of me thinks he was going to say, *Just like I know I love you.*

But that can't be, because we barely *know* one another, and love takes time to grow and blossom.

But maybe this is what the *beginning* of love feels like, and that's what he was going to say.

I steer the conversation in a different direction. "What else do you know about yourself?"

Ron walks up, holding a tray of hot dogs. "Fresh from the oven," he says. "Sorry, Coco, we couldn't get anything fancier on such short notice. Jennifer wouldn't even unlock the controlled-drug cabinet for us."

"First, hot dogs are great. Second, I know you're joking, Ron, because taking prescription medication that isn't prescribed to you is illegal."

He gives me a lopsided grin. "I *am* joking. We wouldn't do that. Jennifer's too much of a professional to even kid about it."

We each take a dog, but once Ron is gone, Stone wrinkles his nose and places his on a nearby table.

I eye the discarded meal. "You're not hungry?"

"I'm hungry, I just hate hot dogs. Can't stand them and I have no idea why. Maybe because they're processed."

He only took the offer to be polite. It makes me smile. "That's a small but notable detail." A shadow passes over his face, and I tug on his sleeve playfully. "What is it?"

"It's weird I can remember those things—what I like, dislike. But I can't remember the important stuff—you, my parents, my brother, my sister. And that's what I want to know. And before you say anything, I want to remember that stuff on my own, just like everything else."

I squeeze his hand. "You'll find the answers."

Before his lips quirk playfully or he gives me a tender look that's stuffed with trust—both expressions that will make my guilt spiral—I glance away and spot Cristina. She scrunches her face and shoots me a look that says, *This is sweet, but we have bigger problems.*

"Do you want to know what I'm most proud of?" I ask, ignoring my friend's look.

"Yes," he says without hesitation. "I for sure want to know this."

"You." When I say it, he flinches. "I'm proud of you for diving into the project headfirst. For believing in yourself. If this happened to me, if I had"—I drop my voice—"amnesia, I'd be a nervous wreck. But you're thriving. You're redoing the resort, and the design is even better. The materials are amazing. The crew is working overtime—for *you*. Not for someone else, but because they respect you."

Stone gently brushes a strand of hair from my cheek. "All I want is to be someone who makes you proud."

Heat floods every inch of my body. My mouth goes dry because I feel the same way. I want to be someone he's proud of, too.

In order to do that, the truth must be told. It's the worst possible time, but better to end things now before I'm in so deep I'll never be able to dig myself out.

"Stone, there's something—"

But before there's a chance to finish, the front doors are thrown open and Brittany appears, her phone in hand.

My sister and my entire family—including my grandmother—step inside the bar and yell, "Congratulations!"

Chapter 29

COCO

Oh my God. It couldn't get any worse than this.

My family. All here. Phones record. Squeals of delight ring in my ears.

My prepper clan sweeps into Sparkle Bar like bad bangs from the '80s. Luckily, my dad is wearing normal clothes for once, probably because my mother made him, which I'm grateful for.

Hey, I'm not going to look a gift horse in the mouth.

In fact, I won't look any horse in the mouth in case it bites my face off.

My mom wraps me in a hug that smells like lavender and mint. "Why didn't you tell us?"

Is this the same woman who said I didn't have the job that I have? What has this stranger done with my mother?

Meanwhile, Brittany gabs into her phone, arms wide, brow scrunched with determination. "We're here at Sparkle Bar, where my sister's celebrating her engagement to Stone Maddox!" She turns to me. "Coco, were you ever going to tell us? Or were you going to let us guess it was your wedding day when you showed up in a white dress, like you did for prom? Except it wasn't white. It was blue. Remember that?"

She laughs like it's the funniest thing ever and then adds, "Just kidding. But isn't this like the time you said you had a boyfriend but it was really a toad?"

"I was three," I reply, my insides curdling.

Brittany gets right in my face. "Well?"

"Um, uh . . ." I start to panic. Can feel the bile surge up the back of my throat. The hot lights, the oxygen-stealing closeness of the crowd, my grandmother insisting Stone give her sugar while he probably wonders why this woman wants sweetener.

My stomach quivers wildly, madly, and I want to run. Worse, though I'm being congratulated, my mother's expression is accusatory—brows knit, lips pursed. My sister's expression is triumphant, like somehow I really screwed this up, and all of it makes me wither into a husk on the inside.

I begin to back up. "Um . . ."

That's when Stone's hand slides across my back, warming my skin through my blouse. He presses firmly, gently, his touch saying a dozen things all at once: *I've got you. Breathe. Let's get through this together. I'm not abandoning you.*

I glance up at him, and he's saying something to my dad, but one edge of his mouth twitches as if it's just for me to see and understand.

Right. I can do this.

I inhale a deep breath and say to my mom, "We were keeping this quiet for a while, but we were going to tell you."

"Now you can tell the world," Brittany announces. To the camera, she adds, "To get the exclusive on Stone Maddox's relationship with my sister, become a member. Members get top-tier access to me and behind-the-scenes bonus content."

She's monetizing this?

Before I can argue that my life isn't for sale, Brittany and Jet zoom away to interview other people in Sparkle Bar, and my mom peppers me with questions about the wedding: What will I wear? When will we dress-shop? Will the wedding be here or in one of his hotels?

Most of my answers are "I'm not sure," and "We'll wait and see," but that doesn't stop Mom from focusing on me in a way that feels alien. There's joy and warmth in her eyes, in how she touches my arm, in how proud she seems.

I can't help but digest this moment, this feeling of standing in the spotlight, for once letting the light hit me.

Stone is still talking to my dad, but he turns and winks. I grin back, so full of happiness I might burst.

For the next hour my family takes over, talking to folks about everything from water-filtration systems to the best way to run a trout line.

It's overwhelming, so when I get a second, I find a corner and plop into it, giving myself a chance to breathe.

Stone is in his element, apparently, talking to my dad, asking him questions about prepping. He seems genuinely interested, and it makes my heart swell.

And my family is eating it up. They fawn over him, dangling on his every word. He's charismatic, explaining how exemplary service is the lifeblood of a hotel like he's giving a TED Talk.

That's when Cristina slides into the seat beside me with a smirk. She nods in Brittany's direction. "This is intense."

My sister keeps the camera on Stone but manages to slip herself into his stratosphere every once in a while. You know, to remind her viewers *why* they've subscribed to her channel.

"I'm surprised Brittany hasn't turned this into a competition where you can win ten thousand dollars by seeing who can outdrink Stone Maddox," my friend says, sipping her beer.

I chuckle. "She wouldn't do that."

Cristina gives me a death stare.

"Okay, she would *definitely* do that."

We both laugh, and it's then that I remember the good news. "I know where Dot is."

"Who?"

"The woman who owned the spell book."

Cristina sits up. "No! When will you see her?"

"Tomorrow, if you want. Maybe she can shed some light on things. There's only one hitch."

"What's that?"

"She's at a nursing home. I don't know if she can receive visitors."

"We'll find out." Cristina pulls gloss from her purse and reapplies a slick pink coat to her lips. "This feels really *real*."

"What does?"

"The way you two are together. It's hard to explain."

"You don't have to."

Her gaze falls on me. "So I'm not imagining it."

"Nope."

"You sense it, too, then?"

"Sense what?"

She shakes her head. "That it's almost like fate, you two. I'm the last person who should be saying this, but you seem really good together. You know, if the circumstances were different and Stone knew who he was, I'd say you had a chance."

"Yeah," I reply, ignoring how her words make me shrink. *Focus on the good, Coco!* "But no worries, we'll get what we need as long as Dot knows about the flower. If her mind is gone, then where will we be?"

"With Brittany shoving a phone in your face and asking Stone if thousand-dollar bills are a real thing."

I burst into laughter. "Stop it."

Cristina gasps.

My gaze tracks hers to the door. Just inside it stands a man with trimmed dark hair, tight jeans, a button-down shirt, and a swagger that's either from false confidence or more cockiness than is legal to own.

In this case, it's false confidence—just my humble opinion.

"What's Jace doing here?" Cristina says in a hushed voice.

"Hmm. Maybe he'll go away in five minutes, once he sees all the people."

"Maybe."

He walks up to the bar. Isaac takes his drink order and then turns and spots Cristina. He gives her a look that silently asks if she's okay, and Cristina nods.

Jace then spots his ex and his jaw tightens. He takes the beer Isaac slides in front of him and swaggers over to us.

The only thing that would be worse right now was if Luke Preston showed up. He works at the bank and is just the worst human being ever.

I nudge her with my shoe. "You don't have to talk to him."

"It's fine. I can do this."

"Before you go all sad-eyes on me, let me remind you what he said: That man, who you think is handsome, said you could be his *first* wife. Not his *only* wife. His first one. Meaning he never planned for anything serious to happen between y'all. Once again I ask, can you be strong?"

Cristina lifts her head. Her chin wobbles for a moment before she grits her teeth. "I can be strong."

Jace reaches the table, takes a pull of his beer, and swipes the back of his arm across his mouth. "Hey, Cristina. Coco."

"Hey," she says.

I don't answer. Jace is a bottom-feeder, the worst of the worst. He stands there, shifting uncomfortably, most likely waiting for an invitation to sit.

Cristina starts, "Jace would you like to—"

I kick the chair closest to us so that it falls over. When Jace reaches to right it, I drop my heels on top, turning the chair into a footstool.

Oops! There goes Cristina's chance to ask if he wants to take a seat. *What is wrong with her?*

"What brings you to Sparkle Bar?" I ask.

He casually glances over his shoulder. "Just meeting some friends." He points to the balloons and lights. "What's the party about?"

"Coco got engaged."

His eyes widen. "You did? That's great. Who's the lucky guy?"

"What do you want, Jace?" I snap. It's none of his business who I'm fake-engaged to.

"Wanted to say hey."

"Hey."

There's a long, uncomfortable pause, and then Jace gives us a nod. "See ya."

He turns and walks off. Soon as he's out of earshot, Cristina smacks my arm. "You didn't have to be rude."

"Yes, I did." Cristina watches him go, and I run a finger over the rim of my glass. "He wasn't good for you. He doesn't care about anyone but himself."

"I know."

"Then why are you staring after him?"

She shrugs. "Because I still care?"

"Girl, there aren't just *more* fish in the sea—there are *better* fish, good fish, great fish, wonderful fish who will love you exactly the way you are. That's the kind of fish you deserve."

Isn't it also the kind *I* deserve?

I look at Stone. He's laughing at something my dad said, eyes crinkling, warm and wide open. Then, without warning, he looks at me—and everything in me tightens.

I like him so much my body throbs with agony at the idea of him changing back, of letting him become the man who hates lambicorns.

The moment he remembers who he is, this all disappears—the laughter, Hercules, the way he touches my back.

"Are you okay?"

No, not even a tad. "Yeah. I'm fine."

Cristina leans forward, and I smell the hops on her breath when she says flatly, "You are so cooked."

My throat tightens. "You don't think he'll forgive me when he finds out?"

"Not easily. Not cleanly."

I could live with him not forgiving me. But what if I can't forgive myself?

Chapter 30

STONE

Soon as things settle down with Coco's family, I grab her, and we talk until the party thins. The world feels new, like there's a chance to experience it all at once, all over again.

I wasn't lying before when I said Coco was an anchor. She secures the Stone ship, and I'll do whatever it takes to protect her.

We talk during the short ride back to her cottage, all the way into the house, and even when I tell Hercules to lie down in his doggy bed.

Coco mesmerizes me at every turn—when she scrunches up her face while thinking, how she lights up a room when she walks into it, how she is a star in the night sky. Luminous.

When we're in the kitchen, she grins up at me. "Thank you for tonight."

"You sure about that? I thought you might curse me after your family showed up."

A flash of worry flickers across her face before it melts into quiet acceptance. "No, they should have been there. My mom would've been upset if they hadn't been invited. And this is a small town. She would've known about the party sooner or later, probably by tomorrow morning."

She laughs, but it's bitter. I ask, "Why do you think your sister is like that?"

A startled look crosses her face. "Like what?"

Coco knows what I'm talking about. I don't understand why she pretends otherwise. "Brittany's obviously jealous of you to undercut your happiness."

"She wasn't undercutting m—"

I wave away her protesting. "Did you hear her? It's a happy day for you, and she brought up something that happened when you were three. She's jealous."

"No she's not."

I take a step forward and cup her cheeks. Coco's breath goes still. She gazes at me like a deer in headlights, like she's terrified.

She doesn't know this new me, so of course she's worried. But I know this new me, and I'm all in.

"Brittany is jealous of you, and I can see why."

"You can?" She cocks her brow slightly as if she's waiting for the punch line to a joke.

There is no punch line.

"Yes." I press my lips to her right cheek, and her breath hitches. "I can."

She pulls back a second and peers at me as if she's trying to decide whether I'm telling the truth, her shoulders tight as if she doesn't believe me. Like she doesn't think she *deserves* to hear this.

Well, she's going to hear it loud and clear.

I press my lips to her left cheek. She smells like cotton and strawberries—clean and sweet, just like her. "Your sister's jealous because you're beautiful."

"Stop it."

"I'm serious. I don't just give out compliments because I want to. You are, and sometimes I wish you could see what I do."

Coco bites her bottom lip as she watches me timidly.

I brush my lips over her forehead. "And you're kind."

Her body goes still.

I kiss her nose. "And thoughtful."

Her lips. "And caring."

My lips hover over her mouth.

"Should I go on?"

There's what feels like an infinite pause. Her gaze flickers between my eyes like she's testing every word, weighing whether or not to believe it.

I brush my lips across the top of her forehead, where the hairline meets her flesh. "I'm not blowing sunshine up your ass."

She laughs, and in that moment she breaks open, and I take everything she's willing to give.

"You can go on if you want to," she admits.

I drop my gaze to meet hers. "I could go on all day about you."

She rolls her eyes, but I keep my focus on her. She squirms a bit, like she's got ants in her pants. But then she looks up at me, and I'm there, staring back at her, not going anywhere.

That's when her body settles, and the room suddenly buzzes with energy.

No, not the room.

She does.

Coco buzzes with electricity. Like there's a firecracker living inside her, dying to get out.

Oh my God. The magic.

There literally *is* a fire inside her.

I'm not sure she even knows it.

But she should. She should definitely know it and celebrate it.

Good thing I'm here to help her.

My mouth drops closer to hers, and Coco tips her lips toward me.

Our mouths meet and it feels like the world has slipped away, that I'm falling with everything I have for this woman, no barriers between us, nothing stopping me.

And then just a thought, a flicker flares inside me. *Betrayal. Having my life ripped away. Knowing I was lied to and it changed everything I knew to be the truth.*

That ache I've felt before, the one that felt intimately familiar, threatens to surface inside me, take over, whisper lies in my ear.

But I push it aside because that memory has no right to invade this perfect moment. I kiss Coco deeply, with everything I have, because I know this will be different, this time everything is different, because a past I don't remember doesn't equal a future that's on the rise.

Because this is real.

Chapter 31

COCO

I melt, dissolving, becoming a puddle under Stone's touch.

His kiss is soft, questioning—*no,* exploring, telling me everything he said in words, but with his tongue, his hands as they slide to cradle my head, his hips as he shifts forward, and oh, wow—there is his erection, pushing into me.

This is a dream, a strange, upside-down dream where I'm kissing Stone Maddox.

Stone. Maddox.

A man who wants to define himself not by his past but by his future. A man who has chosen me. *Me.* And with him I can breathe, I can feel, I can shine, because tonight I did shine even when Brittany tried to dim my light.

I flared into a supernova every time he touched my back, my hand, or slipped me a sly smile.

And I'm still flaring now.

I sigh as heat winds into my core. Stone's lips leave mine and he brushes kisses down my neck to my collarbone. His hands slide down my arms.

I never want him to stop. My fingers entwine in his silky hair and I tug his head up. He looks at me with surprise before rising and claiming my mouth with his own.

The kiss deepens and he moans as I whimper. My nipples are as hard as diamonds, and moisture pools in my panties.

What am I doing? Should we slow this down? Should we stop? But what if in a few hours everything's different? I just want this one night to be perfect, to feel real, to be as real as it can be with him.

Because let's face it, tomorrow I break his amnesia, and then Stone will be different.

He'll hate me, and I'll return to living my little life.

No.

I don't want to live like that anymore. I want to be big. Be seen. Feel wanted.

I don't just want him to forgive me when it all blows up. I want him to see me. The real me. And still want me. But I don't think that's how my story will go.

Stone's kisses become hotter, heated, frantic, and I feel the same energy.

I reach for his shirt and begin undoing the buttons, but his hands take mine and his kisses slow.

Stone presses his forehead to mine. We're both panting. Our chests rise and fall in time. I rest a hand over his heart and feel it thump beneath my palm.

My eyes close and I exhale.

"Since we're relearning each other, we should go slow," he tells me, forehead still against mine. "This doesn't mean I don't want you. I *want you.* But with everything going on, we should pause."

I rock back so we're looking one another in the eye. "Just for the record . . . I would've gone all the way."

He barks out a laugh and kisses me softly again. "For the record, I would have, too."

I want to scream at his honesty, and I want to run because he *is* so honest. So dreadfully, beautifully honest. My lungs squeeze, equal parts longing and ache, and I know he sees all the hidden pieces of me.

But Stone only kisses my palm and murmurs, "I'll take the couch."

The ache inside me deepens. I want this. I want him so badly. Every part of me screams with desire. This whole thing—us—it's a lit fuse, just waiting to reach the bundle of TNT and explode.

But right now I want to explore the fire, the desire I feel, and I know he does, too.

Yet I can't. All I can do is sit in this ache and want him from afar.

I watch him move away, and just when he grabs the blanket and lays it down, he turns and looks at me.

The same want and longing inside me is reflected in his eyes, and I think for a moment his resolve will crack. But he just stands, watching me.

My throat tightens, and all I can muster is, "Good night."

"Good night," he returns, in a voice that drips with want that I shove aside.

Wanting him and being with him are two different things—dangerous things that will lead to my undoing.

But what if I'm already undone?

Stone is magnetic—everything about him is. Watching him work a room, how he gets people to see his vision and be excited about, even how he takes care of Hercules. I'm more than attracted to him. I've fallen for him.

Which means I'm in deep shit.

I don't want any of this to end. I want to wrap myself in the cocoon of this relationship and pretend—even if it's only for a day—that it's real.

Because it feels real to me.

I sigh and make my way to the bedroom, sitting in this feeling I wish would never end.

Chapter 32

COCO

"What do you think she'll be like?" Cristina asks as we approach the nursing home.

"No idea, but I'm hoping she'll at least remember the book."

"Did you bring it?"

I lift it from my purse, displaying one teensy-weensy corner. "Right here."

Her eyes flare with panic and she shoves the book back into the bowels of my bag. "Don't let anyone see."

"You're the one who asked if I'd brought it."

"I didn't expect you to flash it like you're a perv in a raincoat."

I shoot her a dark look as we step inside. An abrasive, nose-wrinkling antiseptic smell permeates the nursing home. Lining the ceiling are bright fluorescent lights that no woman over thirty would ever approve of, and a receptionist sits behind a desk that bustles with nurses.

I tell her we're here to visit Dot Stevens. She and a nurse exchange a quiet, if supercharged, look that makes my stomach fall.

"Are you a relative?" the receptionist asks in a way that makes me feel like I should probably lie and say yes, but if I add one more fib to my conscience, I might break in half.

"We're not related. I brought her a book."

"Let me check if Dot's up for a visit." She lifts a beige phone and punches in a couple of numbers. "Can Dot Stevens see visitors?" There's a long pause before she says, "Okay, I'll let her know."

My hopes plummet because it's obvious she'll say no and I'll go home empty-handed.

The receptionist hangs up the phone. "Dot can have visitors, but you won't be able to stay very long. She's tired."

I nearly jump up and down with glee. "Thank you. Which way?"

She gives us directions and a few minutes later, Dot's nurse meets us in the hallway and knocks on her door. "There's two ladies here to see you."

"Send them in," comes the reply in a raspy voice.

Dot Stevens sits in a chair crocheting a rainbow-colored afghan that's spread over her knees. If I had to guess, she's probably in her eighties. Her skin sags, and brown liver spots speckle her hands and face. She has watery blue eyes and wears thick glasses.

When we enter, she looks up, stares at me, and says, "Who the hell are you?"

So much for the kindly old woman vibe she had going. I wouldn't be surprised if Dot pulled out a cigar and asked if I knew her bookie so she can place a bet on a horse named Winter Fresh.

I nervously tuck a strand of hair behind my ear. "My name is Collette Higginbotham, and this is my friend, Cristina. I took over your old position at land development. Well, it's not really your old position. They made a new one, what with the magic being restored to the land and all. But I got your old office."

"Did that son of a bitch Oscar steal any of my books?" she snarls.

Oh my goodness, I'm so glad I didn't bring cookies. Dot would probably prefer whiskey and a blowtorch so she can break out of the nursing home.

Beside me, Cristina attempts to hold in her laughter. She shakes silently, and I get the feeling that any second now, she'll excuse herself to go scream into another resident's pillow.

"Well?" Dot demands when I don't answer quickly enough about Oscar and the books. "Did he take them?"

"No. He left them, and he didn't even dust the office before I arrived."

"Son of a bitch." She stops crocheting and glares at me. "Do you know I worked with that asshole for thirty years—thirty whole years—and the whole time he gave me the shit jobs, literally. If someone was putting a new shitter in a restaurant, he made me check it out. I told him over and over again, shitters weren't on our list of projects, but he insisted. So you know what I did?"

"Checked out the shitter?" Cristina asks with the most serious face I've ever seen.

"I checked out the shitter," she confirms, deadpan as all get-out.

Before this day is over, I might spontaneously combust from laughing on the inside.

"Sounds like a *crap* job," Cristina adds.

I. Want. To. Die.

"It was more than crap," she screeches. "It was shit!"

"Dot." Her nurse appears in the doorway, voice coated in warning. "What did we say about cussing?"

"We said I can do it every once in a while. Look, Mary, I've been good for a long time. You haven't even heard one 'fuck' from me in, what? Two weeks?"

"Three days."

"Huh? Do you chart it or something?"

"No. I have a memory, and you cuss more than any woman on this floor."

"That's because I'm with a whole bunch of damned dainty Southern belles who think they're too high and mighty to admit they pull up their panties the same way I do. And if Hazel's complaining, she'd better shut her mouth, because do you know what I saw her doing to old Benji in his room?"

The nurse's face turns beet red. "That's for you to know. Just keep the cussing to a minimum, or try not to shout so God and all the angels hear you."

The nurse leaves and Dot stage-whispers to me, "What Hazel did to Benji will give her herpes of the mouth. Everybody knows he's got herpes. Hell, he's given it to half the women here."

Okay, and the geriatric visual was way more than I needed. Talk about finding a way to kill your libido.

"We're here because of one of the books you left in the office."

"Oh yeah? Which one? And it better not be the *Kama Sutra*." She shrugs, seeming to rethink it. "Even if it is, don't pay any attention to the dog-eared pages. They're of no consequence."

A bark escapes Cristina and she scuttles toward the door. "Be right back. Need some air."

"Try not to catch herpes in that hallway! The walls are covered in it."

Cristina's laughter echoes as she disappears out the door.

Dot turns her watery gaze to me. "So. What book is it?"

Here goes nothing. "This one."

I pull the spell book from my purse. Dot takes one look at it, her eyes widen, and then her entire expression shuts down.

"I've never seen that before in my whole life. And what the hell are you doing walking around with it, anyway? Don't you know what people in this town think of someone who keeps a book like that? Do you know what I should do?"

She puts one forefinger over the other, making a cross as if I'm a vampire. "Stay away from me. That book isn't mine, and I don't know where it came from."

I swipe a hand over the cover, removing a few motes of dust that cling to it. "I worked one of the spells," I say quietly.

"And what's that got to do with me?"

"I thought you might be able to help. Things went bad."

Dot exhales a low whistle as she slowly lowers her cross fingers. "Close the door." I do as she requests, and then Dot says, "Sit on the bed. It's a herpes-free zone."

Thank goodness. I was worried, because apparently it's on the walls.

When I'm situated, Dot begins. Her entire demeanor has changed. The crochet hook rests in her lap and her hands are curled atop the afghan.

"I put the book in my office to hide it," she explains. "I knew that son of a bitch Oscar wouldn't touch a thing in there. I'd told him time and again if he ever did, I'd cut his nuts off."

She looks at me as if I should compliment her. I manage to say, "That's very, um, specific of you."

Okay. And these two worked together for thirty years? They either despised one another, or they had hate-sex about a gazillion times.

"Yes, well. That's me. Anyway, the book. I found it years ago, hidden in a house I bought when I first moved here. The magic was beginning to leave then. The unicorns still had some power, but not much, and God knows the piggycorns were cute, but completely useless." She cocks her chin. "Has that changed?"

"Yes, I believe it has. The piggycorns can generate electricity."

"Well, good for those little shits. Anyway, it was funny because I could always do small things—like wish for something to happen and it would. So when I found the book—or when *it* found *me*, rather—I thought I'd gained something special, even though in the back of my mind, I knew what I was doing was wrong. But I thought, just a peek. And so I did. I took a good long peek, and I found a spell that called to me."

Her story almost mirrors mine.

Dot continues, "There was a garden in town, a small community one the widows kept. That year there was a drought, and their garden wasn't doing so hot. I was good friends with one of the ladies, and if she didn't get the food from the garden she needed to can and store, then she'd have a hard year coming up."

I could understand that. Canning is a big deal in my community. People rely on the food they store themselves. Georgia might be in the South, but few people grow winter vegetables, and in some places you simply can't because the soil's too rocky.

"So I thought, what the hell? This damn land is magical."

Why does it not surprise me that this was Dot's thought?

She continues, smoothing the afghan over her legs. "There's damn unicorns all over the place. What's the harm in coaxing a few tomatoes to grow? So I started searching in the book for a spell to help. And I found one. But you know what I did?"

"No clue, but I'm curious."

She lifts one finger. "I ignored the warning."

My stomach knots. "What warning?"

"The warning that told me the spell could lead to disaster. I thought, what does a little book know? I'm smarter than it. So I worked the magic. And guess what?"

My shoulders feel heavy just asking. "What?"

"The damn thing worked. The tomatoes grew big and fast. The cantaloupe ripened quickly. It was all perfect the next day. I thought it was great." She scoffs. "But I was wrong. Because even though the tomatoes were big, if they weren't picked right away, they continued to grow. One got as big as a basketball." She seems to contemplate this before adding, "And that's when the whispers started."

Dot's eyes dim. "People talked about witchcraft. They gossiped about evil arriving in town. They wanted to root it out and destroy it. The things they said about me, not knowing it was me who'd caused it—and these were my friends—well, it would have scared even the strongest man. And don't think I hadn't heard the stories about what they did in the past—people disappearing and all that. So I was scared. But worse, what I did affected the ley lines."

My lungs still. "The ley lines?"

Dot nods as if this is more important than the threat of being chopped into little pieces and scattered in the ocean. "You think magic exists in a vacuum? That you do one spell and nothing notices? Well, you're wrong."

Uh-oh. This isn't good.

"You wanna know what happened to the ley lines after I cast that spell?"

"Not really," I murmur, but she doesn't hear.

"They bent. Warped like a bra strap on a hot day—trying to hold too much for too long. The power in this land, it *tried* to do what I asked. It *wanted* to please me. Just like I always did for everybody else.

"And it broke itself to do it. See, that's what magic does when it isn't used right. It doesn't explode—not always. It *compensates.* Stretches itself thin until one day, it snaps.

"The ley lines started rerouting themselves around people. Skipping over them like stones in a river. Because they could feel the fear, the judgment, the small-town poison people whispered behind their teeth. Magic didn't want to be *seen.* And neither did I. So it disappeared, vanished, felt that it wasn't loved or wanted. Well, so did I."

Dot's hands tremble as she picks up her crochet hook and begins to slowly work on the afghan again.

I frown. "But I thought the magic vanished because of its relationship with starfizz berries."

That's what we were told, that the small berries known as starfizz berries were the reason why magic left Mystic Meadows years ago. They weren't being grown anymore.

It was Rowe Maddox who began cultivating them again, and once she reestablished the bushes at her property, magic returned. The biggest sign of that was when the piggycorns ate the berries and soon after received their power to create electricity.

Dot cocks her chin left and right. "Look who thinks she knows so much. Does one spell in an ancient book and can solve all the universe's problems."

"I never said that," I push back gently.

"For your information," she informs me, "the starfizz berries may have helped the magic return, but that isn't why it disappeared in the first place."

My head tingles as I realize exactly what she's saying. "You mean the magic died in the land because you cast a little spell to make tomatoes grow?"

"Not a little spell. A big spell—a spell so big people turned their backs on the magic, and the magic noticed and began disappearing. So I disappeared, too. Why not? No one would accept me the way I was, so why should I show up with gusto?

"I sat in meetings, took notes on shitters, grinned at my coworker while he handed me every crap job in the county. And nobody ever guessed what I'd done. Nobody *saw* me. Which, back then, felt safer than being burned at the stake with a tomato vine wrapped around my ankles. But let me tell you something, cupcake. If you think for one second you can keep doing what I did—tamping down that shine of yours, pretending you're not blazing from the inside out—you're gonna end up just like me. Angry. Invisible. Crocheting rainbow afghans to keep your hands busy so you don't punch your own reflection. So either let the damn land see you, or prepare for it to start skipping *you*, too."

I try to wrap my head around what she's saying. It seems impossible. But yet, it also seems like what she's saying has a large kernel of truth to it.

"You're telling me it's because of a spell you performed that the unicorns lost their power. It's because of you that Mystic Meadows dimmed, because the spell caused people to reject magic?"

"Bingo! We have a Plinko winner on *The Price Is Right.* That's what I'm saying, and what I'm telling you is, the spell you cast, the one you're trying to act like isn't a big deal, is."

It feels like I'm standing in the very center of a teeter-totter, trying to keep my balance while both feet threaten to fall out from under me.

It can't be. I can't be responsible for the magic dying—*again.* "That's why I'm here. There's a flower I need to reverse the spell, but I can't find anything about it."

Dot lifts her eyebrows in interest. "What's it called?"

"The lunaria bloom."

"Ah, I can see why you're having a hard time. It's practically impossible to find." My stomach drops, but Dot clucks. "Lucky for you, I know where to gather one."

Hope grows in me. "You do? Where?"

"The lunaria blossom grows only during the full moon, in grass that glows with ley line magic. The flower is purple, looks like a lily. You can't mistake it. You'll find it out at Wadley Farms, where the first ley lines manifested. Remember: full moon, purple flower. It's easy enough."

"Thank you."

"Anything else, kid?"

"No, ma'am. Thank you for your time."

"You're welcome." I turn to leave, but Dot's voice stops me. "If you're ever over this way, you can visit me again. But next time bring beer, okay?"

I bite back a laugh. "Of course."

"And there's one other thing."

"Yes?"

"Whatever you've done, you need to fix it. Otherwise, the magic might disappear again in Mystic Meadows—and this time it'll be all your fault."

Chapter 33

COCO

After meeting with Dot, I should be spiraling, worried about the full moon countdown, ley lines warping, magic dying because of me. But instead, I spend time with Stone like the world isn't about to implode. Like I'm not about to be the girl who caused the power in my town to die a second time.

One night, Stone appears at the door holding at least seven board games. At his heels, Hercules bleats in approval.

"What's all this?" I ask as he carries this massive tower inside, somehow keeping it balanced.

He drops the boxes on the small kitchen table that has paper napkins shoved under one leg so it doesn't rock.

With a flourish, he says, "I have brought you a collection, milady."

I giggle.

"What would you like to play? Sorry!? Yahtzee? Clue?"

"Clue, for sure."

He lifts his brows flirtatiously. "You drive a hard bargain. I really wanted to start with Yahtzee."

Before I can stop myself, my arms are around his neck. We shouldn't kiss. This shouldn't keep going. Plus, Dot's words won't stop echoing in my head: *You're gonna end up just like me. Angry. Invisible.*

I want to be chosen. Even if it's just for one game night. So I kiss him. "Then we start with Yahtzee."

"Nope, Clue it is. Especially if it gets me more kisses."

I toss my head back and laugh. "Then let's pick our players."

We spend our evenings playing all the games he doesn't remember as a child—Clue, Yahtzee, Sorry!, Life, Monopoly.

Clue, rather than Yahtzee, turns out to be his favorite. "I claim Colonel Mustard," he tells me one night. "And will you be my Miss Scarlett?"

My lungs expand so much my body hurts. Of course I'll be his Miss Scarlett. I'll just about be his *anything*, take any piece of him.

The best part of this time spent together is that there's so much laughter. Stone makes everything funny. It's a mystery how he does it, but with him, life is easier. It's brighter, shinier, like daybreak after a rain.

And we talk about everything—our hopes, dreams. Whenever Stone remembers a fragment of his past, he shares it. But for the most part, he doesn't focus on what he can't remember. He focuses on the present, the future.

Stone is the best version of all of us—not anchored to a past that poisons him, but always focused on what will happen next, on making the future shine bright.

That's not to say he's naive and innocent, relearning how to navigate the world. His core knowledge is still intact. His common sense, for instance. Stone could, for sure, pick out a pool shark from a lineup and not be taken for all he's worth.

But he couldn't tell you how he knows that. Just that he does.

This is a skill best seen at the resort. His instincts for construction, for design, are amazing, and even though he had to buy all new materials, he's made the budget work so that they're not bleeding money. I'm not sure if Rhett thanked him for that. They spoke after Rhett's big blowup, and Stone convinced him to remain with the project, that he has everything well in hand.

This Stone Maddox is a magician, a person who gets things done with almost no pushback. It's like he has the golden touch, but this touch doesn't destroy. It only breathes life into what needs healing.

Being with him is freeing. And maybe that's what terrifies me most—that he's not just a better version of himself, he's a better match for me. Every time he listens, every time he beams like I'm the sun and the moon rolled into one, I feel myself slipping. This fake engagement was supposed to be temporary. A bandage.

But somewhere between lambicorn snuggles and board game diplomacy, a small, dangerous thought bloomed.

What if I want this for real?

And it's during a particularly rowdy game of Monopoly that my thoughts about this are interrupted by a knock at the door.

Stone jumps up. "You expecting anyone?"

"No. You?"

"Well, I did contemplate having ice cream delivered, but I never made the order." He winks. "No. But wouldn't that be cool if it was ice cream?"

I laugh. "Yes, it would be."

He opens the door and my gaze drops to a girl. The crown of her head, which is covered in spiraling red curls, just reaches the top of his stomach.

She drops her suitcase and tips her chin to look up at him. "Stone Maddox, were you ever going to pick me up, or just let me rot at school all weekend?"

His expression shifts from confusion to joy. "Natalie!"

He wraps her in a hug, one she begrudgingly accepts with both arms at her sides. After a few seconds she melts and embraces him back.

Stone bends so they're eye level. "How'd you find me?"

She strolls in, pulling her suitcase with her. "When I showed up at Sparkle Bar, Isaac told me where you were. And for the record, it's not my job to call *you* when it's your weekend to pick me up. Didn't Pane tell you?"

He grimaces. "Yes, he did. Sorry. I've been busy. Come in. I want you to meet someone. This is Coco."

"Hey," I say.

Natalie scrunches up her face, giving me what I can only describe as a very thorough once-over. "And who are you?" she demands, bossy in a way that makes me grin. "The new girlfriend?"

"Not really." Stone walks over and wraps one arm around my shoulders. "Natalie, Coco and I are getting married."

"Say what?" She does a double take, from Stone to me and back to him.

My gaze drops to my grandmother's engagement ring, and I feel something quiver in my stomach.

Natalie says, voice dripping with skepticism, "Does Pane know about this?"

"I've been pretty busy with the resort."

She points up and down her body. "You think?"

Stone rubs the back of his head sheepishly. "Once again, my apologies."

Natalie cocks an eye at her brother. "I don't think Pane knows. He hasn't mentioned it to me. Have you told him?"

Stone folds his arms and gives her his best scrupulous look. "Would you like to meet a lambicorn?"

Her suspicion dissolves like it's been washed away in the shower. "Did you say *lambicorn*?"

"I sure did."

"Yes!" She throws her arms out wide. "Where is she?"

"It's a he, and his name is Hercules." Stone turns toward the doggy bed. "Come on, Hercules. Meet my kid sister."

As soon as the lamb gets up, Natalie squeals and charges toward him, throwing her arms around his neck.

"I love you, Hercules!" she yells.

Stone and I exchange a look. His mouth tips into a lopsided grin that makes my heart seize every time I see it, and for a single, crystalline moment, the perfection that is this tiny little capsule of our lives melts, because real life just entered, butting its head into our soap bubble and popping it.

I rise from the table. "Natalie, would you like to get some ice cream?"

She stops nuzzling Hercules's neck and turns to me. She grins. "Can the lambicorn come?"

I clasp my hands together and beam. "Absolutely."

Chapter 34

STONE

Natalie reminds me of a gleeful sprite ready to play a prank on anyone at any time—in the best possible way, of course.

She leads Hercules on his leash, guiding him as we walk down the street to the ice cream shop. The evening is cool, so I pull off my jacket and place it around Coco's shoulders before taking her hand and squeezing it.

At the ice cream parlor, Coco makes perfect small talk with my sister, asking if she has a sweetie.

Natalie replies, with all the seriousness of an alligator eyeing its prey, "No. All the boys in my class are dildos. What else would you expect from ten-year-olds?"

My eyes pop open. "What? And where did you learn that word, young lady?"

"Let's calm down. Don't start acting like Pane and being all protective. I know about dildos. My old nanny used to talk about them in her book club."

Coco bites her bottom lip, her eyes shining with laughter. "Well, there you have it. And I agree with you, Natalie, boys your age are dildos."

"Right?" My sister grins wide at me. "I like her. She's got common sense, and she's pretty, too."

Coco's ears turn red, and I embrace the hard thumps as my heart engages in a full-on rock concert against my ribs.

This woman is wrecking me bit by bit, day by day, minute by minute.

As she and Natalie engage in a back-and-forth about school and girl stuff, my heart is full. There's no greater happiness than this moment right here.

A little while later, Natalie's stuffed from eating a large bowl of homemade strawberry pretzel salad ice cream—yes, they make it in ice cream flavor. Don't worry, I bought a half gallon to take home.

Once my sister's finished every last lick, she leans back and groans. "I'm going to be sick."

"Not until we get home."

I grab my sister and lift her onto my shoulders. She squeals in a mix of terror and delight. As Coco grabs the tub of to-go ice cream, I bound from the store and down the street, staying a little ahead of her and Hercules, who we tied to a post outside the shop.

There are things Natalie and I need to discuss.

"Slow down, you're making my head bob. It's worse than brain freeze," she yells.

I lift her by the waist and put her back on the ground. She glares up at me. "I didn't say I was done riding on your shoulders."

"That's okay. I said it for you."

She looks back and sees Coco slowly walking toward us with Hercules on a lead. "You want to talk to me without your girlfriend hearing."

"First, she's my fiancée."

"If she's your fiancée, why haven't you ever mentioned her before? She's not as dumb as the girls you normally date."

A sound of terror escapes my lungs. "Excuse me?"

"You know what I'm talking about." Natalie waves her little pixie hands. "She's got brains. She's smart. I kind of like her." Then she sets her jaw squarely. "But I'm still not convinced Pane knows of her existence. Are you sure you're engaged?"

"Yes. Why?"

"Because you're not being you."

"Define not being me, because last I checked, I'm still the same guy."

I glance back at Coco, brows drawn in what I hope translates into a look that says, *Give us a minute*. She catches my expression and steers Hercules toward a grassy patch in front of a gingerbread-style house. The lambicorn begins to munch happily, and I focus on my sister.

"You're *different*," she answers, emphasizing the word.

Does she know? Can my sister tell? She's a pretty quick kid. It wouldn't surprise me if she opened her mouth and sounded like a fifty-year-old sage. "I'm the same Stone I was when you last saw me."

Sort of. It's not technically a lie because I *am* the same person. I'm just more *me* now.

"No, you're not," she argues.

"And what makes you say that?"

"You're different. Nicer. Not mad at the universe every five seconds. Pane went through this whole anger stage about your dad, too. He's still kind of there, but it's not as bad as it was when he and Rowe broke up for a while. But you"—she slaps her forehead in a dramatic, Oscar-worthy performance—"you were just mad most of the time. Especially at Mom. And now it's like someone pulled that Stone out of you and replaced him with someone else—like a body snatcher."

She leans back, folds her arms, and assesses me. "Has someone stolen your brain?"

I bark out a laugh. "No, of course not. Look, about this whole thing with Dad—"

"*Your* dad. Not *my* dad. Mom didn't tell me my dad wanted nothing to do with me so she could keep us apart for twenty years."

It feels like I'm standing on a tectonic plate while an earthquake hits. But I'm able to keep my legs steady, my feet planted on the ground.

My mother kept my father away from me *on purpose*? I search for this core memory, this piece of me that's missing, the seed of resentment, of anger I know would've sprouted like a weed, but it isn't there.

Of course it isn't. How can it exist when there's no place for it to? When there's no earth for it to be rooted in?

It's hard to explain, and I know I *should* be feeling something, but I can't. It's like that part of me is gone. No, not that *part.*

That *Stone* doesn't exist anymore.

I'm not the same man I was a few weeks ago.

And it's all thanks to a hard hat.

"Listen, kiddo . . ."

"I'm all ears."

I ruffle her hair and she shoos me off. "Even if I'm acting different, I'm still the same big brother you've always had. I'm still me, Stone, someone who wants nothing more than to spend this weekend spoiling you rotten."

She blinks, shocked by my words. "Really?"

"Absolutely. Whatever you want to do, just name it."

Natalie rubs her hands together devilishly. "This is going to be fun. Woo-hoo! Best weekend ever!" She spins toward Coco. "You can come over now. We're done having our little tête-à-tête. It's safe."

Coco strolls over casually with Hercules, who walks slowly, as if he doesn't like being led by Coco. That can't be right. Hercules loves her. He loves everyone.

Natalie bends down and the lambicorn licks her nose. My sister giggles before wiping off the kiss.

"It's safe, huh?" Coco says to Natalie but looks at me. Worry flits across her face until I wrap my arm around her shoulders and pull her into my side.

"It's more than safe." I press a kiss to her temple. "Natalie gets to do whatever she wants this weekend."

"Whatever I want," she seconds, tossing her arms into the air. "And that means tomorrow morning, we tube down the river."

Coco places her warm hand on top of my shoulder. "Tubing? Isn't it a little cold for that?"

I grab her hand and kiss the underside of it. "It'll be fine."

Chapter 35

COCO

"It's too damn cold for this," Stone exclaims the next morning, his breath heaving.

He stands in the chilly water, having jumped in to retrieve the stick that Natalie has lost. *Again.* About every ten minutes or so, the stick she uses to push away from the creek's edge gets lodged between rocks and she drops it, leaving her big brother to jump in and save it.

Natalie presses her lips together, but the sparkle in her eyes gives her away. *The little gremlin is absolutely doing this on purpose.*

Methinks the tiny puppet master is pulling strings just to watch her brother suffer in soggy swim trunks.

He grabs the stick before it can float away and hands it back to her. "Aren't you cold?"

"Nope." She gestures with the stick like she's the conductor of a river symphony. "I'm just getting started. After this, we're having unicorn waffles for brunch."

Natalie floats past us, and Stone rubs a hand down his cheek like he takes waffles seriously. "I could go for unicorn waffles. What about you?"

"I'm just tagging along," I reply, even though it feels like I've been folded into something warm and impossibly perfect. "Today is about y'all. Whatever you want to do, I'm up for it."

He shoots me a firm look. "You're more than just *tagging along*. Hey, Natalie!"

"Yeah?" she calls back.

"Is Coco just tagging along?"

"No! She's with us all the way—from tubing to waffles! She's part of the group. There's no just *tagging along*."

"See? What'd I tell you?" Stone sinks back onto his tube. "Waffles it is. And after that, no more cold river water."

A splash hits the surface and Natalie twists her body to look back at us. "I lost it again!"

He shakes his head and jumps from the tube. "That's it. I'm walking the rest of the way. I'll be the guy dragging a tube and my dignity downriver."

Natalie cackles and I laugh. He turns toward me, fake frustration on his face. "Oh? You think it's funny I'm wet?"

He begins heading toward me and I see where this is going, so I say, frantically, "No! I don't think it's funny! It's terribly tragic. The indignity of it all!"

"That's it," he announces. "I know fake sympathy when I see it."

Before I can paddle out of reach, Stone scoops me up and dunks me into the water. The shock of the cold steals my breath. He lifts me as quickly as I'm put under, and I come up sputtering, clutching his shirt.

"It's freezing!"

"I know! That's what I've been dealing with!"

Our gazes lock and we laugh. I tip my head back, reveling in the sun's warm rays and how luxurious it feels to be held by him.

He kisses me, and all is right in the world.

"Get a room, you two!" A splash yanks us apart, and I look up to see Natalie striding toward us. "You can't leave me out!"

"You want to be dunked?" Stone asks.

"Yes!"

He gently places me back in the tube before he picks up Natalie and submerges her in the water. My heart swells as she shrieks, and we all laugh as we continue down the river.

We finish tubing about an hour later, and true to his word, Stone walks the rest of the way, retrieving Natalie's stick whenever she needs it.

By the time we reach the tubing station, he's shivering, Natalie's laughing, and I'm soaked and blissfully happy.

The unicorn waffles are delicious, and we spend an hour walking among the tourists downtown. All the shops are open, selling everything from hand-carved wax candles to key chains with unicorns on them, to novelty socks and hot sauce. Mystic Meadows is almost like a tiny Gatlinburg, except in Georgia instead of Tennessee.

We take pictures of Natalie standing in front of the unicorn statue, and then Stone pulls me into a selfie—his arm around my waist, my cheek pressed to his shoulder as the sun catches our grins.

Behind us, the bridge crosses over the river. Stone looks down, spots a couple of other people floating, and shouts, "Don't lose your sticks!"

I bite back a laugh at the good-natured bitterness lacing his voice.

I nudge his arm. "Admit it. You had a great time."

He side-eyes me. "If by 'a great time,' you mean slowly freezing my balls off in the name of sibling love . . ."

"That's literally my definition of romance."

Stone snaps his fingers. "I knew it."

Natalie skips over, dragging her fingers across the dozens of tiny padlocks fastened to the chain fence. As they hit the steel, they tinkle and clink. "Why are these here?"

I crouch beside her, pointing to a rusty lock near the bottom. "Couples write their initials on one, then fasten it to the fence and toss the key in the river. It's a promise. Unbreakable love. Forever and ever."

She wrinkles her nose like the locks just confessed to being into autumn-themed Hallmark movies instead of piggycorn cartoons. "Is that supposed to be romantic?"

"*Supposed* to be?" Stone echoes, stepping up behind us. "It *is* romantic, Nat." He reaches into his back pocket. "I brought my own."

I blink. "You did not."

He holds up a small heart-shaped lock. It's incredibly cringe, terribly cliché, and hopelessly romantic.

"Oh my gosh." I grin despite the tightening in my throat. "You've done this."

He shrugs, a little sheepish. "You said you just were tagging along for the morning. I was hoping you'd want to stay."

A breeze lifts the hem of my dress and my hopes with it. Stay. Stay forever? Is that too much for me to want?

What happens when it all comes crashing down?

"Go on," he encourages me. "Write your initials."

Stone pulls a marker from his pocket and holds it out, waiting for me to take it.

I stare at it, trying to decide what to do.

"Hold up!" Natalie yells. "Hang on a second. If you're going to put your initials on that lock, we're doing it right. I saw a glitter marker in that tourist shop. Be back in five!"

She races off.

A knot punches up into my throat and sticks there, heavy and certain, like it never plans to leave. I try not to process the weight of this moment—try to skate past it like a stone skipping across the surface of a pond.

But it sinks. And so do I.

I look up at Stone, studying him, checking for cracks that suggest this isn't real, and find nothing but him watching me openly, studying me as if he's trying to determine whether I'll admit we're not really engaged.

Put on the brakes, Coco!

But I've come too far. I'm in too deep. I'm drowning in Stone Maddox.

He's the only one who can rescue me, and by rescuing me, he pulls me deeper—not to save me but to *join* me. No lifeline. No escape hatch. Just this quiet, terrifying truth that maybe drowning in him is the only way I finally learn to breathe.

I want to stay under, remain submerged and never come up for air, because this is the most real thing I've ever experienced in my life.

And I can't bear for it to end.

"Stone," I whisper, his name barely grazing over my teeth.

His eyes narrow. "What's wrong?"

Words clog my throat, and I want to tell him—I really do—but what comes out is, "Nothing. This moment is perfect."

He leans down to kiss me. I lift up on my toes, eager to accept his offer.

"Quit it, lovebirds!" Natalie jumps between us. "I didn't come here to vomit because you two are making out. You can do plenty of that after you're married. But for now"—she shoves a glitter marker in her brother's hand—"mark your territory and throw away the key."

Stone hands me the marker and says suggestively, "Would you like to mark your territory?"

"I never thought you'd ask."

I may sound brave, but inside I'm quivering. My hand shakes as I write *CH*. Stone's hand does not tremble as he pens his initials. He hands the lock back to me, and I secure it to the fence.

He gives the key to Natalie. "Would you do the honors?"

"Heck yeah, I will!"

She winds up like a pro baseball pitcher and flings the key over the fence, where it sails into the river without even the tiniest of splashes.

Natalie's shoulders slump. "Well, that was anticlimactic."

Stone and I just look at each other, and all I can think is, *She's wrong. She's absolutely wrong.*

Chapter 36

STONE

As Coco walks away with Natalie, the wind whips her ebony hair. She grabs it and pulls it over one shoulder as she talks to my sister.

I wait for her to pull a pencil from her pocket and twist her hair into a bun. Oh, there it is. Coco fishes a pen from her purse, winds her hair around it, and secures it in place.

How does she do that?

She says something that makes Natalie laugh, and I smirk.

If I could bottle this moment and keep it forever, I would.

Hell, who am I kidding, I'll remember it anyway, because of what it means, because of what I'm seeing.

Because of who I am.

For weeks I've been slowly spinning. I've been so worried about who I was before all this, afraid I wasn't good enough for Coco.

She looks back over her shoulder, spots me, and beams like the sun. A jolt of emotion ricochets through me. My ribs loosen and my pulse kicks.

Maybe I've been all wrong. Maybe I didn't forget who I am. Maybe this whole time I've been becoming who I'm meant to be. And it's because of Coco I'm that person at all.

It's ironic. I thought I'd lost myself. But maybe I've been waiting to be found.

Coco points to one of the locks on the fence, and Natalie waves it off as if she's saying, *It's not as cool as the heart-shaped one my brother got you.*

Then my sister turns around. "Hurry up, slowpoke!"

"Coming!"

I catch up and Coco says, "You okay? You looked pretty deep in thought."

"Yeah, I hope you didn't break your brain," Natalie adds.

I mess up her hair, which makes her shriek, and I laugh. "Don't worry, I didn't break my brain. But I was thinking something."

"What's that?" Coco asks, grinning up at me in a way that makes my chest feel like it's on the verge of exploding.

So much I want to say—so, so much. Tell her how beautiful she is. How special. How she fills me with happiness.

Later. I'll say it all later.

For now, all I share is, "I could use a nap."

"Yes!" Natalie cheers. "Three-person pile-on nap! Race you home!"

Coco looks over at me. "I'm not doing that."

I tickle her side and she laughs. "Oh yes, you are."

Chapter 37

COCO

Natalie keeps us very busy for the rest of the day—a nap pile-on, more exploring, and dinner. By the time the sun's beginning to set, I get a text from Cristina.

> Tonight's the night—the full moon. It's now or never.

The joy I've felt all day crashes and burns into a pit of ashes.

If I miss gathering the flower, I won't get another shot for a month. I can't keep Stone from his memory for that long. It isn't right.

My stomach drops like a boulder, and I glance over at him.

He's lying on the couch, attempting to nap while Natalie's sprawled on top of his stomach, peeling open his eyelids.

I watch them—Stone wanting rest, Natalie doing her gremlin best to keep him awake, Hercules curled up on the floor—and something inside me aches with want. I want this. Them. Not just for a day. Not just as a performance. But for real.

"Natalie, you mentioned wanting to see Stella the unicorn, right?"

"Right," she says, blowing on Stone's face. "Wake up, sleepyhead. You still owe me three piggyback rides and a dance battle."

I press my lips together to keep from laughing. "How about we head over to Wadley Farms and you'll get your wish, plus piggycorns?"

Natalie jumps off, hitting Stone in the stomach with her elbow.

He bolts up. "I'm awake! Ouch! Why'd you elbow me?"

"Sorry." She grabs him by the cheeks and kisses his forehead. "Get up, napper! We're going to play with piggycorns."

Stone yawns. "Will they keep you?"

She nibbles the inside of her lip, thinking. "I would love it if they kept me!"

He rises. "Then let's go."

"No fair!"

He picks up his sister and slings her over his shoulder. "Of course they *can't* keep you. Come on, Hercules, let's go play with your nameless cousin."

We reach Wadley Farms right at dusk. The horizon sings as streaks of raspberry and blue ice race across the sky. Piggycorns graze in the yard, and the unicorn stands in the field, watching us with silky black eyes.

Cristina meets us at the door. "Well, hey, Natalie!"

"Cristina!" Natalie throws her arms around my friend. "It's good to see you."

"It's good to see you, too. From what I hear, you came to visit Stella."

"It's been ages since I last saw her. I want to ride bareback!"

Cristina pumps her brows at me. "Really?"

Stone steps up. "Whatever's safe."

"I've ridden her bareback before," Natalie informs us. "We're like this." She twists her middle finger over her forefinger, suggesting they are BFs forever. "May I see her?"

Cristina takes her hand. "Come on. Let's find out if Stella's up for riding."

As they walk away, heading toward the field, Stone glances at me. "I've never met a unicorn. At least, I don't think so."

"You probably have," I tell him, feeling a twinge of guilt. All day, I've watched him with Natalie and pretended to be part of their family. I've never wanted anything more, and I've never deserved anything less. I push away the sorrow and force a smile. "Would you like to be reintroduced to her?"

He winks. "I thought you'd never ask."

Natalie does ride the unicorn bareback, which according to her, is very painful. "Ouch! I should have brought crotch padding!" she shouts.

While she does that, Stone and I walk around the farm, petting piggy-corns and watching as Hercules meets the lambicorn that lives there.

The other lambicorn is really more of a sheepicorn. It's full grown, but that doesn't stop Hercules from trying to play with it as if they're the same age.

The little lambi bends at the knees and jumps to the right, doing his best to entice the larger animal to give chase.

However, the sheepicorn boredly chews on a patch of grass and watches Hercules as if the young lamb has lost its mind.

As the moon rises in the sky, Natalie slides off Stella, and she and Cristina head into the house for a s'mores snack, which Natalie insists Rowe keeps in stock.

"We have them every time I visit," she says with authority. "I know where she hides the ingredients."

"Let's find the goodies, then," Cristina tells her conspiratorially. "If you can pull them out, I'll make the sandwiches."

"But I wanted to play with fire."

"Um. No."

As they walk off, I guide Stone toward the pasture. "Time to get acquainted with Stella."

"I would love nothing more."

The unicorn watches us quietly as we approach. I've met her a few times but have no idea whether she recognizes me. A question that's quickly answered when she walks over and reaches her nose toward my face.

"Hey, girl."

Stella breathes deep, and as she exhales, a blanket of calm drops on me. It permeates every nook and cranny of my being, reaching for all the hidden places—those filled with worry, guilt.

It's like she's telling me I'm on the path of doing what's right, and it's time to release the burden buried deep between my shoulder blades, knotting up the muscles of my body.

Then Stone extends his hand, and the unicorn stretches her neck for him to pet her.

"I've met you before," Stone murmurs as he slides a hand down her nose. He closes his eyes, and for a moment he looks blissfully at peace—and handsome. So handsome, with his sharp, angled features, smooth jawline, gorgeous, thick hair.

His eyes pop open and he regards me. "What?"

"What?"

"Why're you looking at me like that?"

"I'm not looking at you in any way."

"Yes, you are. What is it?"

I sigh. "All right. I was just wondering what it would feel like to rub your chin."

He laughs. "Come and do it. But first, answer a question: What is that feeling I have?"

"Oh, that?" I lean my shoulder on the fence. "I believe that's the unicorn gift. Stella gives them when you see her. I don't know if she gives them to everyone, but I've heard Rowe say she bestows said gifts of wonder on those she likes. Why? What did you feel?"

"Peace, calm," he murmurs.

The unicorn raises and drops her head like she's nodding. "Okay, girl."

I pet her again, and when I do, I feel something slide up my ankles.

When I look down, flowers are growing from the grass—big, tall yellow-blossomed brown-eyed Susans, one of my favorites. The stems rise and wind around my ankles, lifting to brush against my knees. An entire field of them.

"You're glowing," Stone whispers.

"What?"

He nods to my hands.

My gaze falls on my fingertips, which shine with magic. It's not the painful blue sparks I'm used to. No. It's a full-on golden halo of power.

Out in the pasture beyond Stella, the ley lines drum in the same color, as if we're in sync. As if I'm tied to this land and part of it—like we exist in a symbiotic relationship.

"You are magic," Stone whispers almost reverently, as if he's standing before the shrine of the Blessed Zoning Coordinator.

"What do I do?"

"Touch the earth," he instructs.

Fear wobbles my confidence. "What if it explodes?"

He laughs. "Do you really think that's going to happen? Your glow matches the ley lines over there, and you think if you touch the ground you're going to, what? Cross the streams, like in *Ghostbusters*?"

"I mean, maybe?"

"Just try it. Be the brave Coco Chanel I know you are."

I clench my hands, but the glow doesn't die. It only strengthens, and so, figuring that if I don't do this my whole body will look like a giant glow stick in a few minutes, I drop to my knees and lay my hands atop the soft, dewy grass.

Almost instantly, a ripple of magic erupts from underneath my palms. It's small, and fades before it reaches the pulsing ley lines.

Stone drops beside me. "You're holding back. Don't hold back."

"I'm not—"

Before I can tell him I'm not, that he's wrong, he takes my face in his hands and kisses me—*deeply*, with a yearning that sends little tingles spiraling down my spine.

This is not the kiss of a man who woke up from amnesia and is trying to figure out his life.

This is the kiss of man who *has* figured things out—who's strapped into the front row seat of a roller coaster, ready to face every dip, every turn, every loop head-on.

And I'm with him.

Completely.

Utterly.

It's stupid.

More than that—it's *spellbound.*

And no doubt, it's also love.

It's as if his feelings soar beyond the lack of memory, like they're seeded deep inside him and nothing can rip them away.

I give myself over to the kiss, dissolving, melting into it and him.

When Stone pulls away, it feels like the sun's been plucked directly from the sky.

I blink, opening my eyes.

He nuzzles against my cheek. "Now, do it. Show me what you've got."

Something clicks inside me, and I dig my fingers into the earth, grabbing big clumps of grass.

Power ripples from my hands, and this time it doesn't fade out. This time it surges all the way to the ley lines, and when they touch, the earth ignites.

Light erupts from the ground, illuminating the entire pasture as if someone lined it with lights and flipped them on.

I sit back on my heels. My jaw drops.

Stone exhales a low whistle. "Look at that. Just imagine what you could do if you really tried."

Like what? I wonder vaguely before the answer comes. Moments later, the grass grows quickly, shooting up around my feet, and hundreds of tiny pink flowers spread across the pasture, popping up in a wave as they move toward the horizon.

The glow from the earth begins to fade, and I feel myself tiring.

This was a lot of effort, even if it was easy. Because of Stone. All because of him.

I glance at him shyly and see him gently watching me with a warmth in his eyes that makes the tops of my ears heat.

I have no clue why. I'm already fake-engaged to the man. The time for embarrassment is long gone.

"Thank you," I whisper.

"For what?"

It's a good question, and one that has a longer answer than I think he'll ever guess.

"For a long time I've been afraid to let myself shine, because what if I'm tarnished? Thank you for standing up to my family for me. For some reason, I don't. I should, I really should. But I guess there's part of me that thinks my sparkle could never match Brittany's, so it doesn't matter what I say—they won't listen. Worse, they won't hear me. You hear me. You see me, and I don't know what I've done to deserve you."

He takes my hand and kisses each of my knuckles as he speaks. "I think I can only see you because I can see me. I don't remember who I was before"—his voice breaks, but he catches it—"but who I want to be from now on is a man worthy of your love. Worthy of you. I did this once, but I can't remember how it was done, and I can't imagine it being nearly as romantic as this."

He gently tugs the engagement ring from my finger and drops down on his knees. "You are like a star that fell from the sky—you have so much magic inside you. And I know the risks—I know what people in this town believe about those with power. But I'll be damned before I let anything happen to you. I love you, Collette Higginbotham."

The world tips, and I fall off. Loves me? He loves me. I feel the same with everything I have.

So I tell him. "I love you, too."

He rubs the back of his neck bashfully. It's the most humble and gut-wrenching expression. Weeks ago, I was terrified of Stone.

He threatened to expose me to the entire town. Now he's someone different. Someone worth loving.

"So." He lifts the emerald ring. "Will you do me the honor of marrying me? Since I don't recall the first time I asked and all, I want to remember it. I want to live it. I can't miss another memory with you."

My heart kick-starts to life, and I completely understand what he's saying. This time with him has been magical, and I don't want a life that he's not a part of.

I open my mouth to answer, and then, right in front of me, a blade of grass shoots up and unfolds. No. It's not a blade of grass. It's a flower—one with purple petals.

The lunaria bloom.

I'd almost forgotten all about it. Or allowed myself to forget. Take your pick.

"Must be a sign," Stone murmurs.

Of what, there's no telling.

Stone holds the ring, waiting. My pulse thunders with a truth I can't speak. I know this is all about to end—that the lie I've been living is on borrowed time. But for this breath, this heartbeat, I want to believe it's real. That we're real. That love can start in a mess of magic and mistakes and still grow into something worth keeping.

So I nod. "Yes. I'll marry you."

It's like I'm walking through a dream when he kisses me to seal our agreement.

Is it possible to love someone who doesn't know their past? Is the past what makes us who we are?

Or is it the present? Or is it all of it, and even if we forget, the past still weaves into the nooks and crannies of our unconscious?

Whatever the answer is, I know I love Stone no matter his past. No matter his future.

I throw my arms around his neck and sigh into him as the lunaria bloom glows between us.

We laugh. We hug. We live in this moment for a long breath before I pull away and cup my hands under the flower, wondering at the hum of energy that runs up its stem and straight to the top. Magic literally drops from the stamen in golden pollen, and I gently dig around the flower, collecting it from the root and cradling it in my hands.

"What is it?"

Your future. My teeth scrape over my bottom lip before admitting, "It's a lunaria bloom and very rare. I've heard of them."

"Now you have one."

"Now I do."

He kisses me again, and my entire body ignites. Heat pools between my legs and my nipples harden. Stone sweeps his tongue in my mouth, and it breaks me open.

It's anybody's guess what happens when the truth comes out. But for tonight, I needed to believe it. To say yes, even if my head knows better. I needed this dream. Just once.

When we part, he brushes kisses along my jaw, murmuring between each one as he says, "Do you think Natalie will mind spending the night here?"

"With a unicorn in the backyard? I'm sure it's her worst nightmare."

Stone huffs a breath that caresses the shell of my ear. "That was a stupid question. You're right."

I draw back, studying him. "Why do you ask?"

"Tonight I want you all to myself."

This is the perfect time to stop him. But I'm done, tired of focusing on the lie instead of living in what's real. By tomorrow, this might all be over, but for one night, I want to pretend that it's real—before the glass ceiling shatters.

Chapter 38

COCO

Cristina's one step ahead of us, having already tucked Natalie into the bed that Pane and Rowe have designated for her. My friend doesn't give me a hard time. Maybe she thinks it'll all be over soon, anyway, so it's okay to let me have one night with him.

We promise to pick Natalie up first thing in the morning, and head to Stone's SUV.

He holds my hand the whole way to the vehicle and takes it again once he's behind the wheel. He doesn't let go until we're back at the cottage. As we walk to the door, he hugs me into his side, and it feels like his body was made for mine, that I fill the hills and planes of him as we walk in step.

As soon as we're inside, he turns me to him and whispers my name. Then he kisses me gently, and I melt.

We walk in pools of moonlight, heading to my room. Clothes fall aside with each step, and though nothing about this feels hurried, it also doesn't feel like taking our time is the right way to go about things, either.

It's like we both know we're sitting in the middle of a minefield—every step is precious, every moment must be cherished, that we're existing on borrowed time.

At least, that's how *I* feel.

Stone lifts me like I weigh nothing, one arm under my thighs, the other cradling my back. He carries me into the bedroom, eyes never leaving mine, and gently sets me on the bed like I'm precious, breakable. Like this isn't just desire—it's something sacred.

I reach for him, but he catches my wrists, pinning them lightly to the bed above my head. His mouth brushes the pulse point under my neck, and my bones liquefy.

He paints kisses over the tops of my shoulders, down my neck, to the swell of my breasts, sucking on my nipples and lighting my core on fire.

Pressure pools in my groin, and I want to feel him, explore him. I whisper his name, pleading with him, begging for release, and he covers my mouth with another kiss and whispers, "I've been waiting a long time for this. I'm taking my time."

And he does, tasting every part of me, cupping me with his hands, exploring every inch until he's satisfied that he's learned me, memorized me.

He kisses me again and I wrap my legs around his waist. "Not yet," he murmurs.

"No fair. You play dirty."

He chuckles as he moves down to my breasts, taking one nipple in his teeth while he rolls the other between his fingers.

My back arches, a moan escaping me. He growls low in his throat like the sound fuels him.

"You're so beautiful. Do you know what you do to me?"

Before I can answer, his tongue strokes between my thighs, and all I can do is *feel.* He licks me slowly at first, then with purpose, groaning as I writhe beneath him.

"Calm down, little Coco. We're just beginning."

I almost come apart right there. Then he teases me open with one finger, two, and I stretch around him as he flicks my clit with his tongue and pumps me with his fingers.

My own fingers dig into his hair, anchoring myself to the moment, to *him*, as waves of pleasure roll through me.

I whimper his name, but my breath catches on the end of it and the word falls silent.

"Come for me," he whispers. "Let me feel you fall apart."

The climax breaks me wide open—bright and shattering, like starlight exploding behind my eyes. I cry out his name, trembling as he kisses his way back up my body.

"It's my turn to see you," I say.

He lets me explore him, trailing my fingers over his shoulders, down his pecs sprinkled with hair and down to his briefs, which I tug down slowly, freeing his cock.

Moonlight splashes over Stone, creating highlights and shadows, allowing just enough illumination to see him—and want him.

I take his cock in my hand and he hisses. I pump him once, twice, and he growls. "You want me to last, don't you? Stop it."

I bite back a giggle as Stone presses me back onto the bed and covers me with kisses. He whips out a condom from what seems like thin air—even though I think he actually got it from his wallet—and rips the foil with his teeth.

He pushes it down and I'm salivating, yearning, dying for him to fill me up.

Stone complies. He rests between me, and when he first slides in, I whimper and he covers my mouth with a kiss, and keeps kissing me as he slowly fills me up, pumping slowly, making me feel every ounce of love within him.

Love?

That's what this is. It isn't two people yearning to get something out of their system, all passion and lust. This is two people syncing up, letting emotion carry every kiss, every touch, every moan.

I wrap my legs around him, tugging him close, and do the same with my arms. Sweat slicks our bodies, and Stone's kisses deepen as his pace quickens.

There's a moment before he unravels, a slight pause as his tongue probes me deeply and I groan.

Then he snaps, and his kisses become fervent, and he pumps me hard. The headboard slams into the wall over and over.

"Co," he says as he comes apart, and I join him, unraveling as well. Starlight fills my eyes—my body breaks and scatters like a supernova, only to be pulled together once more.

Stone collapses on top of me, his head resting on my breast. He breathes heavily, and my lungs rise and fall, too.

After a moment he pulls himself up until he's beside me, and then he tugs me on top of him and kisses my head.

"You ready to go again?" he jokes.

"No," I murmur. "I just want to stay like this."

"I'll give you ten minutes to recuperate."

But ten minutes later, he's sound asleep and I'm not far behind.

Chapter 39

COCO

I'm on cloud ten, having skipped straight over nine and shot beyond the stars.

Never in my life have I felt so blissfully alive and happy. I've never been cocooned in a feeling like this. Oh, I've had boyfriends before, but there was always a shadow covering those relationships—my fears, my insecurities.

But with Stone, there's none of that. It's absolute freedom.

I never want this feeling to end.

We wake up in the middle of the night and find ourselves tangled in the sheets again. Once more in the shower after we wake up.

Then Stone asks if I'd like to go with him to pick up Natalie and drive her back to school, but I tell him no.

There's a potion I need to make.

That part I don't tell him, obviously. But my knees wobble as I watch him leave the house to take his sister home.

I have one night of perfect memories and an emerald ring that fits snuggly on my finger. He gave me his trust, and I'm going to ruin him with it.

There's nothing to do except move forward.

Soon as he's gone, I text Cristina and tell her I got the bloom. It's sitting in the kitchen window, where I left it last night after I pulled myself out of Stone's grasp long enough to drop it in a vase of water.

Cristina arrives about an hour later with Hercules, who takes one look at me, walks right on past, and heads for his bed.

"What's wrong with him?" Cristina says. "He didn't even greet you."

"He's mad at me, I think, for everything that's happened."

"He'll forgive you soon enough." Her gaze lands on the flower. "Is that it? Is that the bloom?"

"That's it."

"It glows even during the day?"

"Pretty cool, huh?"

She touches one of the petals gently. "Yeah, almost as cool as waking up to a field of pink flowers in the pasture. You wouldn't happen to know anything about that, would you?"

"Me? Whatever are you talking about?"

"Don't lie. I saw you out there last night with Stone," she says in a playful voice. "Coco, what are you going to do? I don't mean about him. I know what we're doing. But what about your magic?"

"I guess I'll keep it a secret as long as I can."

A divot of worry creases the space above her nose. "I don't think you can keep this kind of secret—not forever. You're powerful. It's almost scary."

"Don't worry. I have no intention of dropping a memory-swiping potion on you."

"Thank goodness." She winks. "Ready to start?"

No. "Of course. Let's get this done."

I haven't opened the book since we found the counter spell, and I fear opening it now. The last thing I need is more foreboding wind mixed with a lightning strike to suggest this spell is even more doomed than the first.

But I recall Dot's warning about the land. She never fixed her spell, but I will fix the one on Stone.

I place the book on the table. It hums as if it's anticipating what's about to happen and is excited for it.

I peel back the cover and squint, waiting for a gale to sweep through the cottage.

But what I get is . . . crickets.

This is good. Or terribly bad. Fingers crossed it suggests we're on the right track.

Even Cristina notices. "What? No flickering lights?"

"I guess not."

"Which means we'll probably call Lucifer himself with this spell."

"Stop it."

We locate the counter potion and begin creating it. The bloom's petals have to be ground, so we dry them in the oven and then I pulverize them in an old coffee grinder. We boil the rest of the flower until it becomes a thick syrup, add the petals to it, along with some nutmeg and cotton. The last thing we need is something of Stone's, and I find his hairbrush, pulling out a hair.

This feels like a betrayal. It shouldn't. This should feel right, like I'm doing the best possible thing for him.

If that's the case, then why does my stomach churn? Why does it bubble and boil like the pot of ingredients?

I shove the worry aside and drop the hair in the pot. The ingredients hiss, and steam curls from the very center.

"Well, at least that part was similar to before," Cristina mutters.

I stir for ten minutes, until the potion resembles a light-purple solution. It's pretty, this one, and it looks a thousand times more appetizing than the green goop we made the first time.

"It needs to cool," Cristina says. "Let's sit outside on the front porch for a while."

After taking the pot off the burner and placing it over a cloth on the kitchen table, I pour Cristina and I each glasses of sweet tea and head to the porch to enjoy the sunshine.

"What are you going to put *this* potion in?" she asks when we're rocking back and forth like old ladies on a lazy Sunday afternoon.

"Maybe a cheeseburger? No. Wait. I'll grab some barbecue from Unicorn Tails and put it in that. He likes that place. It's where we shared our first meal, and it's how I'd like to have our last one together."

Cristina scoots closer to me on the porch swing and drops her head on my shoulder. "It's going to be okay."

"I know," I reply, my voice sounding weak even to me.

It's been a great run, but it must end, and however Stone feels when it's over will be how he feels. If he hates me, I deserve it. If he doesn't—then it's a miracle.

Cristina and I swing for a bit, and then she leaves. I walk down to Unicorn Tails and get the food, making sure to order extra corn bread because Stone adores it. Can't say I blame him—add a little honey and butter to moisten it up or crumble it into a bowl of beans, and you've got magic!

I don't order much for myself, just a sandwich because my appetite's gone kaput.

No surprise there.

The sack feels as heavy as a boulder as I return to the cottage. I unlock the front door and sigh. Ready or not, here I come.

The door swings open and I stop in my tracks. The pot full of potion isn't on the table where I left it. My gaze swishes around until it lands on the floor.

The pot is tipped onto its side, and Hercules hunches in front of it. The sound of slopping comes from him.

Oh my God. The lamb is eating the potion.

"No, no, no, no, no!"

I drop the bag of food and rush to the pot. I yank it away from Hercules, hoping that some is left, but when I look in, there's nothing.

Not even one drop. I collapse to my knees. "No!"

Hercules looks up at me. Blinks. Runs a tongue over his lips.

My stomach falls. All that waiting. All that work. All that worry. All for nothing.

This was my moment to make everything right. To fix what I'd broken. To fix Stone. And now it's gone.

How could I have been so stupid as to leave the potion where Hercules could reach it? Well, he couldn't reach it, could he? The lambicorn had to jump on a chair, then on the table, then knock the potion down and lick up every last bit.

I stare at him. "You have been so mad at me because of Stone, and when I want to fix him, you ruined it. What do you have to say for yourself?"

"Baaaaaaaa."

"Not helpful."

What do I do now? Wait another month? Tell Stone the truth? Even if I tell him, will he believe me? Dammit! This potion was going to make it easier because he would remember everything. I wouldn't have to tell him. He'd remember how much he hates me and he'd hate me again.

It would destroy me, but I could live with it, because I've experienced him loving me and that would be enough. It would have to be.

It's a toss-up on whether to scream or collapse. I should call Cristina, but how do I explain this? *Sorry, the magical lamb ate the one thing that could've saved everything?*

I drop my face in my hands.

No, I can't call her. There's nothing she can do that'll help.

I exhale a gusty sigh. There's no use crying over spilled milk. I might as well clean up the mess, even though Hercules has done most of the work for me, then get ready to swallow my bitter pill.

I grab the pot and take it into the kitchen. On my way there, I swipe the barbecue from the floor in case Hercules is still hungry.

Hungry . . .

I whip around. "Hercules, are you feeling okay?"

He cocks his head like a dog trying to understand what I'm saying.

"Come here, little guy."

For the first time in days, the lambicorn pads over. I give him a good scratch behind the ears. "If you throw up, it's not my fault."

"Baaaaaaa."

Hopefully, the potion won't make him sick or change him. Like, you know, make him remember a past he's forgotten or something like that.

The irony of this moment is not lost on me, and it makes me wonder if maybe it wasn't up to me to give Stone back his memory. Maybe it's something he has to do himself.

That still doesn't make me feel better.

I've just washed and dried the pot when the door opens.

I turn as Stone sweeps in, a huge grin on his face. He pulls me into a hug and kisses my temple. "It smells good in here. Did you get barbecue?"

My stomach clenches. "I did."

He tucks a loose strand of hair behind my ear. "Is something wrong?"

Everything. But I shake my head, fighting back tears that threaten to prick my eyes. "No. It's fine. Hercules just got into some food he wasn't supposed to, and I'm worried it might make him sick."

"Oh." Stone turns to the lambicorn. "He looks okay. Has he thrown up?"

"No."

"Then he'll be fine. We'll watch him. So." Stone claps his hands. "I'm starving. Thank you for getting food."

"You're welcome." I wish he'd stop thinking I'm a great person. "How was dropping Natalie off?"

He kisses my forehead. "Fantastic. She told me this weekend redeemed me and I'm not a failure as a brother. Whatever that means."

I laugh. "I think she's joking."

"I'm not so sure." He kisses me again and I melt. This is the perfect chance to tell him the truth. But when we part, his voice is low and his pupils are inky, full of lust. Probably just like mine. "There's something I want to do before we eat."

"What's that?"

He kisses me again. "You."

Before I can protest, he picks me up and, with me squealing, takes me into the bedroom and shuts the door.

Chapter 40

STONE

Everything is good. *No*—it's perfect. So perfect it feels borrowed.

It's questionable if I ever dreamed of this sort of life, but if I didn't, I want it—all of it, every last drop it has to offer.

The resort construction sings. We're back on schedule, and building is going as well as it can be. Almost too well, and that's rare in construction. You usually hit many problems on the way to finishing a project—at least I think so. No, I know so, somehow.

But not here in Mystic Meadows. Here, walls rise with gusto.

For as fast as everything moves forward, something feels off. This feeling that something's going to drop simmers in my stomach.

"It's really shaping up," Isaac says as he comes over to critique my work.

I've been laying out stones in the garden I'm building for Coco. I rise, brush off my hands, and say, "You like it?"

"Yeah. The way you've got the path winding, it's going to be beautiful."

Beautiful. Just like her. "Thanks."

"What are we talking about?" Ron asks, wiping sweat from his forehead.

"How good this garden's going to be when it's done," Isaac tells him.

"Oh yeah. It's gonna be breathtaking."

"Thank you. That means a lot." I step back to admire the work. The path serpentines, and local flora will flank it on both sides, bringing nature into the space seamlessly.

I'm putting everything I've got into it.

My thoughts are interrupted by a sedan rumbling onto the site. My shoulders lift, and I excuse myself from Ron and Isaac to head over to meet Coco.

She kills the engine and gets out, lifting a brown sack. "I brought you some lunch."

I pull her into a bear hug and growl with happiness. "Perfect."

Around us, machines lumber and pneumatic tools hiss and pop.

I take her hand. "Come eat with me."

Her face turns red and she quickly looks around. "I'm not that hungry. Besides, should we eat where all the guys can see?"

"Did you bring enough to share?"

She swats at me. "No."

"They're about to take lunch soon anyway. Come on. I had a couple of picnic tables put in so the guys can take breaks."

"Picnic tables?"

"Yeah. It's the least I could do."

We sit at a table and Coco slides into the seat across from me. She picks at her fingers nervously.

"Something wrong?"

"No, no." Her gaze swivels around. "Nothing's wrong. It's just—"

"Just what?" I open the container and whistle with pleasure. Barbecue, corn bread, sauce. The leftovers are warm. She even heated them for me. This woman makes my body ache in the best way.

"Well, it's just . . . there's something I need to tell you."

"Sounds serious."

She gulps. "It is."

I stop eating and study her. Her eyes are dark with worry, and her forehead is creased. "You can tell me anything. I hope you know that."

A smile ghosts across her lips. My shoulders tighten. Have I done something wrong?

"Thank you for helping me," she says. "With my magic. With my power. It didn't show up until the ley lines strengthened, so I didn't know about it."

"That must've been frightening."

"It was an experience," she confirms.

"But it's still pretty awesome. I mean, I can see ley lines, but I don't have cool powers." I frown. "Why *can* I see ley lines?"

"Oh, well . . ." Her gazes drifts off and she clears her throat. "I . . . um . . ."

"Do I have magic?"

"I don't think so." She takes one of the napkins and twists it with her fingers. "But even though you don't, I'm so appreciative that you can see ley lines." Her gaze lifts to the resort in the backdrop. "It's made all the difference in this building, and it'll continue to make a difference in this town. I can't thank you enough for what you've done." She looks over my shoulder and squints. "What's that?"

"What?"

"That area over there."

I say nonchalantly, "It's the garden I'm building for you."

Her eyes widen. "For me?"

"Yeah. Remember when I told Rhett about it? I wasn't joking. You want a tour?"

"Okay."

I take her over and guide her through the layout, explaining what sort of stones will go where and what plants will be brought in.

She's silent the entire time I talk, looking at me with a mixture of awe and disbelief.

Well, she should believe it.

I love her.

Love her.

And I want to show her how much.

After we've walked through the whole thing, I say, "What do you think?"

She balls up a hand and presses it to her heart. When she speaks, it's in a whisper. "It's going to be gorgeous. Thank you."

"Nothing," I tell her, pushing hair from her face, "could be more gorgeous than you. Look. I know what you want to tell me."

A shadow slides across her face. "You do?"

"Yes. You think because of what's happened, because I don't remember, that I'm not sure of anything. Coco, I've never been more sure of anything in my entire life. When I try to think of the past, it's not *only* that I come up blank, it's that I sense the moodiness I used to have, the anger, and I don't want any part of it. I'm not running toward you to fill a void. That's not why I re-proposed. I asked you because I *am me*. For what may be the first time in my life, I am who I'm supposed to be, and I feel it in every pore and cell of my body."

She looks at me with tenderness. "You really think that?"

"I do. Every ounce of me feels this."

That's it! That earlier feeling I couldn't name? This is the answer. Her. Us. Right here.

Because even if I never get my past back, I've found my future, and it's Coco.

Oh my God. It's Coco.

I mean, I know that, but when the realization hits me, it becomes obvious. Why should I wait to marry her when this is the right thing to do? For me. For *us*. It's what's supposed to happen. She's already said yes. The hard part is over.

I want to get married. To her. Right now. I can't wait one more minute.

But I also don't want her to know this. I want it to be a surprise.

I jerk my head toward the site. "I need to get back. Are you hungry? Do you want to finish my lunch?"

She shakes her head. "No, but, Stone—I know you feel this way, but there's still something I've got to tell you."

I give her my full attention and wait. "Shoot."

She opens her mouth, shuts it. Something wars in her eyes—maybe it's just the effects of the whiplash my speech gave her.

Then she admits, "Just that I'm so grateful for you. For all of this."

Love fills every nook and cranny inside me. "Coco, you own me. Every part of me, and all I want to do is be with you."

I love her. This isn't some high. I've loved this woman since the first moment I saw her. She's grounded me.

"I've got to get back to work, but I have a surprise for you tonight."

Her eyebrows lift. "Surprise? Stone, I—"

I tuck a strand of hair behind her ear. "Don't try to get it out of me. Tonight. Just wait. You're gonna love it."

Her eyes dim a little and she nods. "Okay."

"Don't look so worried."

"I'm not. I'm fine. A surprise?" she murmurs.

I brush a kiss to her cheek. "Yeah. It's gonna be fun."

And it's also going to change your life. That, you can count on.

Chapter 41

COCO

He made me a garden—one filled with river stones and pebbles, one that winds around trees and shrubs, one he's building with his own two hands.

I sit in the sedan, taking it all in. Stone has already told me goodbye, and my excuse for sitting in the car for a moment is that there are emails that need sorting through.

But there aren't any emails.

He's finished lunch and is now laying stones atop each other, lining out the space, studying, shaking his head, rearranging his work.

The whole thing breaks me open.

Because he's doing it for me.

This is why I couldn't tell him the truth. I thought, reveal it to him here, on neutral ground, get it over with. But in the end, this is the truest relationship I've ever had, and it's not even real.

Because my own relationship with my sister isn't even real and it should be. This thing with Stone is more real than that.

And it feels like maybe I don't deserve to have something actual, something that isn't based on a lie.

My God—he's building a space in my honor at a multimillion-dollar facility. He's making it for me, and as much as I should be letting him go, I can't.

What if he rejects the real me? What if the real me isn't good enough?

A fierce lion inside me wants to grab him tight and hold on as long as I can.

The thought of ending things now makes me physically sick to my stomach. It churns at the thought of revealing the truth.

One more month.

Just one more and I'll get the lunaria bloom again, make the potion. Then I'll give it to him.

Besides, it's not as if he'll want to marry me in a month.

That gives me thirty more days to pretend this is real, to pretend that I can keep Stone Maddox forever.

Chapter 42

COCO

When I get home from work, it seems like a cloud has descended over the cottage. It feels dark, drab. Or maybe it's just me and my mood.

I don't expect Stone home for a while, so it's no surprise when he's not there. What *is* surprising is the large white box lying on the rickety kitchen table.

There's a small envelope on top of it. Inside, the card reads: *Please put this on. A car will pick you up at 7.*

A car? What the . . . ?

I open the box and find an evening gown encrusted with crystals. I suck in a breath. Never in my life have I seen such a beautiful piece of clothing. And Lord, is it heavy!

I pull it from the box, and more gasping occurs. It's strapless, with a sweetheart neckline and a fitted bodice that gives way to a silk skirt that flows like water under my fingers.

Holy shit. This is gorgeous. Are we going out on the town—maybe out *of* town? Is this gonna be like in *Pretty Woman* when Richard Gere takes Julia Roberts to the opera and she gets to wear that beautiful necklace?

Is there a beautiful necklace hidden somewhere?

My gaze scours the table. No more boxes. Dang. I really wanted a necklace.

But hell, if there's a driver, there might be a private jet.

He *is* a Maddox, which means he's got all sorts of money.

Giddy about the dress and pushing aside the feeling in the pit in my stomach, I take the box to the bedroom. I quickly shower, put up my hair, apply fresh makeup, and slide into the gown.

It fits like a dream, and the skirt rustles when I spin.

I turn this way and that in the mirror, getting a view from all sides. It's the most elegant piece of clothing to ever have graced my body. It shimmers when I move, sending rainbows of light dancing over the walls.

What does Stone have planned?

I put on heels and am ready to go when, at seven, the doorbell rings.

The last thing I expect is Ron in a suit wearing a chauffeur's hat—but that's what I get.

"Hey, Ron."

"Hey, Coco. You look nice."

"Thank you. So . . . I don't suppose you'll tell me where we're going."

"Mum's the word."

"Hmm. Suspicious."

"You ready?"

"Never been readier." As he escorts me down the sidewalk, I pepper him with questions. "Are we headed to the airport? Is there a jet waiting on the tarmac? There's a jet, isn't there? Is Stone wearing a tux? You're not flying the plane, are you?"

Ron doesn't answer as I jabber at him. He opens the back door of a sleek black limo and I get in, half expecting Stone to be sitting in the back.

Who am I kidding? Stone never would've waited in the car. He would've gotten out and retrieved me himself.

However, even though he's not present, there's another note on the opposite seat. I do a little happy clap. Maybe it's a clue!

I slide out the card and take a look. *I'm sure you're starving, and we'll eat soon. Hang tight just a little bit longer.*

Okay, so are we flying to New York for dinner? Maybe California? Probably California, given the time difference. Oh, this is so cool!

As Ron pulls the sedan away from the house, my gaze skims the familiar streets. Tonight, my town sparkles, and it isn't just because of magic. It's because someone wrapped twinkly lights around the lampposts. It's enchanting, and looks like the set of a Hallmark movie.

Is Hallmark filming in Mystic Meadows?

The lights sparkle all the way to the end of town, where a small white building is decorated with bright pansies popping out from window boxes and tulips sprinkling the front garden.

My excitement turns to horror as Ron pulls up in front of the building.

"Ron," I whisper, "we're not stopping here, are we?"

He doesn't answer, but comes to a halt directly in front of the door. My insides shrivel and die.

Oh no. No no no no no!

Icy dread fills my stomach, and the glowing lights, the ones I thought looked so beautiful only moments before, now mock me.

My core tightens and a charge builds on my fingertips. *No.* I've come too far to lose control of my magic now.

I could run. I could leave this very moment. It would allow Stone to have a future without the wreckage of my truth.

But that wouldn't be fair to him.

I exhale. It's time to face the truth head-on. Maybe this place, this scenario, isn't the curse I think it is.

Maybe it'll be a blessing in disguise.

Or my complete downfall.

Ron gets out and comes around to open my door. I whisper a prayer, asking for strength. I'm about to need every last ounce I can muster.

Within seconds, my door opens and Ron helps me out.

I now stand directly in front of the building, and it's dazzling. Torches line the sidewalk, their flames licking at the night. Pink and red flowers scale latticework attached to the front of the facade.

I inhale a deep gust of air. I'm ready.

Ron walks me to the front door and he pulls it open.

I get my first glimpse and my knees buckle. The air smells like lilies and candle wax and the terrifying feeling of being loved too much.

I thought I was prepared for this, but I'm not.

Inside, the chapel's decorated just as beautifully as the outside, with hundreds of candles lighting up the interior.

The pews are filled with people—Cristina, Clarice, my book club ladies. Even my family is here.

My mom cries quietly.

And standing at the very front is Stone, wearing a tuxedo (I had *that* guessed right), and beside him is Isaac, who is apparently officiating *my wedding*.

Stone brought me here to get married.

This beautiful gown, one I couldn't have picked better myself, is a wedding dress, and Stone has planned the most gorgeous venue, better than I could have imagined—even if it is in Mystic Meadows.

He winks playfully. My throat squeezes. It's all so beautiful that my heart overflows. Would Stone beam at me if he knew the truth? Would I still feel this way? Do I deserve this slice of happiness?

It feels like I've known Stone my entire life, not just a few weeks. It's insane. Absolutely nuts. People only get married when they've known one another for years, when they've had time to witness the ups and downs of a person, see their moodiness, understand what to do when that person has a bad day.

But Stone has unlocked something within me, and I'm more *me* with him than I've ever been. I certainly unlocked something *within* him. It seems the magic potion actually unlocked *his true self*—who he was always meant to be.

Beside him, Hercules bleats, *"Baaaaaaa."*

I completely concur.

Music kicks up. My dad approaches, and he walks me down the aisle as a hundred gazes are glued to us.

"This is pretty fast, isn't it, hon?"

"It sure is."

"Are you really going to do this?" he asks, sounding worried. "I like Stone, don't get me wrong. But it feels a little sudden."

I pat his hand. "Don't worry."

We reach the front and Dad kisses me on the cheek before handing me over. This moment is akin to being on a TV show—the kind where you've only known your fiancé a week and must choose to marry him or end the relationship. Except there are no cameras here.

This is real life.

Stone grins and I force myself to smile back.

Tears prick my eyes. There's so much love in me for this man.

Yes—love.

I didn't think there would or could be. But there is, and for the next few seconds I want to sit in this.

"Too much?" Stone asks, humor lacing his voice.

I burst into laughter. Always, he's so funny. "It's perfectly you," I reply, meaning it. "Surprising me with this is simply . . . you."

"I'm gonna take that as a compliment."

"You should."

Isaac speaks. He doesn't do the whole "Dearly beloved" thing. It's more about two souls joining as one and people finding their people.

Hercules bleats a lot as if to corroborate everything Isaac says.

Then he says, "Stone . . ."

Stone looks at me, his jade eyes filled with warmth, his sharp features softening.

"Coco, I don't really have fancy words for this. I mean, I tried to write some down, but they all sounded like a Hallmark card and not like me."

Everyone laughs. A tear falls down my cheek.

"So I'm just gonna talk to you the way I always do—straight up." Love fills me to bursting as he continues. "Ever since I met you, it's like something in me clicked. Like I didn't know I was lost until you found me. And I didn't even know I could feel this settled. This seen. This stupidly happy watching you laugh at everything you laugh at, which is mostly me."

Chuckles fill the chapel. "You make life feel like a home. Not a house. Not a job. Not a title. But something warm and real and good. With you, I don't feel like I have to perform or earn my place—I just get to be yours. And that's the best job I've ever had."

My heart spasms against my rib cage.

"I don't know what's coming. We'll probably fight. I'll probably say something dumb, multiple times—but I promise this: I'll keep showing up. I'll keep choosing you. Every day. Even on the days when we're tired or grumpy or I track mud in the house after you've just mopped."

His eyes shine and mine blur with tears. "I love you, Coco. All of you. The way you love your job, your life. The way you make me feel like the man I always wanted to be. So here I am. A guy in a tux, totally wrecked in the best way. Ready to spend forever figuring out how to love you better, every single day."

I knuckle tears from my cheeks. Never has anyone said something so gut wrenching and yet so uplifting to me.

And the thing is, I feel the same way—like he sees me, knows me, and is ready to fight for me.

Isaac looks at me. "Coco, do you have anything you'd like to say?"

I nod. "I do. Sto—" His name breaks off in the back of my throat, and I have to push through to keep going. "Stone, ever since you appeared in my life, nothing has been the same. Life has taken on an entirely new meaning. I can truly be myself and let you see the parts of me I've shielded from everyone—except you, that is."

A sob clogs up my words. Oh, God. This is so stupidly emotional.

"But even with all of that, and how much I feel, and how much I love you, there's something you have to know, and it can't wait a second longer. It has to be said."

Stone's face twists in worry. "What is it?"

I exhale a shaky breath. "The day that you—"

The door flies open with a bang.

Heads turn and my jaw drops.

Pane Maddox storms in, his face twisted in confusion and worry. His wife, Rowe, follows quickly behind.

He takes one look at the rows of people, at the two of us, and demands, "Stone, what the hell is going on?"

Chapter 43

COCO

The chapel goes silent. Dead silent. Like if-a-fly-were-buzzing-it-would-be-as-loud-as-a-siren silent.

"What's going on?" Pane demands again.

"Be right back," Stone says nonchalantly, squeezing my hand tenderly while my stomach flattens into a pancake. He moves to greet his brother. "Great to see you!"

Pane gives Stone a stiff hug, the whole time staring at me with fire in his eyes. No doubt this wasn't what he expected to return home to—his brother marrying, the resort materials changed.

"If you don't mind," Stone says, dropping his voice, "I'm a little busy right now. Can we talk after? Better yet, why don't you stand beside me, be my best man? I've even got a ring for you to hold."

A ring? My knees become Jell-O. It's even worse than I thought. It's not just a wedding—there's another ring.

I bet it's got diamonds.

Pane grabs his brother by the shoulders. "I've barely been gone a month, and Rhett calls to say the resort's different and you're getting married."

Stone presses a hand to Pane's shoulder. "Can we please talk about this later? And Coco and I have been engaged for a while. The wedding shouldn't come as a surprise. I'm sorry, by the way, for not officially waiting for you to return before making it legal."

Pane scowls. Behind him, Rowe tugs on his sleeve. "Maybe we should let them finish," she murmurs.

"I can't," he grinds out, then turns to his brother. "What are you talking about? You weren't engaged when I left. You weren't even dating anyone."

Stone shakes his head as if he's thinking, *My wacky brother, always getting it wrong.* "Of course I was engaged. Tell him, Coco."

It's my worst nightmare, this happening in front of the entire town and my family. I think Brittany's even recording. My gaze swivels toward her. Yep. She's recording.

"Coco," Stone nudges.

My ribs crack as I fix my gaze on him—on this beautiful man who's put his faith and trust in me.

My words come out shaky. "It's true."

Pockets of gasps spread out over the crowd. A knot forms in my throat.

"What?" Stone says, taking a step forward. "What's true?"

I close my eyes and exhale. "What your brother said. We're not engaged."

He chuckles. "Yes, we are. Tell them."

For the first time since all this started, there's uncertainty in his eyes. The man I've grown to love with all his confidence and quirkiness, is utterly, completely, totally confused.

I dread what comes next.

"What are you talking about?" he asks gently but firmly, and I know it's all about to unravel, so I might as well get it over with.

"Maybe we can talk privately." I reach for him. "To discuss this."

He shakes his head, confusion scribbled over his features. "Whatever you have to say, say it here."

Several thoughts hit me at once: Dot's warning about being invisible, how the town's magic disappeared, tales of what happens to witches.

There are so many reasons to *not* do the right thing, but it's time for me to stand on my own two feet and stop hiding.

It's the least I can do for Stone.

I lick my lips and steel myself. "Several weeks ago I came to the resort to do an inspection. It was supposed to be run-of-the-mill, but when I arrived, I realized the building was wrong. It was hurting the town's land. When I told you, you wouldn't listen. You called me a bureaucrat, a simpleton, someone wanting to be more important than I was."

Pain flashes through his eyes, but he only nods, silently telling me to continue.

"You wouldn't listen to reason, no matter how much I tried to make you. You threatened to—"

I stop. Can't say it.

"To what?" he asks quietly, his voice reminding me of a pot on a low simmer.

"It's not important." He doesn't need to know about the blackmail. That's one thing I can spare him. "I did the only thing I could think of to help."

"What was that?"

"I found a spell book."

"What?" someone murmurs.

"Witchcraft," another says.

"Everybody quiet down," he commands. "Let her finish."

A bit of hope buoys inside me. Maybe I haven't ruined everything after all.

But then he grinds out in a voice so icy the hard edges of it scrape over my heart, "Tell us what you did."

My insides coil tight, and it feels like my I'm about to crack open. "It was supposed to be a prank," I explain, trying to salvage something of my dignity. "But I . . . I made a potion and gave it to you."

A cold sheen flashes over his eyes. "And then?"

"You lost your memory."

The peanut gallery chimes:

"His memory?"

"He has amnesia?"

"Is that why he came to our book club?"

The candlelight was warm when I arrived, but now the room is stifling. Sweat runs down my spine and sprouts on my palms. I need to get out of here and into fresh air.

"Go on," he tells me in a chilly voice.

When I look up at him, his jade eyes have turn to flint. My throat shrivels to the size of a pea. I'm lost. But there's no going back.

"I couldn't leave you the way you were, so I became your friend. I looked for a cure."

"Then why aren't I cured?"

"At first, I couldn't find it." I pinch the bridge of my nose. "And then I waited." The crowd erupts into gasps again, and I plead with them, "Because Stone was a different person. The potion knocked out his memory, but it also softened something. Before, he was different, rough. But after—he cared about our land, about our town. He changed the materials so the resort wouldn't disrupt the magic."

My gaze locks on Clarice. "He came to our book club. Everyone loved him." I whirl toward Stone. "This whole time, you've worried about who you were, about being someone worthy, and I didn't know you well, but I can tell you the person you were before didn't care for Hercules. You hated him. But now? You don't leave him anywhere. You bought him a bed. He loves you and you love him."

I press a hand to the base of my throat. "I didn't change you. You became *you*, and I fell for that person. Yes, it was my fault, but I've never lied about my feelings. In fact, I tried *not* to fall for you because I was scared to, scared that when you remembered, you'd hate me.

"But, Stone"—the words clog my throat and tears blur my eyes—"the truth is, you helped me see myself in ways I never have. You made me believe I was someone worth seeing, and I'll never forget that."

Stone wipes a hand down his face. "The engagement? It was a lie?"

The word *lie* comes out slowly, like his mind is trying to wrap around it. He gazes at the floor, but when he looks up at me, his eyes brim with hurt, betrayal.

"You lied," he repeats as if he's doing his best to absorb what I've done.

And then I remember what Isaac told me his mother did—took away his father—and I get the sense that even if Stone doesn't remember the details of that, the pain is still real. It haunts him.

And now I've lied to him.

"What about the ring?" he asks.

Oh, God. There's still more to tell him. "The ring was my grandmother's. You saw me wearing it when we first met and commented that no one would marry me, or something like that, and after . . . I think you remembered seeing it on my finger, and that's why you thought we were engaged. I wanted to stop everything, I did. But I was afraid of losing who you'd become."

"And the town," he grinds out. "You were afraid of losing your town."

I nod, ashamed. I can't look at him.

"None of it was real," he murmurs in a voice so broken my rib cage shatters.

"Yes, it was real. I'm real. You're real."

He murmurs, sounding confused, "This whole time I thought it was an accident." He touches his head. "But you did this on purpose. You let me believe this lie, and you had weeks to tell me the truth. *Weeks.*"

"I know what I did is unforgivable."

He stumbles back and Pane grabs his shoulders, catching him before he hits the ground. Stone shakes off the help and swallows hard, his Adam's apple bobbing.

"You let me believe we were engaged. You showed up to this wedding I planned. You would have married me? For what? For money? I don't even know how much I have, but I'm pretty sure it's a lot." He glances at Pane, who nods. His next words come out so cold I don't recognize the man who says them: "You've taken me for a fool."

"No!" I reach for him, but he steps away. "No, Stone. I tried to tell you! I wanted to tell you! But whenever I did, I always got interrupted."

Stone runs a hand down his chest. It's like he's thrown up a thousand impenetrable walls.

And that's when I know there's no coming back from this.

"You had more than enough time to admit you gave me amnesia." He looks at his brother. "Had it for weeks. That's why I changed my cell number, because I couldn't get into my phone. That's why I changed the resort. Because I thought what I was doing was better. But it wasn't." He exhales. "I've been betrayed." Without looking at me, he murmurs, "I never want to see you again."

"No! No, Stone! I tried to cure you. I did. I made the potion from that bloom we found the other night, but Hercules ate it."

He laughs. It's bitter, and it rips me in half. "Right."

"I swear!" I grab his hand, but he jerks back. "Please, you have to listen to me."

He shakes his head. "I've made up my mind. I never want to see you again."

My emotions swirl, ungrounded, untethered, wanting to cling to something. I've never felt so awful in my whole life. Yes, it's my fault. I'm not saying it isn't. But I wanted the lie as much as I wanted him. I just wanted to be seen and loved for myself for a little while longer. Who could blame me for that?

As Stone moves away, power surges inside me. Before I can stop it, blue sparks jump from my fingers, shooting like lightning toward the floor, the ceiling, smashing candles and causing them to explode into fountains of liquid wax.

People scream, *"She's a witch! Get out! She'll kill us all!"*

"No!" I cry. "No! I'm not going to hurt anyone. I'm so sorry! Wait! Please!"

I look over as Stone turns on his heel and leaves with the crowd, who's clambering for the double doors.

His brother puts a hand on his shoulder and Hercules follows behind, kicking up his feet, excited to be going somewhere with his family.

His family.

Not my family.

Never my family.

As people flood out from the chapel, I watch them, all alone, standing in a beautiful dress on what could have been the happiest day of my life.

Who am I kidding? This was never going to end well. The question was, just what degree of awful would it be?

Level terrible is where it ended up.

I'm left standing alone, shunned, just as I feared.

My magic may have been the reason why people are leaving, but it's not the reason I'm alonc.

I did that to myself, and there's no way to salvage this.

Chapter 44

COCO

Ron takes me home, and as soon as I step through the door, the scent hits me.

The whole house smells like Stone—salty air, pine soap, the faint aroma of ocean wind tangled with something warm and clean. After I peel off the dress—which I'll return, of course—I find one of his T-shirts folded at the foot of the bed. I pull it on and crawl into the side he's been sleeping on, pressing my face to his pillow like it might hold the last breath he left behind.

I blink at the dark ceiling hour after hour until sleep finally drags me under.

I awaken the next morning and stare at my ceiling for a good thirty minutes before finally dragging myself from bed to get cleaned up. My entire body aches from the emotional strain of last night, and of course the whole scene is on replay in my mind.

It's like I want to live in this agony. No, not live in it. I simply don't know how to shut it off and move forward.

Maybe I don't deserve to. Maybe I deserve to be haunted by what I did to Stone.

Soon as I'm out of the shower, there's a knock at the front door. My body thrums with hope. Maybe it's Stone and he's forgiven me.

I open the door, half praying it's him, half dreading that it is, because the look of contempt he gave me last night mirrored what I knew he'd feel when he discovered the truth.

But it isn't Stone. It's Cristina. She stands in the doorway with a to-go cup of coffee. "Hey," she says gently. "I thought you might need this."

"More like I could use a bottle of whiskey."

She grimaces. "Can I come in?"

"Sure."

I move aside as she hands me the cup. I'm hit with the scents of cinnamon and vanilla. I take a tentative sip and sigh. This helps. It won't heal. But it will certainly help.

"How'd you sleep?" she asks, placing her lower back against the kitchen counter.

"Like shit. As you'd expect."

She nods. "What are you going to do?"

I shrug. "Hide out here all weekend so I don't have to see anyone. Put a bag over my head if I have to go into town—at least for the first month. Maybe it'll all blow over by then."

Cristina gives me a sympathetic look.

I sink onto a chair. "I made a huge mess of it all and he hates me. He always would've hated me, though."

Maybe I wanted him to, because in the end it'll be easier to release him if he hates me. It's a clean break.

Oh, who am I kidding? There's no easy way to let go of the effect Stone Maddox had on me.

I laugh and it's a fractured sound. "I ruined everything, Cristina."

She crosses to the living room and sits on the couch across from me. "I know you really loved him, and he really loved you. I'm sorry how it ended, but if it makes you feel any better, I'm proud of you."

"What?"

My friend exhales a little whimper of sympathy. "You admitted everything at the hardest time to do it. You could have denied it, but you told the truth in front of the entire town—in front of your parents. That should mean something to you. You should be proud of that."

I shake my head. "Two nights ago, Stone looked at me like he . . ." My throat knots up and I can't get out the words *loved me*, which is what I'm yearning to express. So I blow out a breath and say, "He looked at me like he cared. But last night, he didn't even seem to recognize me. There's nothing to be proud of."

"Hey." She bends until our gazes latch. "You told the truth when it would have been easier to lie. That's brave."

She hugs me, wrapping her arms around my neck, and I sigh into her. I'm broken, shattered into a thousand pieces that are so scattered I don't think they'll ever find their way back to one another again.

But still, I hold Cristina tight. She's probably all I've got left after last night.

When she pulls away, my friend sits and talks to me for a few minutes, but there isn't much to say. After she leaves, I lounge in the living room for a while, reliving the moments of horror from last night until I finally shake it off and take the coffee back into my bedroom, stopping by the kitchen window to peer out.

There, in the distance, sit the ley lines. They pulse weakly, as if they, too, have been drained of the best part of their life—like they just lost the piece of themselves that, when it was locked into place, made sense of the world.

I climb into bed and pull the covers to my chin.

All I want to do is disappear.

Maybe I will.

Chapter 45

COCO

My mom calls later and asks if I'd like to come over for dinner. I simply don't have it in me, but she's got her whole "Mom" voice on, which means if I don't go over there, she might load up the truck and bring herself, along with others, to my tiny cottage decorated in doilies.

So off to their place I go.

When I arrive, it's late afternoon. No one's outside, which is good. The last thing I feel like is being surrounded by my entire family.

I enter the house and call out, "Mom! Dad!"

"We're in here," comes Dad's voice from the basement.

I weave through the house and go downstairs, where I find my dad, Mom, Brittany, and Jet playing pool.

"Just in time," Dad says. "I just whipped Brittany's butt. Now it's your turn to try to take me."

It's impossible not to smile. "All right. Rack 'em up. Let's see if I can do it."

For the next half hour we talk about everything but what happened. The whole situation is soft—no harsh edges. Brittany isn't trying to one-up or embarrass me, or for once make me feel like the little sister who screwed up every day in middle school.

No, it's the easiest conversation I think we've ever shared as a family.

We even laugh. I mean, really laugh, because my emotional walls, which are usually up, have disintegrated. Wow. If I'd known publicly humiliating myself would bring me closer to my family, I might've done it ages ago.

Just kidding.

Even though they're being super nice, there's still a hole in me, an ache that lingers. It feels as if it'll never be filled. So when Mom tells us dinner's ready, my appetite isn't there. I haven't eaten anything since the coffee Cristina brought me this morning, and I don't think I'll be able to manage much.

But still I go up, and stop, instantly hit with the familiar smell of shrimp Creole, my absolute favorite dish on this planet. I look over at Mom, and she smiles with encouragement.

She made it for me.

Nu-Nu walks in when we're sitting down. "Looks like my sixth sense was right. I had a feeling y'all were about to eat. I'm surprised no one called me. Hell, I only live down the road."

"I was just about to, Mama," Dad says, kissing her cheek. "Come and sit."

She takes a long look at the pot. "What? No gumbo?"

"Not today," Brittany tells her.

"Nothing makes a person feel better when your life's been destroyed than rib-sticking gumbo," she mutters.

"Mama," Dad scolds.

And there it is. All the judgment will happen now. My stomach tightens. Whatever my family wants to throw at me, I can take it.

Nu-Nu shrugs. "What? We all saw what happened." They shoot her big eyes, and she glances around until she spots me. "Well, shit. I didn't expect you to be here, Coco."

"Hey, Nu-Nu."

"Come give me some sugar."

The tension melts from me. Sugar. She wants a kiss, not to remind me of all my life's wrong choices. What a relief.

I get up and kiss her, and then I make her a bowl of shrimp Creole and put it on the table. Sweet gulf shrimp lay in a sauce of tomatoes atop a bed of white rice. It's amazing.

There's an awkward silence for a couple of minutes before my grandmother says, "It would have been a beautiful wedding, lambicorn and all."

For some reason that makes me laugh. I chuckle until my ribs hurt, and everyone joins in, the tension that Nu-Nu brought melting like butter in a hot pan.

"It was a beautiful venue," I admit glumly. "The whole town looked great." I take a bite of the shrimp and let the savory tomato sauce linger on my tongue for a moment before I chew and swallow it down. "When did Stone call you?"

"A few hours before," Mom says. "He asked if it was okay. Your dad told him yes."

All eyes swivel to Dad, who runs a hand down his beard. "What? I like the guy. He stood up for you and he stood up to us. Takes balls to do that."

"Yeah, your dad thinks that boyfriend of yours has big balls," Nu-Nu adds, laughing.

We all laugh, and when it dies down, and Mom says, "We liked him. Not because he's a Maddox, but because of how he treated you. How he seemed kind and funny."

"And because he got you to pick a new hiding place," Brittany quips.

I frown. "You want us to keep the same spots. Every year. You tell us to."

"No, I don't."

"Yes, you do."

"No, she doesn't," Jet confirms. "What's the fun in always hiding in the same place? The viewers want it to be different."

"But I thought . . ." I start the sentence but don't finish it, because it occurs to me that perhaps what I thought the truth was isn't what it actually *is*.

"You thought what?" my sister asks.

"I just thought you wanted us to hide in the same places."

"No." She shakes her head. "I didn't want that."

How is it possible to have been so wrong? How could I have completely misunderstood the assignment? Because of my own prejudice? Because I assumed that's who my sister *was*?

Had I ever even really listened to the instructions? Or did I simply make them up in my mind, allowing my own bitterness to take the lead?

All those years, I returned to the same spot, waiting to be found, just like I've been doing with my life.

The irony is real, y'all.

We finish dinner and I tell my mom and sister I'll clean up, so they go outside with the men to sit on the porch and enjoy the evening.

Which leaves me and Nu-Nu. I know my grandmother has things she wants to say. She's had that look on her face through dinner, like there's something on the tip of her tongue. I just have to wait for her to ask it.

"So you have the *touch*," she finally says.

A bitter laugh escapes my throat. I slide the last plate onto the drying rack and take a seat at the table across from her.

"I didn't ask for it," I say, in case she's wondering.

"Of course you didn't. Do you think you chose it? No, it chose you."

I let that sink in. I've never thought about it like that. When the blue sparks began plaguing me, I figured it was a freak occurrence, something that needed to be kept a secret. It never occurred to me the power *chose me*. "Well, now the whole town knows. Any day now, an angry mob will appear, especially after what I did to Stone."

"You know, your great-grandmother was touched, too."

I blink. "What?"

Nu-Nu nods. "She had a little bit of magic in her. Kept it to herself mostly, made little healing remedies for folks. Now, she never gave anyone amnesia that I know of—"

"Darn."

Nu-Nu laughs. "Come on. How bad was it that it happened? Really? From what you said at the church— You're not pregnant, are you?"

I roll my eyes. "We weren't marrying because I'm pregnant."

She claps a hand over mine. "That's real good, *cher*. Not that I would've minded a little great-grandbaby, but you know, I'm old and traditional."

"I know. It's okay."

She draws her hand away and leans back. "What was I saying?"

"About the church—Stone losing his memory and it being my fault."

She shoots me a sympathetic look before continuing. "From what you were saying, it didn't sound all that bad—like he became a better person when he lost his memory. Hell, I'd probably become a better person, too."

We laugh, and light dances in her eyes. "I know right now things may seem hard, but they'll get easier. This'll pass, and even though folks might've been upset because of what you did, no one there pulled a pitchfork out of their butt and came after you, did they?"

"No, I guess they didn't."

"Times are changing, and even if Stone Maddox don't forgive you, I know what you did came from goodness. You weren't trying to hurt no one. Were you?"

"No, I just wanted him to see *why* I did it, and it wasn't for me."

"That's because you've got a good heart. Don't let no one tell you different."

"I'll try not to."

"That's my girl, and if anyone comes to your house looking to burn it down, you call me. I'll come over and sit on them."

I laugh, because Nu-Nu isn't a waif. She's got some weight on her, and knowing my grandmother, she probably *would* sit on someone who wanted to hurt me.

I rise and wrap my arms around her neck. "Thanks, Nu-Nu."

"You're welcome. Now, give me some sugar and get out of here."

I kiss her cheek and head to the front porch. I say goodbye to my family. Even though they don't repeat what Nu-Nu said, that they would protect me, I know they will—they've got my back no matter how this unfolds.

As I head to my car, Brittany says, "I'll walk you."

"It's just right there."

She shrugs. "I know, but I'll still come."

Okay. This is a first. My sister never escorts me to my car. Is she all right? I'm hoping she doesn't want me to cast a spell on Jet or anything. My spell-slinging days are over.

As soon as we're out of earshot, she says, "I'm sorry."

"It's okay. It's not as if you brewed a potion that made Stone Maddox forget who he is."

"Not about that—for everything else."

"What are you talking about?"

"For making you think you had to stay in the same place every time we played Hide from Brittany."

"Huh?"

She scrapes her fingers through her hair. "I'm sorry you feel like you've been playing second fiddle. I didn't realize how pushed aside you've been until . . . recently. My channel requires me to be a big personality, and I guess sometimes I take it too far."

"It's okay." *I'm used to it.*

"No, it's not," she replies, flustered. "When you came along, like when you were born, you got all this attention, and I was jealous. Back then it seemed like everything you did, our parents made it such a big deal—all of it, from the time we were little through high school. Even now, they're amazed because you have magic."

"They are?" I look back at the house. The porch is empty, but the light's still on. "They never said anything to me about it."

"Well, they said plenty to me." We reach my car and Brittany leans against the door. "It's always been like that. They fawn over you."

A laugh bursts from my mouth. My sister gives me a puzzled look, and I explain, "Are you serious? That's how they act about you. All Mom talks about is you and your channel. I'm not kidding. It's all she ever mentions. She's so proud of you, you know that? So proud that she forgot I had a new job. Stone had to tell her."

"Are you sure you didn't *forget* to tell her?"

I frown. *Did I tell her?* Or did I figure she wouldn't remember anyway, so I didn't bother?

Shit.

Maybe I didn't mention it. I look up at the house in disbelief.

Brittany shakes her head. "When we were little, they talked about you all the time. It's why I pushed myself so hard, because I felt like I was competing with you."

Wow. My entire life, I've been comparing myself to Brittany, and she's been doing the same. It never crossed my mind that she might feel insecure about *me*. How could she when she's the one making all the crazy YouTube money?

Is it possible I've been wrong about her? That my sister and I have each suffered in silence, thinking our parents loved the other better, when they loved each of us the same this entire time?

Is it possible we've each been jealous and we didn't need to be?

"I'm sorry," I admit.

She cocks her head. "For what?"

"For years I've been jealous of your success because I thought Mom and Dad respected you more."

"I don't think that's true. They may not tell you how proud they are, but I hear it, Coco. I hear it a lot. I think, if anything, they have a hard time expressing it. But I know they love you. Why do you think they were excited about the wedding? They were worried, of course, like any parent would be. But they want your happiness. More than anything."

My chest expands, filling with love that should have always been there for my sister but was trapped behind the barbed wire of jealousy.

It's hard to wrap my mind around, the fact that my parents have bragged about me to Brittany, when for years it felt like they didn't see me.

Maybe they did see me, it's just that I didn't allow myself to realize it because I was so used to being dismissed.

Just like I'm trying to dismiss myself again. Just this morning, I thought I should disappear because I'd ruined things so badly with Stone.

But that's how I've spent my life—hiding, shrinking, slipping into invisibility because it was easier than allowing myself to be seen.

Stone gave me the power to let myself be looked at. Why would I take that away just because he left me? And rightly so, of course. What I did to him, how I kept up the lie, is reprehensible.

But just because he's gone, does it mean I should allow myself to suffer, too?

It doesn't seem right.

I hug Brittany and she hugs me back. This might be the first time in forever we've actually done this, and it feels right. A lifetime of sadness, bitterness, and jealousy washes out of me, and I allow myself to see things from her perspective.

We've both been trapped in what we thought the world was, but it turns out we were wrong. We've seen each other as the competition, but that isn't the truth. We were never supposed to be against one another.

We were supposed to be on the same side, and I see that now.

Better late than never.

"Thank you," I tell her when we part.

"For what?"

"For telling me. I had no idea."

"Me neither." We stare at each other for a beat before she says, "Now. Go out there and get back your man."

"What?"

"Just kidding. But if you do decide to go after Stone, call me. I'll be your backup."

I laugh and head home. In a couple of days, I return to work.

There's no telling what I'll face when I arrive.

Chapter 46

STONE

Nothing can make me feel better.

Not even Hercules.

Not that I want to. If there's anything that reminds a person they're human, it's pain and suffering.

How could Coco have lied to me for so long?

That isn't love.

It's betrayal.

It's the depth and breadth of the lie that hurts. For weeks she could have revealed the truth, but she let me fall in love with her. She let me *believe* the lie . . . and that's unforgivable.

It's Monday morning and I'm back at the construction site, ready to dig into work, get things moving.

I stayed the rest of the weekend with Pane, who helped me break into my phone and laptop. Man, did I have a few thousand emails to sift through. Answering them kept me busy all of yesterday and helped keep my mind off Coco.

Mostly.

She got in there every once in a while, like when Hercules wanted to be petted.

All the best memories of him are tangled up with her.

But I'm not some softy who gets taken by a woman and played for a fool.

There's a knock at the door. "Come in!"

Pane enters and grabs a hard hat from a shelf. "Hey."

"Hey. You ready to walk the site?"

"Let's do it."

I push up from behind the desk and head out with him. Hercules is still with me. Even though he reminds me of her, I can't get rid of the lambicorn.

He's only a baby, and I'm not a monster.

Pane says good morning to the guys as we pass them. All I can offer is a nod in greeting. This isn't a good morning. I don't see myself experiencing a "good" morning for the next hundred years.

Not without Coco.

Not without my sun.

Stop it, Stone. She lied to you. Repeatedly. *Even when she had the chance to tell the truth, she still lied—happily, so that she could save her town and apparently her own ass.*

Those two things were always more important to her than I was. And that's what hurts most of all. I gave her every part of me, and all she wanted was her town.

I don't miss her. In fact, I'm better off without her. I was fine before her, and I'll be fine again. Maybe. At least that's what I tell myself over and over until it's almost believable.

Much as I've tried repeatedly to push these thoughts away, they continue to creep in.

"The build's going great," Pane says. When I don't answer, he sighs. "You okay?"

"Fine," I reply curtly.

I'm such a liar. The ley lines thrum happily. Well, maybe not happily, but they're pulsing and alive thanks to the changes we made to the resort.

"I was worried when I first heard about the materials shift, but this looks good. It's strong."

"How's Rhett?"

"He still not talking to you?"

I grunt.

"He'll get over it." Pane kneels and runs his palm over the limecrete. "This is perfect. Not one crack. It's hard to find that. Well done. Looks like the materials switch was worth it. Otherwise, if you'd kept using the other stuff and this town lost its magic, we'd be screwed. No tourists, no need for the resort."

I rub the back of my neck. "Yeah, I guess."

"You should congratulate yourself." He rises and slips his hands in his pockets. "Mom called me."

My mom. Pane explained that whole clusterfuck to me, too. "Yeah?"

He nods. "Yeah. She's sorry. I think she really wants to try."

"Good luck to her." I'm too raw to even consider talking to anyone about emotions or feelings or their long lost cousin who's been living in a swamp.

Hercules runs past, kicking up his hind legs with glee. Glad someone's happy.

He munches on grass that sprouts on top of the ley lines, and when he turns around, his horn is glowing this weird iridescent purple. It reminds me of the color of that flower Coco picked in the meadow during the full moon.

"Is he okay?" Pane asks.

"Hell if I know. Hercules, come!"

The lambicorn leaves the grass and trots over. Pane watches him closely. "Does he have magic?"

"Not that I know of."

"That's what the piggycorns did when their magic first showed up. Their horns glowed."

I bend down and pat the lambi on the back. "You feeling okay, bud?"

"Baaaaaaa."

He lowers his head, touching his horn to my wrist. A line of light flashes under my skin. At the same time, I feel the ley lines throb with power.

I exhale a gusty sigh. Electricity surges through my veins, burning like lava. It hits me—hot, sharp, like my insides might explode.

The air's knocked from my lungs, and I struggle to catch my next breath. Everything in my head goes silent, still, like I'm suspended in midair, waiting for gravity to grab me with its unyielding hand and drag me back to Earth.

Then my veins open. Air surges into my lungs. Blood rushes in my ears.

And I remember everything.

Who I was before the amnesia. The pain my mother caused by keeping our father from us. My initial rejection of Hercules and all his sunshine.

And I remember how I threatened to blackmail Coco.

My body hurts, the muscles *aching* from losing her. Coco's voice echoes in my mind—how she felt *seen*. I remember the night in the meadow, and feel her breath on my neck, taste how she kissed me like she believed in us.

I remember the lie my mother told and how much pain it gave me, and how Coco's betrayal hurts all the more because of the past that's chained around my ankle like an iron ball.

All that pain crashes down, threatening to choke me.

So I wall it up because I know who I am now, and I remember everything.

What happened with the lambicorn hits me. Hercules ate the potion Coco had made to fix me, and somehow harnessed its magic. Now I'm free.

Am I? Or am I chained to the past?

The past is what made me who I am. The past is an anchor that doesn't shift or change.

So many emotions and thoughts flood my mind. It's like I'm two different people—the *before* me and the *after* me. The person I became because of Coco, because of the amnesia, is compromised. He believes people too easily. He trusted the wrong person. That Stone was a sucker who doesn't deserve respect.

So I shut the door on him.

"You okay?" Pane asks.

"Never better."

My gaze washes over the site, and all I see is limecrete, red earth, and grass. No more ley lines. They've vanished from sight because the spell Coco cast no longer strangles me.

I'm glad they've vanished. I didn't need them anyway.

"The materials," I tell Pane.

"What about them?"

"What would you think about changing them?"

Chapter 47

COCO

I've been fired.

It was inevitable, but seeing the letter on my desk hits differently than envisioning it, because it's real.

Word travels fast in a small town. No surprises there. To be honest, the one thing that *is* surprising is the fact that I didn't receive a call over the weekend informing me of the town's decision.

Looks like the mayor held a private meeting after the wedding fiasco.

Oscar Rutledge, the man Dot couldn't stand, hovers in the doorway, waiting for me to pack up my stuff and head out. It takes all of five minutes. I've only had this job a month. It's not like I started squirreling away ramen noodles in my drawers for late-afternoon pick-me-ups.

"Sorry, Coco," he says.

My shoulders sink. Oscar's old, with gray-streaked hair, bushy eyebrows, and a permanent frown. I can see how he and Dot would've butted heads, but I've barely gotten to know him.

"It's okay," I tell him, dropping the last of my things into the cardboard box they provided.

I leave the office and hit the parking lot. Folks walk the streets, heading to the shops.

A few of them are locals—like Mrs. Malfree, who's walking her pug. She spots me and I wave, but she lifts her nose and looks the other way.

Looks like the shunning has begun.

What they don't realize is that I've put my town first. I never would've dabbled in anything if not for my love of Mystic Meadows. Well, that and self-preservation.

The birds chirp as I unlock my car. In the park across the street, kids play on the swing set. Life goes on, doesn't it? Even when one person falls apart, life still continues somewhere else.

I'm not sure that makes me feel better, but it certainly puts things in perspective.

"Why are we here?" I ask Cristina several nights later.

"Because you need to get out. You can't stay in your house alone every night."

I glance up at the exterior of Sparkle Bar. The swinging wooden placard portrays a smiling unicorn. If only I felt like smiling on the inside.

"Come on," she says. "You've got friends there."

She tugs on my sleeve, but I stay put, both feet glued to the sidewalk. "Stone sometimes comes here."

What if he's in there? I haven't seen or heard from him in a week. He hasn't even called about his things. He's rich, so it's not like he needs the shirts and pants. He can easily buy more.

But still . . . I'd hoped he would contact me.

It's no less than I deserve, I suppose.

"Stone's not here," she says. "I already made sure."

That's good. I guess. Exhaling a deep sigh, I say, "Okay. Let's go."

We head inside, and to my relief, the bar is busy. The jukebox plays, and people laugh as they toss darts and shoot pool.

This week would have been unbearable if Dad hadn't called. My parents needed someone to fulfill prepper go bag orders, so they hired me. It's not glamorous, but it's work, keeping me busy while I heal.

Don't worry, there's still a hole in me the size of a fist.

So yeah, there's some self-pity going on.

I'm able to easily slip into the crowd with Cristina, going unnoticed and disappearing into the throng of people. This is good. It feels normal. I've returned to being someone no one sees. It's my comfort zone. We all need one of those.

Cristina orders us a couple of beers and we sit at an open table. "What about the book?" she asks, brows pumping.

I sigh. "Well, I didn't take it with me to work on Monday, so it's still at my house. You think Dot wants it?"

She laughs. "Can you imagine us showing up with it to the nursing home?"

"Can you imagine us *not*?" The book isn't mine to keep. It belonged to her. "Think she'll take it?"

"Hard to say. Maybe. Maybe not." Cristina eyes me while she sips her beer. "Probably not."

"You're right, but I still need to check, because it doesn't feel right to keep it."

A commotion from the other side of the bar makes the crowd hush into the kind of quiet only reserved for when really bad things happen.

"Who let *her* in?" a man growls.

I hear Isaac say, "She's free to go wherever she wants. There aren't any locked doors in this town. I let you in here, Luke, and we all know how you cheated your *friends*—me included—in poker."

Cristina sits up and peers around me. Her lips part as her eyes widen. "Don't look now, but Luke Preston is at the bar, and he's looking over here."

Oh, crap. Luke Preston. The scourge of this town, the man who runs the bank and who co-owns the unicorn farm, Happy Trails, with his wife, Sally Ray.

"I say she leaves," he demands.

I turn around, and Luke is nose to nose with Isaac, who stands behind the bar.

"Nobody wants *that witch* in here."

Luke's gaze locks on mine, and his eyes are inky dark with anger. Everyone's gone quiet, and their eyes are either fixed on me or on Luke.

"Let's calm down." Isaac pats the air. "She's not hurting anybody."

"Yeah? Well, how do I know she's not going to cast some spell like she did to Maddox?" Luke sneers at me. "What were you planning to do, Coco? Spell all of us? Turn this entire town into a bunch of zombies?"

My insides tighten. *This.* This is exactly what I was afraid would happen.

Luke Preston is not my friend. He's a jerk, and one who holds a lot of clout in this town.

My cheeks heat. The tops of my ears burn. This is literally the worst position I could have found myself in, and there's no one to blame but myself.

If I hadn't made that potion, then none of this would have happened.

My shoulders tighten because I *also* know that if I hadn't made that potion, then I wouldn't have had the very brief and wonderful experience of being loved by Stone Maddox.

And that made it all worth it.

I don't think I've realized that until this exact moment, when an angry mob is about to burn me at the stake.

Once again, better late than never.

"We should go," Cristina says.

"No." Don't ask me where that word came from. It shot out of my mouth of its own accord, deciding to take charge.

"Coco," Cristina warns.

"No. I'm tired of hiding," I murmur. "I've been doing it all my life."

It's a strange thing to go from feeling small and nonexistent to being seen. Stone had a lot to do with that, and so has my family lately.

I knew the firing was coming, and of course it's risky to be out in public at a bar. But it's time I face the music.

Luke stomps over, the heels of his boots hitting the floor so hard it sounds like the boom of a shotgun.

He reaches the table and glares down at me. He really is intimidating—angry eyes, big, muscled shoulders. This man is no shrinking violet.

I *should* be shrinking, but I'm done with that.

Luke raps his knuckles on the tabletop. "You need to leave this town. Get the hell out of here and never come back."

"Why?"

He drops his head back and laughs. "*Why?* Are you kidding me? Because of what you did. Because of what you are. There's a lot of things we'll accept in Mystic Meadows, but devil-worshipping is not one of them."

"I don't worship the devil."

He spins around, arms wide. "She doesn't worship the devil," he shouts to the crowd, people he clearly sees as his loyal supporters.

"Did you hear that, folks?" he adds, trying to get a response from the crowd. "Coco says she doesn't worship the devil."

"I'm warning you, man," Isaac tells him.

"Warning me about what? I'm not hurting her. I'm not even touching her. I'm just telling her like it is—that her kind is not wanted in this town. She'd do best to vacate the premises and leave Mystic Meadows. For good."

Knots of worry twist inside me. This whole scene makes pressure build in my hands.

Several weeks ago I would have shoved my hands in my pockets, knowing that blue sparks would come and that they'd hurt.

But that was before, and I'm not the same person I was then.

"I'm tired of what this town believes," I say quietly.

"What's that?" Luke says, cocking his ear.

"I said, all my life I've heard what you said: Creatures with magic are good. People with magic are bad. But I didn't have a choice in this.

When the ley lines came back, when the magic returned, it entered me, too, and I refuse to believe it's wrong."

"It *is* wrong," he sneers.

"How can this be wrong?"

I lean over and place a hand to the floor. With an exhale, I push all the power building in my body through the floorboards. My body glows from the inside out, down to my hand and into the floorboards.

The room goes quiet.

Folks might be about to jump me. I don't know—I'm not looking.

The magic inside me flows into the ground. I feel it talk to the land, mingle with it, coax it lovingly as if the two are meant to be partners and not combatants.

That's what took me so long to learn. I'm not separate from this land. I'm part of it, someone who needs to work with it and help it. Protect it.

"Stop," Luke warns.

"No," I whisper.

"She's going to kill us all!" he screeches.

"Quit your whining. I'm not going to harm anyone."

A second later, I prove this as long-stemmed flowers pop up from between the cracks of the floor, unfolding into beautiful irises with bold blue and gold petals.

I pull my hand away and stare at the flowers. "Sorry, Isaac. They probably won't last too long. Maybe a day."

He scratches his head but doesn't speak.

It's okay. I wouldn't know what to say, either.

But that doesn't stop other people from figuring out what to do. They stare at the flowers in surprise, until a woman bends over and starts picking them.

"I'm gonna put these in a vase at home. You know how much irises cost at the store?"

Then more people pick the flowers, and more, until almost all of them have found homes, and I sit up, watching in awe.

No one condemns me. No one says I'm evil.

People simply pick flowers until they're all gone.

"Y'all are sick!" Luke storms out of the bar, yelling about devil-worshipping.

It's funny. He's the only person who seems to think that.

This is proven when a petite redhead comes over and says, "Can you make some more?"

"Isaac?" I ask.

He nods. "Make as many flowers as you want."

Chapter 48

COCO

The next morning, I feel a thousand times better than I have in days. Maybe what happened at the bar last night has gotten out, but if it hasn't, that's okay.

Eventually, it will.

There are bills to pay, and since the utility buildings are just down the street, I decide to take a walk. It's cloudy outside, heavy with humidity. Rain is coming.

The streets are bustling with early-morning joggers and a few tourists looking for breakfast. I spot Mrs. Malfree walking her pug and expect the woman to turn up her nose like she did last time we crossed paths, but as she approaches, she reaches for me.

"Good morning, Coco."

My brows lift in surprise. "Good morning."

"I'm so glad I ran into you."

Mrs. Malfree is the quintessential Southern woman, with big blond hair, large hoop earrings, and just about everything she wears is monogrammed. Right now, she's sporting a light rain jacket with her initials emblazoned on the left breast.

"Oh?" I ask. "Did you need me to tell Mom something?"

"No. I found this in my cupboard today and thought you could use it." She pulls out a small mason jar. "It's the strawberry jam I made last year. I don't think you got any. Is that right?"

"Um, yeah. That's right."

She pushes it into my open hand. "Take it, and let me know how it is. Tell your mama I said hey."

"Will do," I reply as she walks off.

My gaze drops to the glass jar. Jam? Mrs. Malfree gave me jam? Isn't she supposed to tell my mom when I've done something wrong? Spy on me? But here she is, giving me jam?

"Oh—and, Coco?"

I turn around and she gives me a thumbs-up.

"Good job."

Good job? Is she talking about last night? But before there's a chance to ask, Mrs. Malfree has rounded a corner and disappeared out of sight.

Huh. That was weird.

As I continue down the street, a few folks I recognize but don't really know wave. I wave back.

Is this all because of the flowers?

The more I walk, the more people grin, wave. Until one girl, who's maybe eight or so and walking with her parents, runs up and hands me an iris.

"Can you make more?"

A slow smile spreads across my face. "Yeah," I tell her. "I can make more. I can make a whole field of them."

Which gives me an idea. A great big glorious idea.

One that I hope my parents will go for.

When I get home, there's a note inside my mailbox. Worry knots my stomach for a moment. Is it a challenge from Luke Preston? Does he want to duel?

But when I unfold it, the handwriting is in cursive. It's feminine, unsigned.

You made things bloom. That's not what evil does, and this town will remember it.

Warmth spreads through my body, the feeling lingering like a heated cloth on my skin. So I won't be kicked out or shunned.

I'll be accepted by the folks of Mystic Meadows, which is all I've ever wanted my whole life anyway.

Chapter 49

STONE

I'm miserable. Completely miserable. Hercules can't make me feel better. Not even the resort can.

The reason I'm miserable—I won't say her name. I *refuse* to say her name.

I rub my eyes before staring at the computer screen, going through the last of my emails, cleaning up the inbox.

Someone knocks on the trailer door. "Boss!"

"Yeah?"

"Delivery!"

I yank on my hard hat and meet Isaac outside. A flatbed truck has arrived filled with steel beams, a material that will probably kill a few ley lines. Hell, there's a lot of them running under this resort. A few pieces of steel in one area couldn't hurt . . . that much.

I tell them where to unload the metal and turn to go back into my office when Hercules barrels past, bleating and basically being a happy baby.

Must be nice to have that kind of innocence.

I reach down to pet him as a black SUV with tinted windows rolls up. I frown, because it's not Pane's vehicle.

Maybe it's Rhett.

But when the passenger door opens and I get a glimpse of white, I know it's not Rhett. It's definitely not Pane.

It's Sylvia, my mother.

She steps out wearing her signature white pantsuit. Her dark hair is secured at the nape of her neck, and the one gray stripe that's woven into her otherwise ebony locks is whiter than it was last time I saw her.

She takes a look at the resort, drinking it in, and for a moment, I stand there wondering whether I should go into the trailer or greet her.

Decision made, I cross the red clay while Hercules runs alongside me. My mother sees me and smiles stiffly, as if she's had to train her face how to do this trick.

I frown and her lips slowly dip into a frown.

"Stone," she murmurs.

"Sylvia," I spit.

Her green eyes—eyes that match mine—linger on me for a moment before they swish to the resort. "It looks good. I knew you boys had the skill to build on your own. Of course, you could have done it within the company. You didn't have to . . ."

"Leave?" I finish when she can't.

She nods, mouth tight. "Is there someplace we can talk?"

I want to tell her no, we can't talk. We can *never* talk. But she's come all this way, and it's loud, and I don't like scandals or spectacles.

"You can come inside. Pane isn't here."

"I didn't come for Pane. I came to speak to you."

Something about that makes my stomach coil tight.

I lead her into the trailer, and when we're inside, I point to a chair. "You're welcome to sit."

"Thank you."

I take a seat behind my desk. "You thirsty?"

"No, I can't stay long. I'm on my way to Palm Beach."

"Building a new hotel?"

"Yes. It would have been a good one for you to oversee."

"I'm tied up for the foreseeable future." I pick up a pencil and twist it between my fingers. But the stupid pencil reminds me of Coco, how she would stick them in her hair, so I drop it on my desk.

My mother sits ramrod-straight in the chair. I don't think I've ever seen her relaxed in my entire life.

"Stone, there are things I didn't get a chance to say before you left. The competition with Pane—you were both so close to becoming president I couldn't decide."

"So you pitted me against my brother head-on? This is how you nurture friendly competition?"

Her voice hardens. "What was I supposed to do? Pick one of you to become the next CEO?"

"Yes, Sylvia." My nostrils flare in anger. "You were supposed to pick *one* of us to lead the company. We shouldn't have competed against one another." I exhale and lean back in the chair. "Pane won fair and square. I don't have hard feelings about that."

Her shoulders sag slightly. "But you have hard feelings about other things."

"You mean about the fact that you kept my father from me for my entire life? Yeah, I've got some feelings about that."

"You don't understand—"

"Yes, I do!" I explode.

She blinks, stunned by my response.

Everything that's been building up in me—my anger at Coco, the agony I suffered because I loved her, discovering her betrayal—I've kept it all bottled up tight for weeks. But seeing my mom, this is the cherry on top, the moment that breaks me wide open.

"Stone . . ." she says feebly.

"Since you don't seem to understand that what you did was so horrible, let me break it down for you." I drum my fingers on the desk to give me a way to focus on something other than how torn apart I am. "When you divorced my dad, you made me think he didn't want to have anything to do with me or my brother. You perpetrated that lie, fed it, and stoked it until Pane and I were so full of bitterness toward him there wasn't room in our hearts for anything else. Then you know what happened?"

She shakes her head slightly.

I lean forward. "One day I ran into him on the street. Instantly recognized him. It may have been twenty years since I'd seen him, but I knew my dad. He explained what you'd done, how you told him if he attempted to see us, you'd destroy him financially. Now you tell me this—what kind of mother does that to her sons? What kind of mother shields them from a father who loves them?"

Sylvia cringes. "I assure you, Stone, there were reasons."

I slam a fist on the desk. "No, there weren't. There were no reasons strong enough for you to do that. He's not an awful person. He didn't abuse you, or us. The one fault he had was that he wasn't a Maddox. Hell, you didn't even let us take his last name. We took *your* last name." I lean back in the chair. "The bottom line is, he wasn't good enough."

"And what do you know about good enough?" she demands, clutching her purse so hard her knuckles become pale hills. "What do you know about raising two boys and making sure they keep the family name strong and won't let the company die a sad death? Do you know how many companies fold when the head family member dies? Do you know how many don't survive? Maddoxes are survivors, and I needed my boys strong enough to carry that name into the next generation."

"And now you don't have either of us. You did this, Sylvia. *You.* You pushed Pane and me away. We will never run the Maddox Group. We're forging our own path, one that isn't based on lies."

The corners of her eyes tighten. "I know from your perspective, this is hard to understand. My goals, my motivations must seem so foreign to you." She rubs her forehead, and this may be the first time I've seen what appears to be vulnerability from my mother. She's an ice queen through and through. The whole time we were growing up, she never shed a tear, not even when her father passed away.

"All I wanted was for my boys to grow up strong and be ready for the world. But I see now what I've done."

"And what is that?"

Her gaze latches on to mine, and regret swirls in her eyes. "I thought I was protecting you."

"From what?"

"From him. From him leaving, because when you have money like we do, people only want you for so long before the shine wears off."

"What? That's not true."

Wait.

If anything, I should be agreeing. I should say, *Yes, you're right—all anyone ever wants us for is money.*

But Coco didn't. She never asked for a dime.

Don't think about Coco now. Not here. Not yet. This is about Sylvia.

"I realize now I was training you to leave before anyone could leave you, and I suppose I deserve it."

I frown. "What are you talking about?"

Sylvia unsnaps her purse and pulls out a tissue, blotting her eyes. "Your grandfather was a cold man, and I suppose I inherited much of his temperament. Though it may have looked like my actions were done to keep love away from you, I was only trying to keep you from heartbreak."

My voice softens. "How?"

"Because it's inevitable. No matter what we do in life, we wind up destroyed. My marriage would have ended. I just did it on my own terms. I did it to keep us safe, to protect you."

"But it didn't protect me or Pane. It destroyed us."

She shattered us, and on purpose. My mother, thinking she was protecting me, only made my life worse.

She lowers her head in shame. "Pane and I have talked, though I doubt anything will ever fully heal the rift between all of us." She sniffles. "I didn't want you to be like me, always waiting for the other shoe to drop, so I taught you to let go first."

Her words are a punch to the gut. She taught me how to let go first, how to distrust first, how to leave *first.* How to ignore what someone's saying and abandon them before they have a chance to abandon me.

Just like I did with Coco when I left her in the chapel, all alone, when she tried to explain why she'd let me be an amnesiac—for the town, and for me, because of who it made me.

She stood there in that wedding dress trying to tell me the truth, and I left her.

A heaviness sets in my chest. It weighs me down, like someone has rested a boulder on my heart.

It's familiar, almost cozy, a feeling I've embraced for years, but for a few short weeks I didn't have it. I was lighter. Honest. Open. I want that again. Not the man trained to leave, but the one brave enough to stay.

I want to be who I'm supposed to be. It's what I deserve.

The weight that's been pressing on me suddenly lifts, and I feel a hundred pounds lighter.

"You may never forgive me," Sylvia whispers.

It's almost a question. My answer comes swiftly. "I can try."

"What?"

"I can try . . . Mom."

Her eyes well with tears and she nods. "Thank you."

I nod back. It's all I've got in me.

"My plane taxis in half an hour. I must go."

I rise and walk her to the door. "Thank you for coming."

She gives me a timid grin and opens her mouth to say something, but then throws her arms around my waist and hugs me.

The last time my mom hugged me, I must've been ten years old. For a split second, I'm not sure what to do, but then I relax and pull her tight, hold her close and feel how small she is, how frail, how she smells of jasmine.

I don't think I've realized how fragile she is until now. She's a small, thin woman who won't live forever, one who wants to have a relationship with her children.

Something inside me breaks as she holds me. Tears fill my eyes until one falls, dripping onto her head, and I gently brush it away.

She looks up. “Is everything okay?”

I nod, feeling my lips tipping upward. “Everything’s just as it should be, and there’s some steel beams that need to be returned.”

Chapter 50

COCO

When I knock on the doorframe, Dot puts down her crochet hook. There's a new afghan in her lap. It's a patchwork of mermaid colors—aqua and purple.

I love it.

She squints. "Look what the cat dragged in. You gonna tell me what the hell happened, or are you gonna make me guess?"

I nearly laugh at the welcome. I really didn't expect anything else. Or more, actually.

I take a seat on the herpes-free bed and drop my purse beside me. "I did what I was supposed to."

My voice must betray sadness, because Dot cocks her head, studying me. "What did you lose?"

"The love of my life."

"Could have been worse. You could've lost your purse to a street gang." She picks up her hook again, and almost as an afterthought, she asks, "But what did you gain?"

My shoulders tighten. "I gained my family and the respect of the town."

She tips her head from side to side, considering. "So it's a wash, huh?"

"Almost." Even with everything that's happened, I find myself smiling. Not because I'm healed. I still hurt. A lot.

But I'm growing through it, and at some point it'll feel better. I'll be able to look myself in the mirror and recognize that I did what I could. I tried to free Stone, even if it was too late.

The ball of yarn Dot's using falls from her lap and unwinds, landing at my feet. "Son of a bitch," she growls.

"I heard that," the nurse calls from the hallway.

"Fix my yarn and I won't have to cuss!"

"Here." I pick up the ball and move beside her. "I'll hold it for you."

"You will, huh?" She shoots me a suspicious look. "Why? You after my money?"

I throw back my head and laugh. "No. But do you have any? Some that's not covered in herpes?"

She clucks. "Look who learns so fast. Grab that chair over there and sit beside me. You can tell me everything that happened."

So I do. I tell Dot the whole thing, from start to finish, even the wedding. Surprisingly, she's a great listener. She doesn't judge, just nods and laughs in all the right places.

By the time I'm done, she pats my hand. "You did good."

"Thank you."

"Now, take a look at this throw. Pick it up. Let's see if it's big enough."

I grab hold of one edge and lift it. The afghan is beautiful.

"It's gorgeous. Who's it for?"

"You," she deadpans.

"What?"

"It's for you. Go on. Take it."

She starts to push it into my hands, and I shake my head. "No. There's got to be someone else you can give it to."

Her lips form a grim line. "You want me to give this here throw I made with my own blood, sweat, and tears to one of these ingrates? To someone who does naughty things in their room?"

"But you worked so hard . . ."

"Just take it."

It is beautiful, so I relent. "Thank you. And now I have something for you."

"Oh? Is it a man? One whose pecker isn't about to fall off?"

"Um. No." I pull the spell book from my purse. "Since it came from your office, I'm giving it back to you."

Dot stares at it, and I'm not sure if she'll actually accept the book. But after a moment she opens her hand.

"I suppose someone needs to keep it safe."

"I suppose so, since I don't need it anymore."

"I don't need it at all."

"You never know. You might find a cure for those herpes walls."

Her eyes brighten. "You know what, you got a point. Come back next week and check on me. If I've found a potion, we'll do it together."

"Uh . . . how about we start slow and read all the fine print?"

She nods. "Good point."

"I'd like that, and I will come back next week."

"You'd better, or else I'll hex you. I know how."

I laugh. "You sure do."

"Hand me those scissors and I'll finish up the throw."

As she works, Dot says, "So what will you do now? You know, with your magic?"

A bubble of excitement fills my stomach as I reply, "I'm going to make flowers."

Chapter 51

COCO

"You ready for this?" Mom asks as I unlock the front gate.

"I'm ready."

Dad grabs one side of gate and swings it open. "It looks great, honey."

A knot of worry pushes up into my throat. "Let's see if they come."

My gaze brushes over the field of tulips I created. It took weeks of planning, weeks of course correction to make sure I could grow the flower I really wanted—and I wanted one that withers in the heat but, with magic, could bloom.

So I picked tulips.

"All the social media's done," Brittany says, coming up beside me. "Lots of folks selected they're interested in coming. So maybe they will."

"Hopefully so." I grin at my family. "Let's get ready for them. Even if they don't come. It's okay. We tried."

I turn back to the field—rows and rows of brightly colored tulips stand in straight lines. They look like a rainbow, one I'm so proud of because growing the right flower proved harder than I thought it would be.

And luckily, it doesn't take long for cars to start rolling up. People park and exit their vehicles. As soon as they spot the flowers, their eyes flare, their mouths part into bright smiles.

"Morning," I say, welcoming them. "Pick whatever you'd like. Everything's free."

"Free?" a woman asks.

"Free," I confirm. "Completely free."

My family and I spend the day helping people pick and load up baskets of blooms. It's the least I could do for Mystic Meadows—give back to the town that has embraced me with open arms.

By the end of the day, I'm sweaty. My pits are stained and there's a line of dirt beads clinging to my neck. It turns out that giving away free flowers is a lot of hard work.

It's when I'm cleaning up that Brittany calls out, "Coco."

"Yeah?"

She nods to the driveway. "Someone's here to see you."

I look up and my lungs squeeze. Stone gets out of his SUV. He opens the back door, and Hercules jumps out. The lambicorn has gotten so big he's nearly a sheep.

Stone grabs a bucket from the back seat and strides over. My stomach leaps at the sight of him. He looks amazing in Carhartt jeans and a blue button-down shirt that's rolled to the elbows. He's clean shaven, and his hair's brushed to one side. It's a little longer on top than it was before, and thicker.

"Hey, Stone," my mom calls.

"Hey, Mrs. Higginbotham," he replies, his voice friendly.

He reaches me and I can't move. I can't believe he's here.

"So, um." He scratches the back of his head. "I heard there were some flowers to be picked."

"Yes." Brittany's gaze swishes from me to Stone and back. "You can pick all you want."

"Yes, let's help—" Mom starts.

Brittany grabs her by the hand. "Oh, wow. I hear Nu-Nu. Sounds like she needs something. Let's go."

I barely notice them leave because my eyes are glued to Stone. I absorb every inch of him, and as I do, I remember his warm touch, his protective hand on my back, his soft lips.

Oh my God. This is torture, and he's not even doing anything.

I have to say something. "I'm sorry—"

"Look, I—" he says at the same time.

I laugh and drop my head.

He shifts his weight from one leg to the other. "You first. This time I won't pretend to know what you're going to say, maybe because I actually don't." His voice is warm and inviting.

I've practiced this a lot. I've had weeks to think about what I'd say if he ever asked for a deeper explanation than what I gave him at the chapel.

I clear my throat. "I never should have used the spell on you. I didn't think it would work, but that's no excuse. And then, after it did work and we became close and I fell for you, I was afraid that once you knew the truth, you wouldn't love me anymore."

My throat shrinks. This is harder than I expected it would be, but I push on. "I thought the real me wasn't good enough for you, that you'd reject me. And that thought"—the words crack as they tumble from my lips—"broke me. I was going to tell you at the chapel, and then Pane came in, and if you hate me, I understand. I would hate me, too, and I did for a while.

"Stone, I never—" My voice falls, and he takes a step toward me, but I hold up my hand to stop him from interfering. "I never wanted you to hate me, and I'm so, so sorry for all of it. For what I did. All I ask is that you forgive me, but if you can't do that, I understand."

The words leave me in a rush, and the burden I've carried for weeks—almost two months—is finally, finally gone. I inhale a deep, cleansing breath and look at him.

His jade eyes sparkle with a twinge of amusement I can't place. He grins, and my own mouth quivers as I try to smile back.

"Coco Chanel," he says.

And it breaks me. I half sob, half laugh.

He takes a step forward and winds his fingers in mine. "I'm so sorry."

"For what?" I whisper, looking at his feet.

He hooks a finger under my chin and tips my face until I'm looking up at him. "I'm sorry I didn't listen to you. Time and again, you tried to tell me, but I didn't hear it. I told you what you were going to say instead, and for a long time I was angry. Not because of the spell, but because the spell forced me to see myself, to really look—and do you know what I found?"

I can barely get the whisper out. Too much hope hangs in this moment. "What?"

"That I was a real miserable son of a bitch."

His words are so surprising that a laugh bursts from me. So does a tear.

He thumbs the tear away and keeps his hand on my face, slowly rubbing his thumb over my cheekbone. "That spell stripped away who I was, the part of me that was vindictive, who planned to blackmail you. Blackmail you!" He tips his head back in disbelief. When he drops his chin and looks at me, my insides pulse. "What an asshole I was, and it took *you* to show me I'd been living without love, pushing it away. And I'd been doing it a long time."

My ribs hurt just hearing these words—that Stone, a man I'd grown to love, had chosen to be miserable.

Memories can bind us. They can chain us. But who we decide to be is up to us. Do we let the bad experiences, all the painful moments that get saddled to us, define who we are?

Or do we create ourselves by pushing through the bad and letting it fall away?

He shoots me his lopsided smile, his jade eyes filling with a warmth that just about undoes me right then and there. "The spell didn't strip me of who I was. I see that now. It made me who I needed to be. You even said that, but I didn't listen. Coco, I never want to be that person again. *Ever.* I refuse to be Stone Maddox: *asshole*. I want to be Stone Maddox, a man worthy of your love and someone who loves you back.

"You didn't break me. You *made* me. You showed me who I could be if I stopped trying to be someone else. And I like who I am when

I'm with you. Maybe magic started it—but it was your love that made it real. *Your love.* It changed me, and I'm forever grateful."

I've spent so long thinking I'm forgettable, and Stone just reinforced that I'm not.

Another tear slips from my eye and he thumbs it away again. "So I guess I'm here because I want to say I'm sorry for how I acted."

I take hold of his wrist and squeeze. "You had every right to be angry."

"I know." He says it lightly, and we both laugh. "But seriously, I would have destroyed this town if it hadn't been for you. And you're right, I never would have accepted Hercules, and who doesn't love that little guy? Maybe not so little anymore." He looks over at the lambi, who stops munching on grass to lift his head and bleat. "Yeah, I'm gonna need a bigger SUV."

I laugh at that, too.

His gaze drops to mine and he murmurs, "I guess what I'm asking is, can you forgive me for leaving you at the altar and for not listening? For not hearing you when you tried to tell me the truth? Can you forgive me for all of that?"

"Let me ask you this first: Can you forgive me for potioning you? And my potion days are over, by the way. But can you forgive me for that?"

"I already have." His voice is so tender it rocks me to my core. "I was never angry at you. I was always angry at *me*, that I backed you into a corner. That you saw no other choice. So can you forgive me?"

His eyes are so clear and green, with small flecks of gold in them. "I already have," I reply, repeating what he said.

His gaze drops to my mouth, and I tilt my face up until our lips touch. Both of his hands are on my cheeks, sliding into my hair and cradling the back of my head. I let go of all the worry and regret, allowing myself to truly be in this moment and melt into Stone's arms.

This kiss—we've kissed so many times, and so many emotions have flowed between us through our lips. But this time, the sense I have is that this kiss is a promise not to break one another, to be gentle with each other and to give grace when sometimes giving grace is the hardest thing to do.

When we break apart, he takes my hands and kisses them. Then he lifts a brow and says, "Tulips?"

I laugh. "Tulips."

"Were they hard?"

"They were so hard! It took me weeks to get it right."

He twists away, still holding me, to survey the landscape. "Well, I'd say you got the whole town on your side."

"It wasn't the town I wanted. It was you."

He kisses me again and murmurs onto my lips, "Well, now you have me."

The bang of a door grabs our attention, and I look up toward the house. Brittany, Mom, and Dad stand on the porch. It's my mom who speaks.

"Does this mean Stone's staying for dinner?"

I cock a brow. "I bet my dad will let you put on some vinyl."

He rocks back like I've punched him. "You drive a hard bargain, Coco Chanel."

"It's not so hard."

"No, it isn't." He squeezes my hand and calls up to my mom. "Yes, ma'am. I'd love to stay for dinner."

"'Ma'am'?" I ask, eyebrow crooked.

He shrugs. "What can I say? When you're in the South, you learn to speak Southern. Come on. Let's go up to the house."

My parents greet Stone with hugs, and as we're walking inside, he says to my dad, "Sir, that's a pretty amazing jazz collection you've got."

"Thank you."

"You wouldn't happen to know a CollectorPrep561 on eBay, would you?"

Surprise flits over my dad's face before he says, "Why do you ask?"

Stone leans in. "I've been looking for you. You're a hard man to pin down. I've got a proposition you might be interested in."

Stone tugs me to him and we go inside. My heart is so full I think it might pop.

Epilogue

COCO

One year later

Since Stone and I got back together, I've had the best time of my life.

"Are you ready?" he asks as we pull up to the resort.

He's wearing a slate-gray three-piece suit with a blue shirt. His sandy hair is brushed to the side, and he's clean shaven, his eyes sparkling.

I'm wearing a flowy pink dress and heels I might break my neck in, but it's worth it for this moment.

"I'm ready," I tell him.

He kills the engine and gets out of the SUV, coming around to open my door. The parking lot is already half full. We're running late, which is pretty typical of us.

But that's okay. Why rush when you want to live?

It's been a few months since I've been up to visit the resort, and the place is stunning.

It sits on twenty-five acres of gorgeously landscaped trees and grass, and features a pasture for visiting unicorns, luxury cabins, a farm-to-table restaurant. There are also magical gardens, several pools, and nature trails perfect for hiking.

The place is enchanting, and I'm thrilled to be a part of it.

Pane and Rowe are already outside. Rhett's here, too. So's Natalie, who runs up and hugs me when we arrive. Stone's mother is also here. She stands by Pane, looking regal and terrifying at the same time.

"You sure *you're* ready?"

He winks. "Yes, I am."

An hour later, we're in front of the entire town, and Stone walks up behind a lectern. He taps the mic to make sure it's on and then says, "First, I want to thank everyone for supporting the build of the Summit at Mystic Meadows. This town has come to mean so much to my brother and me. It's where we've made our homes and where a new generation of Maddoxes will grow up."

He nods to Rowe, who is clearly pregnant. She shoots a tender look of love up at Pane, who beams down at her. They're great people. After Stone and I got together, I was able to explain everything to Pane, who was more understanding than I thought he would be. His position was simply that he'd wanted to protect his brother, and I understood that. They love each other so much. Watching their relationship has helped me improve my own with Brittany.

Stone continues, "Our hope was always to keep the magic in Mystic Meadows and help it flourish, and if it wasn't for one particular person in Zoning and Development, we would have failed that. I'd like to thank Coco Higginbotham for her contribution."

Everyone claps and I nod, smiling. My gaze washes out down the hill, where the ley lines hum with strength. Magic flares inside me and the lines hum in unison. We're connected, and that's how it should be.

"So, without further ado," Stone adds, "the Summit at Mystic Meadows is officially open. I welcome all of you to enjoy the gardens and the restaurant, and if you brought your swimsuit, you're welcome to jump into one of the pools. They're heated, so you can enjoy them even in the colder months."

People laugh and clap while Stone cuts the ribbon and moves aside so that folks can wander the premises.

I stand next to him, smiling and greeting people. Cristina approaches with Clarice and some of the book club ladies in tow.

Clarice eyes me up and down, leans over, and says, "I still woulda fixed you up with a Collins boy. But I see now you don't need it."

"Thanks, I don't."

Cristina hugs me. "You look beautiful. I'm so glad things worked out with you two."

"Same here." My gaze slides to Stone, who's talking to the mayor. "Thank you for coming."

"Of course. I brought my swimsuit." Her gaze lands on Rhett. "Who's that?"

"Stone's cousin. He's a bit prickly."

She winks at me. "I can handle prickly."

"Good luck," I reply as she walks off to meet a very prickly Rhett.

My parents are in the crowd, and I greet them, as well as Nu-Nu, who requests sugar before going inside.

Brittany and Jet are here, too, and my sister doesn't even have her phone out recording.

"I left it at the house," she says, shrugging. "You don't always need to document every moment of your life."

I couldn't agree more.

As the crowd makes their way inside, Stone turns to face me. "There's something I want to show you."

"Sounds mysterious."

"Not really."

He takes me to the side of the property where a rock entrance welcomes visitors to the garden. He gestures to a plaque hanging on the wall.

My hands fly to my face as I read the inscription. "Coco's Garden?"

He nods. "I told you I was building this for you. Here it is."

I squeeze his hand as tears prick my eyes. "Thank you."

"You're welcome." He kisses my forehead. "Would you like a tour?"

"I would love one."

Blankets of flowers line the winding stone path, making the whole place magical. I wipe tears from my eyes as Stone guides me. I'm so full of love as my gaze skips over benches and hedges, flowers climbing lattices and beds of brightly petaled peonies and tulips.

"Tulips," I exclaim.

Stone slides his hands into his pockets. "Tulips."

"Thank you." I kiss his lips and sigh into him. "Nothing could make me happier right now. Nothing."

"Maybe one thing."

"What?" I tease. "What could make me happier?"

Stone kneels and my knees quake. What is happening right now?

He pulls a box from his pocket and opens it. Inside sits, not my grandmother's ring, but a new one, a different emerald cushioned with diamonds.

"Coco, will you do me the honor of becoming my wife?"

Is that even a question? "Yes!" I yell. "Yes, I'll be your wife!"

He slides the ring on my finger, and out of nowhere, my family appears. So does his family. I'm surrounded by everyone I love, and so is he.

Stone kisses me lightly and murmurs, "I love you."

"I love you, too."

Then he quirks a brow. "So what do you say to eloping?"

I shake my head, laughing. "No, sir. This time, we're doing it right."

Acknowledgments

Writing a book about magic and being truly seen feels fitting, as I've been blessed with people who see and believe in me.

To my incredible editor, Maria Gomez: Thank you for continuing to believe in my little stories and for supporting my vision, even when it is a bit harebrained. Also, to my developmental editor, Lindsey Faber—your insight makes these books shine.

To my agent, Jill Marsal: Thank you for your wisdom, your advocacy, and for pairing me with Maria in the first place. I couldn't ask for a better champion of my work.

To the entire Montlake team: Thank you for turning my words into beautiful books and getting them into readers' hands. Your expertise amazes me.

Thank you to my early readers, Eryn Scott, Sarah Laughmiller, and Alex VanKoughnett, who've been with me for years and who don't pull punches. It only makes the book better when you tell me the truth. Keep doing it. And to Kelly Figh—for your friendship and help with this story. You have excellent insight. Thank you.

To the Moxies: Thank you for always being willing to have an emergency plotting session.

Big thanks to Bambi Crivello, Jean Hovey, and Stephanie Jones for your friendship. It's because of y'all that a magical creature farm even exists at all.

To Mark and the girls—thank you for your endless support, for helping decide which magical creature comes next, and for understanding when I disappear into fictional worlds. I love you all.

To my readers: Thank you for taking this journey with me to Mystic Meadows, for embracing Coco and Stone (and Hercules!), and for loving these characters as much as I do.

And finally, to everyone who's ever felt unseen—this book is for you. May you find your magic and someone who helps you shine.

About the Author

Photo © 2022 Christy Stahlnaker

Amy Boyles is the author of the Stupid Love series, *How to Fake It with a Fae*, the Sweet Tea Witches mysteries, the Bless Your Witch series, and the Magical Renovation Mystery series, among many other novels. A resident of northern Alabama, Amy loves antique shopping, cooking for her family, and watching K-dramas. When she's not chauffeuring her two kids to after-school activities, she can be found reading a good romance. For more information, visit www.amyboyles.com.